Praise for the works of

Justice Calls

I must admit that I was sucked in from the first sentence because Ann Roberts has a way of crafting a story to keep her readers captivated. I definitely got a realistic portrayal of the gut-wrenching pain, frustration, and anger that Ari and her father felt as they worked tirelessly to find out who killed Richie. I can't believe that I went through a gamut of emotions with every word I read and I just couldn't let Ari, Molly, or Jack go even when the story ended. If you're looking for heartfelt moments, character growth, timeless love coupled with an understanding that knows no boundaries and a compelling mystery, then this story is certainly for you!

-The Lesbian Review

A Secret to Tell

This is surely one story you should not miss out on reading. I can assure you, this story has the right amount of angst, mystery, comedy, and romance to keep you up way past your bedtime. From the first page I was completely sucked into the story due to the nonstop action and the steady flow of angst and excitement. The characters were realistic and the dialogue between them was fantastic!

-The Lesbian Review

Deadly Intersections

June, 2011, RLynne - Roberts has given her reader a wild roller coaster ride in a plot filled with dead bodies, intrigue, lies, and corruption. Her characters are very real with flaws and baggage, and very likeable. Set in Phoenix, Arizona, juxtaposes the bright sunlight with the very dark underbelly of the city. This is a book full of surprises with an exciting cliff-hanger of an ending.

-Just About Write

Vagabond Heart

The story starts off with a bang and kept my interest all the way through. It's been forever since I picked up a book that I had trouble putting down. This one could easily make it into my read-again pile. Both Quinn and Suda are interesting characters and their interactions didn't feel scripted or overplayed. The author managed to weave in several real-life xenophobic/ bigotry issues which just made the characters feel like they were operating in real life without detracting from the story. In fact, I'd say it enhanced the story because we need to call more attention to these things. I've never been on Route 66, but based on the descriptions and the adventure it's on my bucket list moving forward.

-C-Spot Reviews

Beacon of Love

This is a well-written book about love, loss, redemption, and parenthood. Roberts intertwines her characters like a helix and slowly unveils the truth about each one... This is one of those books that sneaks up on the reader. There aren't a lot of bells and whistles, it doesn't shout at you, nor does it hit you over the head. It is, however, well written and in a quiet way, the characters and their story will stay with you long after you finish the book and put it aside.

-LambdaLiterary.org

Dying on the Vine

AN ARI ADAMS MYSTERY

Other Bella Books by Ann Roberts

Romances
Brilliant
Beach Town
Root of Passion
Beacon of Love
Petra's Canvas
Hidden Hearts
The Complete Package
Pleasure of the Chase
Vagabond Heart
Screen Kiss

General Fiction
Furthest From the Gate
Keeping Up Appearances

The Ari Adams Mystery Series
Paid in Full
White Offerings
Deadly Intersections
Point of Betrayal
A Grand Plan
A Secret to Tell
Justice Calls

Dying on the Vine

AN ARI ADAMS MYSTERY

ANN ROBERTS

BELLA
BOOKS

2020

Copyright © 2020 by Ann Roberts

Bella Books, Inc.
P.O. Box 10543
Tallahassee, FL 32302

All rights reserved. No part of this book may be reproduced or transmitted in any form or by any means, electronic or mechanical, including photocopying, without permission in writing from the publisher.

This is a work of fiction. Names, characters, businesses, places, events and incidents are either the products of the author's imagination or used in a fictitious manner. Any resemblance to actual persons, living or dead, or actual events is purely coincidental. The publisher does not have any control over and does not assume any responsibility for author or third-party websites or their content.

Printed in the United States of America on acid-free paper.

First Bella Books Edition 2020

Editor: Katherine V. Forrest
Cover Designer: Judith Fellows

ISBN: 978-1-64247-122-9

PUBLISHER'S NOTE

The scanning, uploading, and distribution of this book via the Internet or via any other means without the permission of the publisher is illegal and punishable by law. Please purchase only authorized electronic editions, and do not participate in or encourage electronic piracy of copyrighted materials. Your support of the author's rights is appreciated.

Acknowledgments

When I began this journey, I knew only the most basic things about wine: how to remove the cork, that it was made from grapes, and that wine from a bottle beat wine from a box. Once I was deep in the research, it was hard to believe that something so complex, so reliant on back-breaking work, and so dependent on the whims of nature had survived thousands of years.

Winemaking is one of the most difficult professions, combining science, business, and artistry. I am indebted to Pamela Adkins of Adrice Wines in Woodinville, Washington, for schooling me on the intricate and highly complex process that turns grapes into the fruit of the gods. Once Pam told me some stories, I was certain a murder could happen in a vineyard. If you're ever traveling in the Woodinville area, stop by and see Pam and Julie, or check out their website https://adricewines.wine/.

The winemaking community near my home of Eugene, Oregon, was incredibly receptive to my emails, and while I would have loved to interview all of them, I chose two very different situations, the first being Rainsong Vineyards (http://www.rainsongvineyard.com/).

A completely family affair, winemaker Marcus Hall is the son-in-law of the owners. Family and friends have picked the grapes, made the wine and marketed the product for over three decades. It is a shared family tradition, like making Christmas cookies or hosting the 4th of July barbeque, except it takes all year and tests the patience and tenacity of each family member.

Marcus met with me for two hours, answered multiple emails and gave incredibly detailed answers, which helped me create authentic scenarios.

General Manager Angela Jaquette and Head Winemaker JP Valot of Silvan Ridge Winery (https://silvanridge.com/) the largest vineyard I visited, gave up time during the height of harvest to answer questions, show me their winemaking process, allow me to taste their newest creations, and explain how a larger winery works. Angela was also kind enough to review some of the book's content.

My dear friend, Catherine Maiorisi took a break from her own novel writing (plug here for the Chiara Corelli mystery series) to beta read a later draft, catching all the "nits," as she calls them, before I submitted the book to my editor, Katherine V. Forrest.

I learn things every time I'm privileged to have Katherine as my editor. Her suggestions always enrich the story, and I'm grateful for her caring but demanding approach to quality fiction.

Fifteen years ago, I got a phone call from Linda Hill, the publisher of Bella Books, that changed my life. As I reach this milestone of 20 books, I'm forever grateful for the support of the Bella family.

The pups, Chip and Hattie, and the cats, Bean and Simon, reminded me constantly during this process that it's important to take breaks and play ball or sit quietly and "listen to the purr."

My wife Amy has traveled by my side down the road to #20, providing support when there's a deadline, reading the early drafts, and puppy sitting so I can finish writing a chapter. I'll forgive you for not being a "wine person."

And to all the readers… Whether this is your first or your eighth Ari Adams mystery, I'm grateful and humbled that you're here for the ride.

Cheers!

Dedication

For my dear friend, Patricia
Your passion for wine was contagious and your love
and friendship are forever in my heart

CHAPTER ONE

The vineyard was as dark as a rich cabernet. Dion Demopolous stopped and gazed west, across the sprawling sixty acres. At night, deep in the heart of the Willamette Valley, the land belonged to the creatures and critters. The vineyard was at their mercy. The wind rustled the leaves and the trellises creaked under the heavy weight of grapes ready for picking. He could barely see anything in front of him as he trudged up the gravel path toward the behemoth structure that housed Sisters Cellars Vineyard.

It was harvest, the most exciting time of year for a vineyard. Usually several cars would still be parked in the lot, the bay doors open to the deafening hum of the machines working in tandem with the efforts of the growers. Automation meets authenticity, Mina always said. Usually he wouldn't have been able to hear the crunch of gravel under his feet.

But tonight wasn't usual.

He'd left his car on the highway outside the front gates. The night was as quiet as it was dark, and a rumbling engine most certainly would've awakened Berto, the aging winemaker who lived in the quaint cottage at the base of the hill. Harvest was exhausting for everyone, but more so for someone in his seventies.

Everyone else was gone except for the owner. Mina's house sat on the opposite side of the production building, and for now, she was asleep. She'd spent the evening watching her beloved Oregon Ducks women's soccer team playing their rival, Oregon State, but before she retired for some much needed shuteye, she would've checked the fermenting grapes, "her children," one last time.

As for Mina's wife, Cleo, Dion knew she'd taken a lover and was away, at least for a while.

Twenty paces more and he halted, confronted by his own smiling visage emblazoned across a banner advertising the Wine 101 class that he conducted as the premier sommelier for Sisters Cellars. He looked good, his sandy brown hair parted on the left and his goatee expertly shaped to hide his double chin. They had even managed to highlight the brown of his eyes.

When Mina unveiled the banner, he'd been stunned and a little uncomfortable that his face would greet every visitor. But his mother had joked he had wine in his veins instead of blood. And he was named for Dionysus, the Greek god of wine. When he was a teenager, his brother Apollo (who told him "Apollo" meant "boss,") told him Dionysus was also the god of fertility. Dion had focused on the wine aspect since he was rather certain the fertility piece wouldn't be a strength. But the wine, yes the wine…

He was likely to gain the title Master Sommelier after he passed the last section of one of the hardest exams given in any profession, and the idea brought a smile to his face.

Then a strange noise, like the snapping of a branch, halted him once more. He looked off into the trees, moonlit silhouettes playing on the trunks. Was one of those silhouettes a human form?

He blinked and shook his head. He'd enjoyed a few belts of whiskey from his flask before he left his car, needing the proverbial liquid courage for this mission. He glanced again at the ridiculously large banner, guiltily. He'd toyed with the idea that once he passed the test, he'd leave tiny Cheshire, Oregon, for Portland, a doorway to a lucrative and significant career. But now he was reconsidering for many reasons.

He crept around the outside of the production room, passing the enormous grape press, breathing in the distinctly rich aroma of the latest batch, grapes destined to be cabernet.

He veered to the far side of the building to the tasting room door. It was unlocked—as promised. He slid inside and shut the door quietly. Two sconces provided enough light to navigate the room successfully. The lingering cologne and perfume of the day's last visitors assaulted his acute olfactory senses and he made a face. A Gen X couple had appeared just five minutes before closing, promising to hurry the tasting and vowing to purchase at least three bottles of wine. He shook his head and tried to clear his senses. Why would anyone sabotage one of life's true pleasures—tasting wine—for a ridiculously priced fragrance that garnered hateful looks from the scent-free crowd?

He flipped on his cellphone's flashlight as he entered the event room. The enormous Sisters Cellars logo of the three mountain peaks known as "The Sisters" sat in the center of a sprawling mural of the Willamette Valley. It was beautiful art and effective PR. He walked a circuitous route, necessitated by the round tables placed precisely six feet apart for ADA compliance. A bridal shower was scheduled for the next night, one that would net him big bucks in tips as the bartender.

His hip caught the edge of a staging table, toppling several crystal vase centerpieces and sending a few dozen sachets to the floor. "Shit," he hissed and swayed slightly. Perhaps he'd taken one belt of whiskey too many. Fortunately the linen tablecloth muffled the thudding vases. He quickly righted them and plucked the sachets from the floor, grimacing at the ungodly lavender smell.

He glanced up to the balcony that sat above the tasting room where the executive offices were located, as well as the guest room. No lights were on. Tomorrow Mina's childhood buddy was due to arrive, but tonight everything was quiet, empty and dark. Tonight no one had any reason to be in the building. Mina had forbidden it.

He took a deep breath and pushed through the steel doors that led to the production room. Unlike the public areas, the corridor was well lit since work happened at all hours—but not tonight. He knew tonight would be the only night everyone was gone during harvest.

As he approached the large accordion door, he glanced up at the security camera, its green light flashing hello. No one ever checked the footage unless there was a problem, and it taped over itself every few days. Since his little covert operation would go completely unnoticed, he wasn't worried. Everyone was far too busy right now with harvest.

A laminated sign had been haphazardly stuck to the door with a magnet. KEEP OUT - HIGH CO_2 LEVELS. CO_2 was the natural byproduct of adding yeast to the grapes. At least once during each harvest they experienced a day when there were so many grapes fermenting at once, the CO_2 levels became unsafe. Work shut down until the grapes completed the most critical step to becoming wine.

Before he pressed the door control button, he visualized his route. He'd grab a mask from the wall and would be in and out in less than three minutes. The door ascended and he ducked inside, heading straight for the safety equipment. Odd, he thought. There was only one mask on the rack. He strapped it over his face and closed the door to contain the CO_2. There was no way to smell the natural and odorless gas, which was why at this level it was so dangerous.

As he started across the room, he marveled at the equipment necessary for turning grapes into wine. Two massive steel tanks flanked the left wall. He imagined the pinot gris that would eventually flow out of the tanks and into the bottles. It was some of the best he'd ever tasted and a great success for a winery literally brought back from the ashes. He debated grabbing a glass for just one more taste, but he didn't want to risk it.

In the center of the room sat the eight fermenting bins, each housing approximately a ton of grapes that would become pinot noir, cabernet, syrah, and malbec. He couldn't help but take a peek inside at what currently could only be described as a science experiment. Thousands of grapes, still possessing their skins, mixed with various yeasts chosen by Mina, the owner and winemaker. Currently the consistency of oatmeal, the grapes were undergoing a carefully monitored chemical reaction that involved sugar levels, acidity, brix scores, and pH levels. He understood some of it after spending fifteen of his thirty-five years in the industry, but only Mina and Cleo, the viticulturist, understood all of it. Cleo made sure Mina had the best product possible for her part—making the wine and blending finished wines for new products.

He shook his head and chastised himself. For some reason the production room was like Disneyland. He was in complete awe of the winemaking process and easily distracted by all of the machines and tools.

He needed to get moving and get what he came for. He stepped away from the bins, realizing he was parched. He swallowed—and his throat burned. It was worse than any case of strep he'd ever had. He gasped and pulled off his mask. *What the hell?* He found a slit in the respirator, rendering the mask useless. He swayed and grabbed one of the fermenting bins for support. New plan. He had to get out of there. Now. What he'd come for would have to wait.

He held the compromised respirator to his face, hoping it provided some protection, and stumbled toward the back door. He pushed the control button repeatedly but the door didn't open. He looked over his shoulder, back at the large accordion door where he'd entered. It seemed so far away. He swallowed again and winced, rusty nails lodged in his throat.

He focused on the red door button that would once again raise the accordion door. He stumbled forward, unsure if his legs were actually attached to his body. He pressed the button again and again but nothing happened.

"Damn it!"

He no longer cared who heard him. In fact, he couldn't remember why he was in the production room. His phone! He reached into his pants pocket. Empty. He checked the rest of his pockets. Where was it? He closed his eyes and groaned. He'd used the phone's flashlight in the event room—and left it on the table. He'd forgotten it after he picked up those stupid sachets off the floor. He was starting to sweat and felt terribly nauseous. He imagined he'd soon vomit the whiskey. Or worse.

There was a phone in Mina's office. He had to cross the room yet again to reach the far corner. His feet tangled and he tripped on himself. He grabbed the corner of a fermenting bin to stay upright. He took short breaths to prevent the CO_2 from overpowering the remaining oxygen in his body. He needed every bit of it if he was going to save himself.

But all he wanted now was sleep. No use fighting it. And as the CO_2 dropped a shroud over his mind, he remembered his plan and knew who had done this to him. He just wished he'd used his final minutes for something meaningful—taking a final taste of that pinot gris.

CHAPTER TWO

The long security line wended left and right as the weary passengers shuffled forward, a few gulping final sips of coffee before the stoic TSA agent confiscated their cups. Ari Adams sighed as she and her best friend and fellow real estate agent Jane Frank joined the line. "I really wish you'd sign up for Pre-Check," Ari said. "As often as you fly to Cali to see Rory, I'd think you'd want to skip this part."

"Nuh-uh," Jane replied. "And miss the chance to be frisked?"

"Are you serious? We're in this line at three thirty in the morning because you want to get felt up by a cop?" Jane just smiled. "Don't you think that's a little ridiculous since we're headed to the location of your *wedding*?"

Jane picked some lint from the shoulder of her black jacket. "Hey, Rory and I aren't married yet."

"If you're suggesting—"

Jane held up a hand and gave her stuffed carry-on bag a push forward with her Louboutin heel. "I'm not suggesting anything. I'm totally committed to Rory. My days of lewd remarks to women in uniform and committing sex acts in nearby restrooms because of said uniforms…are over."

Ari rolled her eyes. She'd lost track of how many times they'd almost missed a plane or caused a flight delay because Jane had disappeared with a member of the crew.

"But Rory gave the green light for flirting," Jane continued. "She knows it would be impossible to completely stifle my overactive libido."

Ari shook her head. "Rory is a good woman."

"Indeed she is. And she reaps the benefit of my libido frequently." She turned on her heel and sauntered forward.

Ari didn't share Jane's worldview of women despite them being as close as sisters. According to Jane this trip would finally introduce Ari to the other woman Jane considered a "sister," her childhood friend Mina Sommer. Over the years Ari had learned tidbits of Jane's youth in Southern California, which she described as her wild years. On dozens of occasions, usually when she and Jane were consuming a good bottle of wine, they would Skype with Mina, and eventually, once Mina married, her wife Cleo joined the call as well. After their first Skype session, she'd asked if Mina was an old flame and Jane replied, "Weren't they all?"

Ari had become virtual friends with both of them. With Jane's prompting, she had shared many of her escapades over the last few years, like finding a dead body in a real estate listing, catching Jane's stalker, and most recently, solving the murder of her own brother. Mina and Cleo were fascinated with her stories, maintaining that nothing interesting ever happened in their tiny town.

Meeting them in person would hopefully solidify the "friend" title. Ari was a bit nervous, having read many articles about virtual friendships that fizzled after disappointing face-to-face meetings. She doubted that would happen as she knew their respective biographies, which were nothing less than incredible.

Mina had received her bachelor's and master's degrees in chemistry, and after amassing a small fortune working in private industry, she bought her uncle and aunt's failing vineyard in tiny Cheshire, Oregon. Around the same time, Mina met her soulmate, an environmental engineer named Cleo Vidal. After four years they were thriving and winning awards for their wine.

Jane easily convinced Rory they should marry at the vineyard, and this trip would only confirm what was already decided. Rory had wisely chosen to stay away, giving Jane and Mina reminiscing time. Ari was happy to accompany Jane and fulfill her maid of honor duty, meet Mina and Cleo, and sample the winery's award-winning pinot noir cleverly named Phoenix.

They finally reached the head of the TSA line. Ari eyed the one female officer—a trim, young thing with short, jet-black hair smoothed back in a ducktail. *Most likely family.* Ari absently threaded her fingers through her own shoulder-length dark hair, remembering a time when it fell to her waist. Although her girlfriend Molly swore she loved it just as much now as she did when it was long, Ari still wasn't sure she'd made the right decision to chop off six inches.

The young agent wanded a woman who'd set off the metal detector. Ari shook her head. Jane lived for this.

They each grabbed two gray bins and performed the required FAA ballet that allowed them into the airport's inner sanctum. Ari assumed the hands joined overhead position and exited the scanner without incident. She gathered their things and moved outside the immediate security area, waiting for what would undoubtedly be a show starring Jane and the poor, unsuspecting TSA agent. The only thing missing was the popcorn.

Jane, wearing a crisp, tailored white shirt that clung tightly to her large chest, stepped into the scanner and locked her arms above her head. She closed her eyes, shook her blond mane left and right, thrust her chin to the sky, and froze in place like an actress in a bondage film. When the young female motioned for her to exit and step to the side, Jane's eyes grew wide.

"Is there a problem, Officer..." She leaned closer to read the agent's badge. "...Cassidy?"

Cassidy cleared her throat and stood ramrod straight. "Yes, ma'am. I need to check here, here, and...here." Her blue-gloved hand motioned toward Jane's left and right hip, as well as her abundant cleavage.

"Do your duty, Officer Cassidy. I don't mind." Jane grinned and young Officer Cassidy turned completely red. She patted Jane's hips so lightly that Ari wasn't sure she'd actually made contact. "It's okay, Officer," Jane coaxed. "I won't break."

Cassidy shifted from one foot to the other, unsure how to approach the issue with the cleavage. "Ma'am, are you wearing a bra with a wire?"

"No."

"Have you had any surgeries or augmentations—"

"Honey, everything up here is grade-A, one hundred percent real. Wanna see?"

"No, no," she replied quickly. "I believe you." She stared at her breasts. "Are you wearing a necklace?"

"Of course," Jane cried dramatically. "I forgot. I'm so sorry." She undid the next button of her shirt, pulling apart the fabric so the agent got a clear view of her maroon bra. She withdrew a funky medallion from between her breasts. "Might this be the problem?"

Cassidy cleared her throat again. "Uh-huh."

Jane reached behind her neck, undid the clasp and freed the necklace. She held it out to the agent, who stood there mutely, her jaw dropped. "Why don't you keep this?" Jane suggested. She took the agent's hand and placed the medallion in her upturned palm.

Officer Cassidy whispered a slight, "Thank you," as Jane swaggered away and took her carry-on from Ari. She threw the young agent one final look and said, "Do you think she'll remember me?"

"For a long time."

Their flight to Eugene, Oregon, proved uneventful and their drive through the verdant Willamette Valley toward tiny Cheshire was beautiful in the early morning light. Sprawling acreage went on for miles, mostly farmland or vineyards, and the reds and yellows of the maples and dogwoods announced fall had begun.

According to GPS, Ari was driving up a major state highway, but periodically a dirt road would intersect, an artery to a large farmhouse in the distance. Ari had always wondered how people arrived at those solitary structures, ones surrounded by only field or forest. At these crossroads were often smaller signs for wineries, and Ari noted directions for at least twelve—Mina and Cleo's competition.

The scenery was relaxing and hypnotic, and Ari found her eyelids drooping. She wiped a hand across her face to stay awake. She glanced at Jane in the passenger seat of their rented Range Rover. Her eyes were closed and she was lightly snoring. Ari poked her arm.

"Hey, it's your job to keep me awake. And you're missing all the lovely scenery."

"Huh? Oh." She stared out the window for a half second. "Yeah, beautiful."

"You don't think this is pretty?"

Jane snorted. "City girl through and through."

"Then why are you getting married out here?"

"Rory wanted something charming and quaint. And she wanted the ceremony outside California so most of her family would skip it."

"That's rather warped logic."

"You haven't met her family."

"Have you?"

"Only a few of them. They're...medieval."

"Is she going to like living in Arizona?"

"I...think so. She's tired of California."

Ari heard the hesitancy in her voice. "How many times has Rory visited Arizona. Twice?"

"No, three times. Granted, the third time we went to Sedona the minute after she stepped off the plane..."

"Ah, that's right. I just remember a few heated discussions about Arizona's backward ways."

Jane faced Ari. "There wasn't anything to discuss. She's right. When it comes to ridiculousness, especially regarding social issues, there's no place more back asswards than Arizona. Did you hear about that legislator who wants to outlaw the word homosexuality in schools?"

Ari groaned. "Yeah, I read that."

"I hadn't…until Rory sent it to me."

The seriousness in Jane's voice was unusual. Jane was the joker, the optimist, the one who lived life as large as possible. Ari was the serious one.

"What are you thinking?" Jane asked.

"Nothing," Ari lied. When it came to Jane and Rory's relationship, she saw some red flags other than Arizona, but she didn't think they were serious enough to warrant conversation. "Tell me more about what Mina and Cleo have been up to. I missed the last few Skype calls."

"They're up to their eyeballs in harvest."

"Should we really be visiting?"

"I asked Mina the same thing. She absolutely insisted that we come now. She knows we need to finalize the wedding venue and she's really excited that we're getting married there."

"I just hope we aren't in the way."

Jane picked some lint from her jacket and said, "I doubt it. She's a complete workaholic who gives a hundred and ten percent to everything she does. What she accomplishes in a day takes most people a week. We'll just be one more detail. She'll probably put us to work."

"I'm game."

Jane laughed. "You say that now. Winemaking is hard! It's tough physically and mentally, but you know Mina. She's completely driven."

"Agreed. It's not surprising her winery is successful. I've read that most aren't."

"That's true. A lot of boutique wineries have popped up over the last decade, especially ones owned by retirees. It's their life dream," she said melodramatically, clasping her hands. "What they don't realize is that it's incredibly expensive and a ton of hard work. Most fold within the first year. But not Sisters Cellars."

Ari heard the pride in Jane's voice. "Mina's made some great wines. I love that cabernet she sent you."

"Hmm, yes."

"And Cleo is the... What is that word for what she does?" Ari asked.

"I can't remember her official title. She's the one who takes care of the grapes. The grape mom. I wouldn't be surprised if she gives names to all of them."

"That's smart. They divide the work in half. And Mina got the vineyard from her aunt and uncle?"

"Sort of. The land was originally owned by them for decades and Mina spent her childhood summers up here helping them—until she turned into a teenager."

"You corrupted her," Ari concluded.

"Ha, more like the other way around. Anyway, Mina's aunt and uncle didn't have any children or other heirs, but they weren't happy about Mina's choices. They told her that someday they might leave the winery to her but only if she got her act together. She got her degree, went to work in the private sector, and when they passed—"

"They left it to her."

"No, actually. Her uncle made some bad decisions and there were gambling debts. Right about that same time she met Cleo on a blind date. Mina showed her the vineyard, which the bank had foreclosed on by then, told Cleo she dreamed of owning the vineyard, and Cleo said they should go for it. By then they'd fallen in love and decided to get married. It took a few years, but they're finally reaping some rewards. The cabernet is their second wine to win an award and there's talk about their upcoming pinot gris which hopefully you and I will get to sample. *And* they were just named best up-and-coming winery in the Willamette Valley."

"Impressive, but it still sounds like a ton of work."

"Yeah, but they're living their dream. They even brought a couple of Mina's childhood friends into the business."

"Well, I'm excited to finally meet them."

"Yeah, me too," Jane said with a genuine smile.

They spent the rest of the drive discussing a frustrating real estate client who wouldn't compromise on the features he wanted. Ari had shown him dozens of listings but none of the houses in his price range met all of his requirements. "Thank goodness for the Internet," Ari said. "At least he's been doing most of his vetoing by email."

"Ah, yes," Jane said. "Here's to not spending hours driving around for no reason, wasting gas and contributing to climate change." She sat up and pointed. "There it is, up there at the top of the hill."

Ari peered down the ribbon of highway—and saw flashing red lights. "Jane, this doesn't look good."

CHAPTER THREE

Ari pulled up next to a young uniformed sheriff's officer standing at the entrance to Sisters Cellars. He quickly put away his phone, tipped his hat and said, "Good morning, ladies. Unfortunately, the tasting room is currently closed."

She smiled and nodded. "We're not here for a tasting. We're out-of-town friends of the owner."

Jane leaned across Ari. "What's going on? Are Mina and Cleo okay?"

"Uh, um…"

"Officer! Mina and Cleo!" Jane shouted. "What's their ten-twenty?"

Ari put a gentle hand on Jane's arm and pushed her away. She glanced at the gold name tag above his shirt pocket. "Officer Silas, can you help us, please?"

He nodded and scratched his head, Jane's "ten-twenty" police jargon apparently a mystery to him. He leaned on the driver's door and looked at Jane. "Mina and Cleo are fine, but there's been…" He exhaled. A former cop herself, Ari felt for the guy who was probably a rookie since he'd been assigned guard duty on the road. He looked around before he said, "Go ahead," and stepped back.

"Thank you, Officer."

"Moron," Jane mumbled once they'd pulled away.

"Don't, Jane. He was just doing his job. Mina and Cleo are fine. Focus on that."

Ari followed the narrow strip of asphalt that cut the property in half. The grandeur of the enormous building before her would be enough to pique the curiosity of any tourist out for a drive. Rows and rows of grapevines surrounded them as they ascended the hill and pulled in front of a French chateau constructed entirely of stone, with unique gables, a variety of windows and a front breezeway that would've been quite welcoming, except for the presence of several police vehicles and a large van marked CORONER.

Jane scowled. "Well, Mina and Cleo might be fine, but somebody isn't."

They parked in the adjoining guest lot to stay out of the way and left their belongings for later. Jane walked as quickly as she could, but Ari had no trouble keeping up. Her six-foot frame's long strides easily matched Jane's gait, and she'd opted for loafers. An enormous banner across the entrance announced that Sisters Cellars was the home of the award-winning pinot noir, Phoenix. Below it was a smaller banner announcing Wine 101 taught by Dion Demopolous, whose pleasant-looking, grinning face stared at her.

Another officer stood at the front door, adeptly holding coffee in one hand and tapping his phone with the other. Jane veered in his direction but Ari grabbed her arm.

"Come this way. I'm betting he won't let us through and the action isn't in this part of the building anyway. When we drove up I saw a commotion on the south side."

They followed the perimeter of the chateau until they came to a narrow path that led them to a gate, but a female officer was stationed there as well.

"Terrific," Jane said. "I guess I'll have to use my charms." She began unbuttoning two buttons on her shirt while Ari searched for another way.

"There's Mina and Cleo," she said, pointing to a very fit blonde and her equally trim wife, a brunette with a ponytail that stuck out the back of her baseball cap. Seeing skin that was a rich tan, Ari remembered Cleo was from Argentina. She was Mina's physical opposite with dark, wild hair, a solid toned physique, and exotic features. Mina was a Scandinavian beauty with straight blond hair, freckles, and delicate hands that Ari always noticed whenever Mina gestured during their Skype calls.

"Mina! Cleo!" Jane shouted.

Mina saw Jane, yelled to the officer to let them through and then flew into Jane's arms. Cleo joined the group and pulled Ari into a hug. She kissed her cheek and said, "It's so good to finally meet you."

"You as well." She felt something brush against her leg and looked down at a cute black and white terrier. "Dexter!" she cooed. Whenever they Skyped, Dexter sat on Mina's lap and stared into the camera as if he were listening to the conversation.

Cleo scooped him up and brought him face-to-face with Ari. He licked her cheek and wagged his little tail frantically. "I'd say he's very happy to meet you too."

Ari was in love. Dexter's limpid dark eyes were the sweetest she'd ever seen. *If only Molly would let us get a dog.*

Mina turned to Ari and gave her a fierce hug. "Ari! I'm so glad you came."

"Me too." She stepped away and saw Mina had been crying. "What's happened?"

"I'm sorry for not calling this morning and warning you both." She gestured to the chaos surrounding them. "But this…"

Her voice broke. Cleo pulled her close and said, "One of our employees, Dion, our sommelier, died during the night and was found this morning by another employee. We don't have a lot of details yet. They haven't even let us inside."

Jane's hand flew to her mouth. "Oh, my God. I'm so sorry. How awful."

"Denise arrived first as usual. She's our assistant. She found him on the floor in the production room," Mina said.

"It's standard to keep people outside," Ari said. "They have to preserve the area until they determine whether it's a crime scene."

Cleo nodded. "You're a former cop, right?"

"For a brief time," Ari clarified. "Dion's the guy on the poster outside?"

"He is…was," Cleo said.

Mina's gaze drifted to the production room. "I understand preserving the scene and I'm heartbroken over losing Dion, but I'm also very concerned about preserving our harvest. That's our entire income for the year. We're introducing our malbec, and the pinot gris will be the best it's ever been."

Cleo reached for her hand. "It's okay, babe. They promised they'd let us back in by nine." She looked at her watch. "That's only twenty minutes from now."

"Is the time really important?" Ari asked.

"Yes," Mina said. "The grapes are fermenting. They have to be carefully nurtured during this process. There are crucial steps if they're going to turn into wine."

"It's like a lot of food," Cleo added. "If you don't follow the recipe, your dish doesn't turn out well. Our label is finally rising to the top. This year's harvest is critical to solidifying the reputation we've *finally* cultivated." She stopped herself and shook her head. "I'm sorry if I sound callous. We're both incredibly distraught about Dion. All we know is they found him on the floor. I'd guess he's a victim of CO_2 poisoning."

Jane made a face. "CO_2? You mean like the gas a car gives off? Like when people commit suicide in their garages?"

"No, honey," Mina said. "You're thinking of carbon *mono*xide. We actually exhale a portion of carbon dioxide. It's natural and in small doses, it's not harmful. However, if a room is filled with CO_2, then that means there's little oxygen."

"So you can't breathe," Jane concluded.

"Right. During the fermentation process, CO_2 is released in the air. It's a byproduct of adding yeast to the grapes. Yesterday we had several tons of grapes fermenting at the same time, so there was a lot of CO_2 in the air."

"Can you work in those conditions?" Ari asked.

"No," Cleo said, "which is why no one was allowed to work in the production room until this morning. Dion knew that. Everybody knew that. Work had to shut down, it was unavoidable."

Jane cleared her throat before she asked gently, "Do you think Dion did this intentionally?"

Both Mina and Cleo shook their heads. "Absolutely not," Mina said. "I can guarantee this wasn't a suicide. Dion had everything to live for. He was probably going to become a Master Sommelier, one of only two hundred in the world."

"A sommelier is the person in a restaurant or liquor store who knows everything there is to know about wine, right?" Ari asked. "They recommend pairings?"

"Amongst many things," Cleo said. "Somms are vital to the industry, especially the high-end restaurants. When customers are paying three hundred dollars for a meal, they want the right wine to accentuate the whole experience."

Jane looked up from her phone. "Holy crap! It says here that a Master Somm has to pass some wickedly hard test?"

"Three tests, actually," Mina corrected. "It's one of the most difficult exams in the world." She glanced at her Apple Watch and the production building. "Babe, I've got to get in there. Now. Those rosé grapes are gonna get stuck."

"What's stuck?" Jane asked, still tapping on her phone.

"During fermentation we have to keep an eye on the levels," Mina explained. "If we're not watchful, they'll get stuck in the fermenting process and that entire batch is worthless."

"Can't you just restart the process?"

Mina offered a little smile. "No, it's not like jumpstarting your car battery."

"Well, sometimes you can restart it," Cleo disagreed, "but usually not."

"Jane? Is that you?"

A handsome man in his late thirties flashed a gorgeous smile and opened his arms. "C'mere, kiddo."

Jane floated toward him, but Ari noted the hug was much stiffer, at least on Jane's part.

"Hi, Eddie," she said. "How are you?"

"Doing well, except..." He gestured to the building and shook his head. "It's awful."

"I'm so sorry. Were you close?"

"We knew each other pretty well." He turned to Ari and extended an enormous hand. "Eddie Navarro, CFO, winemaker-in-training and general pain in the butt."

Cleo pointed to the side door of the production building. "There's my assistant Denise with Sheriff Jerome."

A tall, lanky man dressed in a tan uniform with a white Stetson towered over a short-haired redhead with a pasty-white complexion. He looked unfazed and she looked ill. Ari guessed he was mid sixties, graying temples, with pronounced jowls from the deep creases on his face. His nose was red and Ari wondered if he was a drinker. His gaze was studious and swept past all four of them as if inquiring how Jane and Ari were connected to the vineyard.

Denise ran into Mina's arms. "It was horrible," she said. "He was lying there on the floor. He was holding a respirator, Mina." She looked young and was clutching a clipboard and a purple pen. It was clear she was fighting to remain professional when she just wanted to burst into tears.

Sheriff Jerome motioned for Mina and Cleo to follow him away from the crowd, and Mina pushed Ari and Jane along with them. "Ladies, we're just about done inside. Coroner has determined the time of death as somewhere between midnight and three a.m. Were any of your employees working at that time? I know during harvest you people work all night."

"That's true," Mina agreed, "but we had eight fermenting boxes going so the only person who came in and out was me."

"And when was that?"

"I'd have to check for the exact time, but it was around midnight. I would've seen him if he were there, but he wasn't."

"So no one else went in or out?"

"No," Mina confirmed. "We'd closed down the production room yesterday. There was a sign posted on the accordion door. Did you see that?"

"Yes, Denise showed it to us. It's still there. She's been very helpful. I don't know that we'll need to speak with her again, but we will need to talk to your other employees." He gestured toward Ari and pulled a notepad from his back pocket. "I could start with you, ma'am. What's your name?"

"I'm Ari Adams, but we just got here from Phoenix."

"Jane and Ari are visiting," Mina offered. "We're hosting Jane's upcoming wedding."

Sheriff Jerome smiled cordially. "Congratulations." He cleared his throat and asked Cleo and Mina, "Do you require safety equipment when working around the CO_2?"

"Of course," Mina snapped. "Always."

"And do you have security cameras?"

Cleo and Mina exchanged an anxious look. "We have two, one at the main gate and one outside the production room entrance," Mina said.

"I'll need to see that footage."

He made a note in his notebook and looked past them. He motioned for someone in the back, and a female officer clad in a matching tan uniform approached carrying an iPad. She looked Hispanic and was short, but her erect posture gave the illusion of height. Her dark brown hair was pulled back in a tight bun, making her serious expression that much more severe. As she drew closer, Ari saw the gold shield over her left pocket read *Deputy*. Ari wouldn't have been surprised to see her salute. Her entire presentation screamed ex-military.

"Yes, sir," she said with a nod, staring up at him.

He wiped a hand over his face and looked away. "Okay, so here's what we need to do, or rather, what you need to do."

"Yes, sir," she repeated, opening the iPad and withdrawing the stylus from her breast pocket.

"We need to review the security footage. Mira—"

"Mina, sheriff. It's *Mina*."

He raised a hand and looked at her. "My mistake. If you could provide us with the victim's HR file as well as a list of employees, that would be helpful."

Mina stepped forward into his personal space and Cleo put an arm on her shoulder as if she might need to be restrained. "Sheriff, can you please tell us what's going on? Why the heck was Dion in there? What's with all the questions, why do you need to interview the other employees? This was an accident, right?"

He scratched his head. Ari got the impression Sheriff Jerome was unaccustomed to handling serious crime since it occurred infrequently in sleepy Cheshire, Oregon. And she was certain she knew which crime had occurred.

When he finally met Mina's stare he said, "We'll need to speak with everyone. I'm nearly positive that someone else was nearby or in the room with Dion, and I'd bet my measly pension that someone murdered him."

Jane slammed the rented Range Rover's cargo door shut. "Okay, so you just need to solve this murder ASAP so we can get this weekend back on track."

Ari gazed at her dumbstruck. "Excuse me?"

Jane grabbed her suitcase and they headed for the guest quarters in the main portion of the chateau. "I don't mean to sound callous, but I know Mina and she's about to lose it."

"Finding a dead body at your business can do that to you," Ari said mildly. "I speak from experience." When Jane didn't reply with a witty comeback, Ari asked, "What else is going on?"

"A lot. Besides the incredible pressure of running a relatively new business, they've been worried about the harvest because of all the rain. Apparently it's been super hard on the grapes. That malbec they're making? They got a much smaller amount of those grapes from the grower, and they can't make as much wine. And on top of all that, Mina and Cleo have issues. Cleo's having an affair and Mina thinks it might be serious."

Ari stopped. "So, the second part of that last sentence is more concerning than the first part? Not in my world."

"Well, you and Molly don't have an open relationship."

"Uh, that's true. We don't. How did I not know this about Mina and Cleo? After all those Skype calls…"

Jane waved her off. "They don't discuss it much. But it works for them as long as both of them mind the ground rules."

"Which are?"

"Well, I don't know all of them, but a few really important ones are no traveling with that person, no kids involved, and either of them can call off the openness anytime they want."

"Meaning either of them can tell the third person to take a hike."

"Exactly. Mina's on the edge about this one but she's not said anything. It only became obvious in the last month, and with harvest going on she didn't want to deal with it, especially since the other woman is an employee."

Ari took a deep breath, remembering her own love life woes when there was a third—and fourth—person in the picture. "So did Mina name the other woman?"

"No, she wanted me to observe everyone this weekend and then tell her my thoughts."

"What?"

"She figures if I can correctly guess which woman Cleo is bonking, then it's probably too intense and she should reel Cleo back in. And if I can't, she'll just let it go."

Ari shook her head. "I don't get it, but that's okay."

Jane nodded. "Here's the context. Last year Mina had a short-lived relationship with someone from her past. That guy, Eddie, the one you just met."

"The one you knew from school?"

"Yeah. He and Mina were hot and heavy years ago, and I guess there were some unresolved issues."

"So Mina's bisexual."

"Yeah."

"And Cleo knew?"

Jane looked at her as if she were stupid. "Of course Cleo knew! Open relationships are just that. Open and honest." She groaned as they reached the back stairs, her gaze tracking the steep steps that led to a private guest entrance above the tasting room. She hefted her suitcase and said, "Just solve the damn murder."

By the time they'd finished unpacking, the vineyard had come alive. Their front door opened upon a hallway that overlooked the tasting room. A handful of employees in black pants and white shirts scurried about, preparing wines, stocking glasses, cleaning tables. Through the expansive glass doors was the grand patio where visitors could enjoy the light breeze, the crisp air, and the comfort of a padded chair. Ari imagined the doors remained closed during the chilly winters, but today promised to be a gorgeous fall day. Mina had all but guaranteed Jane pleasant weather if she came up this weekend.

Ari glanced at the office doors along the upper floor, the closest of which bore a gold plaque—*Emily Mills, General Manager.*

The lights were on but Emily wasn't in the office. Ari imagined she was dealing with the ongoing presence of law enforcement, allowing Mina and Cleo to focus on the harvest. Ari resisted the urge to test the door handle. She knew if it wasn't locked, she would likely step inside for quick snoop while Jane played lookout. Curiosity was indeed a blessing and a curse.

"Wanna take a peek?" Jane suggested.

Ari met her grin with a frown. "Am I that transparent?"

"To me? Yeah."

"It's a little too soon to be snooping through a stranger's desk." She pointed to the left. "Let's just stroll down this way and see what we see."

The next door was Cleo's office and next to hers was Eddie's. All of the offices had full glass fronts instead of walls, which Ari knew was supposed to promote transparency and collegiality between supervisors and employees, but in her experience, they also led to assumptions and paranoia when conversations could be seen and not heard.

"Where's Mina's office?" Ari asked.

"Maybe it's down with the production room?"

At the end of the hallway—and without a glass front—was the conference room. The door was ajar so Ari poked her head inside. The deputy was setting up a video camera for the interviews that Ari imagined would begin right away while everyone's memory was still fresh.

She looked up and said, "Hello. I'm Deputy Lacaba."

Her appearance was spit-shine, nothing out of place. Her warm brown eyes seemed lost in a stoic face just shy of hardened cement. Ari knew any attempt at humor would fall flat in the space between them. Sheriff Jerome had deputized a female cast in his own image.

Ari held out a hand. "We're Mina's friends, Ari and Jane. I don't think there's anything we could contribute. We just got here."

Deputy Lacaba crossed her arms. "On the contrary. I took a moment and Googled you, Ms. Adams."

"Please, call me Ari. And why would you Google me?"

"Let's just say that life in a small Oregon town isn't nearly as interesting as what happens in Phoenix, Arizona, especially in your life. Mina and Cleo have shared your…escapades for years."

Ari glared at Jane, who was busy studying her shoes. "I'm surprised to hear that, Deputy Lacaba. I'm not usually one to tell stories."

"From what I've read, you've helped the police solve many cases."

"No, not many. I'm a real estate agent."

"Well, Sheriff Jerome asked me to run point on this investigation."

"He must have a lot of faith and trust in your abilities."

She offered only a nod. "He's retiring next year and he wants me to get the job. We're just a small department but we have our pride. This is our jurisdiction and we're not gonna invite the big guns in until we hit a wall. Sheriff J will be *royally* pissed if that happens."

"I imagine so."

Jane looked up from buffing her nails. "Maybe Ari could help you?"

Ari gave her an elbow and Deputy Lacaba stood straighter, her hands resting on her gun belt. "That won't be necessary. My training as an MP as well as the sound procedures of the Lane County Sheriff's Department will guide this investigation." She studied Ari and Jane. "Are we clear?"

Jane's eyes grew wide and she returned the nail buffer to her purse. "Wow. You're all about taking charge, aren't you, Deputy…" She tried to read her nameplate.

"Lacaba," she replied. She looked at them tentatively and said, "I learned that you, Ari, were with Tucson PD for a year, and I inferred from some of the articles that you interfered with an investigation that led to your dismissal?"

She couldn't contain a laugh. "Not quite how that went, Deputy Lacaba, but it was a long time ago."

"Ms. Adams, just to be clear. You need to let me run the investigation and you go about your personal business this weekend."

"Absolutely," she said with a smile. "I guess we'll be going." She looked at Jane. "Off to plan the wedding."

Once they were in the hall and headed down the front staircase into the tasting room, Jane said, "She's something else."

"She just wants to get it right. Nothing wrong with that."

"Yeah, but she's gonna need your help."

Ari shook her head. "I think the only thing my help will do is get me a trip to a jail cell."

"No," Jane scoffed. "I didn't get that vibe from her."

"I'm not surprised."

Mina and a curvy blonde in a plum suit came around the corner. The blonde's hair cascaded over her shoulders effortlessly, but Ari guessed it took at least twenty minutes of effort to get it to look that natural. Chunky black glasses cut across her heart-shaped face, hiding her pretty blue eyes. She wore eyeliner and no other makeup except lipstick that matched her suit. Ari guessed she'd seen her thirtieth birthday but not much more. "It'll work," she said to Mina.

Mina sighed and shook her head. "Ari and Jane, this is my general manager, Emily Mills."

They all shook hands and Emily said, "I feel like I already know you, Jane. I went to college with Mina."

Jane nodded. "Yes, you're the Emily that broke into the frat house."

Emily shook her head and waved her red-painted pointer finger. "None of that was ever proven." She smiled at them and then said grimly to Mina, "If we close, it's at least a thousand bucks in tastings, vineyard merchandise, food, and of course, wine. That's the monetary cost, not to mention the lost goodwill. We have no way of telling the public we're closed today. A few dozen people will drive twenty miles from Eugene, find our front gate closed and start reviewing us on Yelp. It won't be pretty."

Mina sighed. "As you can probably guess, I'm trying to decide if we should remain closed today." She glared at Emily. "Given the fact that one of our employees, a well-known employee, has passed." She smiled again at Ari and Jane. "Care to weigh in?"

"That's a tough one," Ari said.

"Did I mention Facebook?" Emily asked. "Upset customers will be happy to write negative posts."

Mina groaned. "I hear you." She looked up to the second floor and held up an acknowledging hand. Everyone else followed her gaze. Deputy Lacaba stood outside the conference room looking down at them, a displeased expression on her face. "Shit, she's waiting to interview me." She turned to Emily. "Do what you think is best."

Emily smirked. "Exactly," she said, turning on her heel and heading up the stairs.

"Is everything okay with the grapes?" Jane asked.

"Yes, thank goodness," Mina said. "Everyone's back to work." She looked at Ari. "Any chance you can help Deputy Do Right?"

"Who?" Ari asked.

"That's what we call her. She's so by the book it's not even funny. I'm pretty sure she hasn't told a single joke in her life."

Ari shrugged. "That's okay. She just might be a very serious person."

"Yeah," Jane interjected. "She practically threatened to throw you in jail. Definitely serious."

"Really?" Mina asked. "Look, I'm really worried. My friend at the sheriff's department says she can't close a case unless Sheriff Jerome steps in."

"Does he favor her?" Ari asked.

"I guess. They're both ex-Marines."

"Once the Corps, always the Corps," Jane said, standing at attention and saluting.

Mina held back a laugh, and Ari stole a glance up at Deputy Lacaba who didn't look amused at all.

"It's not just that. There are stories. She might've been dishonorably discharged. Not sure about that one."

"How long has she been in the area?"

"Only a year. She started as a patrol officer, but she's moved up quickly. Literally saved a kid in a burning building."

Jane stole another look upstairs. Deputy Lacaba had returned to the conference room. "I take it you had dealings with her before?"

"One time. About six months ago. Had a drunk guy on a Friday night who wouldn't leave. She and another officer came and collected him."

"Doesn't sound too bad," Ari said.

"Look, I have to go talk with her, but Ari, I'd like you to come with me. I'll just say you're my moral support. Okay?"

Ari felt the acid churning in her stomach, unsure if it was hunger since she and Jane had skipped breakfast to make the flight, or if it was the idea of stepping anywhere outside the clearly demarcated lines Deputy Lacaba had drawn for her.

"Go on," Jane nudged. "I'll start checking out the venue and get us something to eat for when you come back."

"Okay," Ari said, "but if she kicks me out, I'm going willingly."

"Understood," Mina said as they climbed the stairs to the second floor. "I want to share some information with you about Dion before I go talk with her. I had a really interesting conversation with his brother a little while ago."

Mina marched up to Deputy Lacaba and stated, "I need twenty minutes. I've got two phone calls to return to vendors as well as retrieving the information that Sheriff Jerome asked me to get for you. Okay?"

Deputy Lacaba took a long inhale, possibly a breathing strategy to stay calm. "Fine. If you're going to be a while, then perhaps I could speak with someone else?"

"Sure," Mina said. "I'll have you talk to Peri. She's the other sommelier here so she worked closely with Dion."

"That would be fine," Deputy Lacaba said, wandering back into the conference room.

Mina looked down into the tasting room, grabbed her phone and tapped a contact. Ari heard Melissa Etheridge's voice over the workers' noise. Behind the bar, a woman with spiky maroon hair answered her phone.

"Hey, come on up here to the conference room and give your statement to the deputy, okay?" Peri looked up at Mina and nodded. Mina glanced at the closed conference room door and added, "Take your time getting up here." Peri offered a thumbs-up and Mina disconnected. "Come with me," she said to Ari, "into Cleo's office."

Without the nameplate on the door no one would know this was Cleo's office as there was only a computer desk and chair, two guest chairs and what looked like a very comfortable sofa. The only personal touch: a picture of Mina and Cleo next to the computer. Ari guessed Cleo spent most of her time outdoors with the vines and this office was just an open space, but Cleo, as the co-owner, deserved an office even if it was just to lie on the sofa and take a nap.

Mina slid behind the desk and woke up the computer. "I learned some things today that truly pissed me off. I didn't kill Dion, but if he was still alive, I'd think about it."

CHAPTER FOUR

They watched Peri pass by the glass front with a wave for Mina and a long appraising gaze at Ari. "Okay, come look at this," Mina said. "It's the security footage for last night." Ari came around the desk and knelt by the computer. "So here's Dion entering the production room and there's the time stamp that reads 1:05 a.m."

They watched Dion look nervously over his shoulder, pause, and then press the red control button on the side of the large accordion door. When the door was high enough, he ducked inside. Ari saw the inside of the production room for only a second as the door descended immediately.

"And that's it," Mina said. "I watched this three times and no one else comes in or out until Denise arrives. And here's where it gets interesting."

Mina put 6:14 a.m. in the search bar. The video forwarded and the time stamp whirred until it reached the moment when Denise came into the frame, shouldering a backpack, holding a travel mug of coffee in one hand and her phone in the other.

She had AirPods in her ears and she was singing "Hey Jude." Obviously it was just another day at work. She removed the laminated sign that warned people about the CO_2, pressed the red button, and nothing happened. It took her a few moments to realize the door hadn't ascended, so she pressed it again. And again. She swore, put her phone in the backpack and studied the button's metal housing.

"She's looking for the little light on the bottom of the box and checking to see if it's glowing. That shows her that electricity is still reaching the box."

Denise found the light wasn't glowing, swore again, and disappeared from view. "She's going to the breaker box which is located at the other end of the hallway." Mina pointed to the screen. "See the light is back on. Now she presses the button and it works."

The door ascended and she ducked inside.

"She doesn't bother to close the door because the danger has passed and we always leave it open. Now, this is the part that makes me feel so bad," she said sighing, on the verge of tears.

Mina moved the mouse and forwarded the timeline by a minute. Ten seconds later, a scream pierced the air and Denise ran through the open production door, a look of sheer terror on her face.

Mina sat back and covered her eyes. The tears came and Ari found a box of tissues in a drawer. Soon she had composed herself again. "I'm sorry."

"You've got no reason to be sorry. I'd be really worried about you if you didn't cry. It's obvious you care for these people. That's part of what makes you a good leader."

"You're very kind." Mina continued to dab her eyes. "I'm just sorry that you're seeing me like this. You hardly know me."

Ari nodded. "I'm not sure how long Peri will last in there, so you should probably tell me everything else you want to say before Deputy Lacaba comes looking for you."

Mina sniffled and said, "You're right. Part of the reason I picked Peri to go next is that I know where she was last night. She was in Salem fixing her mom's plumbing. She's got nothing to say. And I know she didn't have anything to do with this. Let me show you one more thing." She re-entered Dion's time, and he appeared back on the screen again with his backpack. "He goes in, but now watch what happens to the light under the button housing."

Within thirty seconds of Dion disappearing under the door, the light went off.

"Someone turned off the breaker after he went inside," Ari said.

"Yes. Someone else was there."

Ari scratched her head. "What'd you find out that made you so upset?"

"Not upset. Angry." She took a deep breath, dropped the tissue in the can and opened one of the desk drawers. "Okay, I had Denise make two copies of Dion's personnel file. One is for you."

Ari's eyes grew wide. "Oh. Okay."

"This will give you a little bit of history on him. Denise knew him fairly well, so she added some bio. Thirty-five, came from Paso Robles, California, parents were Greek immigrants who came to the US in the sixties. He worked at a vineyard with his brother, Apollo, before he came to Oregon. Apollo has a family and Dion adored his nephews and niece."

"Has someone told him?"

"Yeah, I talked with him just a little while ago and the Paso Robles sheriff had already been out to personally tell him. We didn't get very far in the conversation because he kept breaking down and saying how sorry he is about everything. He said that like ten times. I finally asked, 'What is this *everything* that you're sorry about?' He said, 'Well, you knew he was leaving your winery, right?'"

Ari held up a hand. "Wait. Dion was leaving Sisters Cellars?"

"Yeah," Mina said. Ari saw the fire smoldering in her green eyes. "After everything I've done for him." She took another cleansing breath. "More on that later. Anyway, Apollo told me he wanted to think about it some more but he had some ideas about who might be behind Dion's death."

"Really?"

"Yeah, and I told him you'd call him later."

"I...I would be calling him later?"

"Yeah, I figured it would be best for you to talk with him rather than hearing it secondhand from me. I need to be out in the production room. I've got nine tons of grapes out there!" She closed her mouth when she realized she was shouting. "I'm sorry. I know this isn't why you came here but I just can't trust the deputy to figure this out. Maybe she will. Maybe she won't. I'm just hoping you can ask some questions that might help her."

"I'm not sure she wants any help."

Mina grabbed her arm. The desperation in her eyes was obvious. "Please."

Ari nodded. "Well, it can't hurt to ask a few questions. I just don't want to step on her toes."

"I don't think it would matter," Mina snorted. "I'm pretty sure she wears steel-toed work boots."

Peri exited the conference room a minute later. She offered a thumbs-up to Mina through the front glass of Cleo's office and gave Ari a dreamy smile. Ari couldn't help but smile back. As she approached forty, it was nice to think that a youngster would find her attractive. Not that she would ever again do anything to jeopardize her relationship with Molly, but it was nice to know women still noticed her.

Deputy Lacaba strolled out of the conference room and spotted Mina and Ari in Cleo's office. Ari saw her wheels turning. Fortunately, the tableau looked innocent and not nearly as incriminating as it had fifteen minutes prior when she and Mina were huddled together by the computer. Now she sat in the chair across from the desk texting her boss Lorraine about a real estate transaction, while Mina was stretched out on the couch talking to Denise who was in the production room. Ari had no idea what Mina was talking about—something about a brix score. One thing for sure, the art of winemaking was far more complicated than she had ever thought.

When Mina saw the deputy, she rose from the couch, put on her shoes and slowly headed toward the door while she wrapped up her instructions to Denise.

"I'll be back in thirty minutes, tops. Hang on until then, okay?"

She pocketed her phone and the two of them met Deputy Lacaba in the hallway, who held up her hand in front of Ari. "This is a private interview."

"Uh, no. I've asked Ari to come for emotional support."

The deputy snorted, "What the hell are you trying to pull?"

"I'm not pulling anything. I am very concerned about your lack of sensitivity to me and my employees and this situation so I've asked Ms. Adams to join us. I don't see what the problem is since she had nothing to do with what's happened here. Are you going to tell me you don't allow other adult witnesses to have moral support during an interview? Or is this an interrogation?"

The challenge caught Lacaba off guard. She opened her mouth and then closed it when Mina continued her tirade.

"Do you really believe that I killed Dion to elevate my business? You think I killed him at the busiest and potentially most lucrative time of the year because it would somehow improve my bottom line?"

Ari set a hand on her shoulder. "Mina, Deputy Lacaba most likely wants to interview you so you can provide information no one else can provide."

Mina blinked at Ari and then looked at Lacaba. "Is that true?"

"Partly," Lacaba admitted. She gestured to Ari. "Now, if this were your wife—"

"My wife is busy making sure we can eat next year. My best friend is with my general manager doing what she came here to do, make her wedding plans. I'm sorry if my choice for supporter is unusual to you."

Lacaba was doing her best to hold it together. Ari noticed she flexed her hands, looked away, and breathed deeply. *Definitely a woman with anger issues.* When she finally met Ari's gaze, Ari said, "Look, I'm not here to jam you up."

"No, you're trying to steal my case," she whispered.

"No. I'm here because I'm the maid of honor. I'm right here standing next to Mina because we're friends."

"You're not friends."

"We most certainly are," Mina said. "We've been Skyping for...I don't know how long. Seven years?"

"Something like that."

Lacaba raised an eyebrow. "You really know her?"

"I do."

She hunched her shoulders and sighed. "Fine, let's do this."

Once they were situated in the conference room, Lacaba made introductions for the recorder and said, "Please state your name and position."

"I'm Mina Sommer, owner, winemaker, and CEO of Sisters Cellars Vineyard here in Cheshire, Oregon."

"And how do you know the deceased, Dion Demopolous?"

"Dion was my employee, and, I thought, my friend."

Lacaba glanced up from her notes. "Can you explain your last comment?"

"I just learned during a condolence call with his brother, Apollo, that Dion was quitting his job here after he passed the Master Sommelier test to take a position in Portland. I'm a little miffed about that since I've employed him for the last few years, given him time off to study, *paid* his registration to take the somm test, bought his plane ticket, and paid for his lodging in Dallas where the next test will be given."

Lacaba tapped her iPad, her gaze flicking between Ari and Mina. Ari guessed the sheriff's department had learned of Dion's job change when they talked with the officer who made the home visit to Apollo. And that Lacaba had assumed Mina knew, giving her motive to kill him.

"So you're saying you had no idea he was leaving until just a short while ago."

She nodded. "That's exactly what I'm saying. He told me nothing of the sort. Didn't even hint about it."

Lacaba grimaced and said, "You've explained that yesterday the production room was closed because most of the grapes were fermenting, creating unhealthy amounts of CO_2, correct?"

"Yes. We're always prepared for when that occurs, but it isn't something we can always predict. We don't know exactly how many grapes we'll pick, and we don't always know the transportation schedule of the grapes we buy elsewhere."

"But everyone knew the production room was closed yesterday."

"Yes. Everyone, including Dion, knew that no one was to enter the production room without my permission." She shifted in the chair and poured some water. "Someone, usually Cleo or myself, has to check on the grapes several times during the day but that person wears safety attire, and someone almost always accompanies her and waits outside. When the CO_2 is like it was yesterday, nobody is in there for longer than three minutes. That's it. From what I'm piecing together, I went in around midnight and did a check. He certainly wasn't in there or I would've found...his body."

"Did he know when you'd check the grapes during the night?"

"Yes. It's always the same. Every four to six hours. We fudge a little on the overnight check because we're usually exhausted. I went in at midnight and then Denise showed up around six a.m."

"Did someone—Cleo—accompany you?"

Mina stiffened. "For that check, no. Cleo was already gone for the evening. I did it myself."

"For the record, you had no knowledge that Dion had entered the room."

"Absolutely not. I don't even know how he got in."

"Who has keys to the building?"

"Only four of us: myself, Cleo, Emily, and Denise."

"Has there been any occasion when a different employee might be issued a temporary key?"

After a long drink Mina said, "Not really a temporary key, but we've given our keys to other staff to run an errand, retrieve something that was left in the office...that kind of stuff. We have a level of trust established with our employees." She shrugged. "If we can't trust people, and some of these people I've known most of my life, then we'd go out of business."

"Do you have any idea how Dion would've gained entrance to that room?"

"The only thing I can figure is that someone set her keys down and he picked them up."

Lacaba looked up from her notes. "Can you think of a reason he would risk his safety and go in the room despite your direct order not to?"

Mina broke her hard stare and looked away. In a haggard voice she said, "I've thought of nothing else all morning. I don't understand. I thought he and I had a great relationship. If there was something he needed, like something for his studying, he could've just asked."

Lacaba reached for a box of tissue and set it next to Mina. "I know this is a tough question, but is it possible Dion might've been doing something…something to harm the business?"

"No. I have no clue why he was going in there and I don't understand why he took a job in Portland, but I can't believe for a moment that…" She covered her mouth with her hand and regained control of her emotions. "He and I had a special relationship."

Lacaba raised her hand. "Let's talk about that for a moment." She pulled out a framed photo and handed it to Mina. "Do you recognize this photo?"

"I do," she said with a sad smile. "This was the day our pinot noir won the Willamette Valley Invitational. What a great day that was. Put us on the map." She looked at Lacaba, puzzled. "Where did you get this? What does this picture have to do with anything?"

"I don't know that it does," Lacaba said slowly, "but we did a search of Dion's cottage an hour ago, and he kept it on his nightstand. I thought the location was…"

"Unusual for a gay man?" Mina concluded. Lacaba took a deep breath and looked embarrassed. "My relationship with Dion was complicated. About five months ago, Cleo and I asked Dion to be our sperm donor. After harvest we were going to try and start a family."

Mina glanced at Ari—and her surprised expression. Jane had never mentioned Mina and Cleo wanted children.

Mina added, "Nobody knew about that—the sperm donation—so please don't discuss it with other employees."

Lacaba's pause was thoughtful. Then she asked, "Is that the *only* reason he had this picture on the nightstand?"

Mina shook her head. "After we asked him to be the donor, he confessed that he had a crush on me. He knew I was bi, and he knew that Cleo and I, to some degree, have an open relationship. He asked me if I could ever feel the same for him. I said no. I was only interested in him as a friend. It was awkward for a couple months, and then I thought we just worked through it. He didn't mention it again and there wasn't any awkwardness until…well, until I picked up with Eddie again."

"Eddie Navarro, your CFO?" Lacaba clarified.

"Yeah. We had a thing a long time ago and we both knew there were some residual feelings that we never handled. I won't give you the whole story, but we had an affair for about three months. That was when it was weird for me and Dion. I rejected him but I didn't reject Eddie." She raised her hands. "I get it. As a spouse or partner, I'm not so great."

"Did you and Dion ever talk about his feelings?"

Mina nodded. "Somewhat. Everyone may not like my choices, but I own them. I'm proud to say I'm honest. With Dion, I tried to be a great friend. I saw his potential. He had one of the sharpest palates I've ever seen. He could taste a wine and name all of the ingredients, even the subtlest additions. I supported him as he prepared for the exam and he was going to become a Master Sommelier, which would've been a huge deal." She stared at Lacaba. "Do you know anything about the Portland job?"

"No," she replied. "We don't have any details. We just know he'd been making trips to Portland."

"Son of a bitch," Mina murmured. She laughed mirthlessly. "Well, I feel like a complete fool. Let me just take back everything I said. Apparently our relationship was about to take a different turn."

Lacaba remained silent and Ari sensed the interview had stalled—without her asking the most important question.

Finally Lacaba said, "I know you're very upset, but I need to ask where you were at one a.m."

Mina looked as though someone had just fed her rotten meat. "What are you suggesting? You think that I… I can't even finish that sentence."

"I'm sorry to ask."

Mina ran a hand through her hair. "I was asleep—alone. Well, Dexter was home too."

"Was Cleo there?" Lacaba asked casually.

Mina stared at the table and said quietly, "I'd guess she was with Emily Mills, the general manager, but you'd have to ask her."

Lacaba glanced at Ari, who had schooled the surprise off her face. *So Emily is Cleo's lover.*

Lacaba cleared her throat. "Can you think of anyone who has threatened Dion or would want to harm him?"

"Not really. I mean the sommelier study group is always going at it, but I think that's about energizing each other as much as it is about criticizing one another. Dion was known for helping people with the test." Her gaze flitted between them. "Have you seen his blue notebooks?"

"I have."

"He started making those as a study tool for himself and then shared them with others. I think there was even talk about him publishing a lot of his stuff as test prep materials. A few of the Master Somms used his ideas and it increased their pass percentage." She folded her hands on the table and leaned forward. "May I ask you a question?"

"Of course."

"Do we know the official cause of death?"

"The ME strongly suspects CO_2 poisoning since he had no wounds and there was no sign of struggle. We also found a half-filled flask on his person. Was he a day drinker?"

Mina shook her head and looked surprised. "Wow. No, he never drank anything else. Said it messed up his palate, which is totally true. If he did that all the time he'd probably fail the tasting portion of the Master Somm test."

"Understood," Lacaba said. "Any other questions?"

"None right now." She shook her head again. "Wow. I just can't believe it."

Lacaba reached under the table into a briefcase and withdrew a red binder. "Have you ever seen this?"

Mina cocked her head to one side. "No. Does it belong to Dion?"

"It does." Lacaba pushed it toward her. "Can you take a look at it and give me your impressions?"

Mina flipped through the pages. "It seems like a sample book of resources so that test takers would have an idea of what a weight tag looked like or the list of yeasts available to a vintner. There are some mockups for labels as well. Here's one for our soon-to-be-released malbec, Sabrosa." A purple splotch filled the center of the label, the word Sabrosa printed in the center with a fun font. "This was an early design. Cleo thought it looked too much like a Rorschach test. In the end we went with a fancier look."

She picked up the Respite label. "Not sure why he's got the competition in here, but whatever…"

"Any idea how he would've acquired that?"

"I'm guessing from Racy. He's in the somm study group that meets here four nights a week, sometimes more."

"You let the competition in your house? That's very generous."

"I try." Mina leaned back, looking completely unraveled. "Look, this business is hard enough without enemies. I avoid bad relationships if I can, but sometimes I can't."

"Who are your enemies?" Lacaba asked with a shrug.

"I only have one I can think of. John Graham, and even then I'd call him a frenemy. We need each other so we stay connected. He's the one who sells me my malbec grapes."

"So what's the problem?"

Mina rolled her eyes. "So ridiculous. He got angry because Dexter was chosen as the cover dog for the Vineyard Dogs of Willamette Valley calendar—two years in a row. He thought his golden retriever, Chardonnay, should've been picked." Mina held up her hands. "Now she's a pretty dog, but Dexter is an all-American mutt cutie pie." Mina looked at Ari who smiled in agreement. Ari would put Dexter on any calendar cover every year.

"But seriously," Lacaba said, "you can't get past that?"

Mina shrugged. "I could, but Eddie, my CFO who picks up the grapes, said John's not over it and that John would prefer that Eddie and Berto, my other viticulturist, continue to be the intermediaries between us. So, fine." She glanced at her watch again. "Wow. The day is going fast. How many more questions? I know my alibi isn't great, but I'm not worried because I didn't kill him. I had too much invested in him to wish him harm. Since I didn't know he was shafting me, I don't see a motive here."

"That's all I have for now." Lacaba glanced at Ari and said, "As Ms. Adams mentioned, I see you more as a resource. It's likely I'll need to ask you further questions to help with context."

"Of course." Mina rose and started for the door, then turned and said, "Here's one more thing: when Dion finally told me he was leaving, I would've thrown a huge guilt trip on him and used my most persuasive tactics to change his mind, including the carrot that he'd hardly see his child. I'm not so sure he would've ever made it to Portland."

CHAPTER FIVE

"Walk with me," Mina said as she and Ari hustled down the stairs and through the tasting room. "There's a little more I want to share with you."

Ari put her hand on Mina's arm. "Wait." They stopped and Ari said, "Does Jane know about the baby? About Dion?"

Mina looked guilty. "Not yet. We were waiting until you got here. I wanted Jane to meet Dion because otherwise I would've gotten a shitload of grief from her."

Ari laughed. "True."

"Please don't say anything."

"I won't. That's yours and Cleo's story to tell."

"Thanks." Mina gave her a quick hug and they continued through the tasting room. "While you and Jane were unpacking, Cleo and I walked the property with the sheriff and deputy." She gestured to the vineyard. "The first thing you need to know is how dark it is out here at night. You can barely see in front of you." She headed to the French door that led outside. "Denise found this door unlocked this morning. Once Dion got inside the main building, he had access to the production room since everything is connected. This whole place is a Frankenstein amalgamation of my uncle's eclectic visions."

"And you really don't have any idea why he was in there?"

"Not the slightest."

"So either he had a key or someone let him in."

"Well, Emily is hawkish about those keys. If I lose a key, she has permission to yell at me. More than likely it was intentionally unlocked so he'd have a way in."

She looked at the double-sided deadbolt. "So he couldn't have locked it either."

"Right."

"Which means someone could've followed him in, and the door would've remained unlocked until the person with the key returned to lock it."

Mina nodded. "Or that person just could've left it unlocked through the night. We don't have a lot of set procedures during harvest. There's too many people in and out."

Ari followed her into the event room. "We found a mess in here," Mina told her. "That corridor leads to the production area. Emily does double duty as the event coordinator and she'd laid everything out here for the bridal shower that's happening today. But this morning, some things weren't on the tables correctly—and stuff was on the floor. Plus, they found Dion's phone in here."

"What? His phone?"

"Well, everything is completely picked up now, but it was a mess this morning. The crime scene techs found it on the table. I'm thinking he kept all the lights off but he came through here and knocked stuff over. He used his flashlight app to pick everything up but he left it accidentally."

"That's really unfortunate since it would've been very helpful when he got locked in the production room."

"My thought exactly."

Ari followed her down the hallway. Mina pointed out the electrical box and they went down the corridor and into the production room, stopping next to a wall of safety equipment.

Ari saw a row of masks on pegs, wading boots on the floor, goggles in a box, and rubber jackets on more pegs.

"We have a lot of safety equipment. But last night there was only one mask."

"Where were the rest of them?"

"Denise found them in a plastic bag in my office, which was locked—and someone had plugged the lock."

"What?"

"No one could've opened that door except the person with the plug puller. She had to break the glass to get in. And the topper? The one safety mask that was up here, the one Dion put on, had a gash in the respirator."

"So it was worthless."

"Completely."

Ari studied the vast building with large aluminum tanks, huge plastic boxes, and steel machinery. It was too much to take in all at once. "Was there any other way out?"

"There's the back door to the production room but if the electricity was off, it wouldn't open."

"Someone made sure he had no way out."

"Yes," Mina agreed. "Someone made sure he was trapped."

"That's called premeditation. This was a meticulously planned murder."

Mina had to get back to harvest, but she gave Ari the address of Dion's cottage. Apparently he lived with an elderly divorcee named Frankie Smith. Mina had already called and Frankie was expecting Ari. She asked about Jane, but Mina assured her that Jane was busy and happy.

Ari was relieved to climb into the Range Rover and just sit for a minute to absorb the morning's events. She rested her head on the steering wheel. *How did I get into this mess?* She programmed Frankie's address into the GPS, and once she was rolling, she tapped her Bluetooth and called Molly.

"So how's the case?" were Molly's first words.

"Wh-What?" Ari asked. "How did you know?"

Molly groaned. "You're serious? I was kidding! Oh, honey, really?"

"Yes. Do you have a few minutes?"

Ari shared with Molly everything that had happened, Dion's background, all the facts, her encounter with Deputy Lacaba, and Mina pleading with her to help. "I couldn't say no."

"I really don't want you to wind up in jail."

"I would like to avoid that as well. Help me. What are your thoughts?"

"Well, first off, why would anyone want this guy dead?"

"Maybe someone was jealous of his future. Maybe he knew something." Ari leaned back in the seat. "There's definitely some drama happening in this place."

"Like what specifically?"

"Well, maybe I'm just being a traditionalist, but Mina and Cleo have an open relationship. What do you think of that?"

"Are you asking if I want *us* to have an open relationship?"

"No!" Ari's voice reverberated about the vehicle. "Please, never."

Molly laughed. "I guess it's up to the couple."

"Yeah, that's my opinion, but they've been involved with employees. I just think it's straining the work environment."

"No doubt. You're right about the drama then."

"Dion's behavior doesn't make any sense. Why would you willingly enter an area that was quarantined? An area you knew was hazardous to your health? According to Mina, the fermentation process completed this morning. Everyone's back in there right now. Why not wait until then?"

Molly thought while Ari listened to voices in the background—Molly's security employees arriving for work. Eventually she said, "Unless you didn't want anyone around. Maybe Dion wanted to be there when he was sure he'd be alone. Maybe he planned to sabotage the harvest, somebody learned of his plan, and they took revenge on him before he could execute it."

"Would someone really kill over a bunch of grapes?"

"Uh, yeah. You haven't met Beige. He's a new guy on our team."

"And his name is Beige? Seriously?"

"It is. And his family has been involved in the wine industry in Napa for decades. He's got all kinds of stories. Here's the thing about the wine industry. It's one of the hardest, most unpredictable and expensive industries there is. These owners put their lives—and usually their life savings—into these vineyards. At least fifty percent of their success depends on the whims of Mother Nature, so they are fierce about controlling what they can. So, yes. People would kill to protect their grapes."

"Huh. What you just said gives Mina and Cleo motive. Couple that with the fact that Dion was leaving. Mina was completely in shock about it so I don't think she knew. But one other thing. Dion had agreed to be their sperm donor."

"Well, that adds to the drama," Molly deadpanned. "But what about Cleo? Did she know he was leaving?"

"Not sure."

"If she did," Molly continued, "she may have made certain he couldn't leave."

As a motive for taking someone's life it was hardly rational, Ari thought as she signed off with Molly, but nothing could be discounted at this stage.

CHAPTER SIX

Ari relaxed and enjoyed the scenery as she headed to a residential area on the outskirts of Cheshire. Long stretches of green space separated the homes, and she marveled at the individuality of every property. While all the houses were made of the same sturdy siding that could endure the wet Oregon winters, each boasted its own charm via the eclectic taste of the owner. One expanse of land was a museum of rusted and rustic tractors that looked as if they'd just stopped working one day and were left where they stalled. Another farmer was clearly a master of the chainsaw and his life-size tree carvings of bears and birds were available for sale. And two cannabis growers made their presence known—with enormous signs and the strong smell of weed.

An abundance of animals enjoyed the early fall weather. A herd of cows lounged in a green field. Flocks of sheep dotted a hillside and a murder of crows lined a wooden fence. But she squirmed at the roadkill—first a raccoon and then a squirrel.

Suddenly she realized something was in the road ahead—a lot of somethings. She slowed and then stopped in front of a rafter of turkeys. Most of them seemed to understand the objective was to cross the road, but a few continually veered left then right, finally making it across by the sheer momentum of their peers pushing them forward.

"I'm completely amused," she said as she accelerated again.

She pulled up in front of a well-kept gray and white Craftsman home complete with an inviting brick walkway, wraparound porch, gorgeous dormer windows that ensured a bright and airy second story, and a teal front door. *Not a color I would've thought a man like Dion would pick.*

She was climbing the stairs to the porch when the teal door swung open. A short white-haired woman in jeans, a fuchsia top and polished cowboy boots said, "Well, hello."

Ari bit her lip. *Not like any elderly divorcee I've ever known.*

"Hello, Ms. Smith."

Frankie's handshake was powerful and her deep gray eyes matched her house color. Her all-white hair was coiffed in a chignon and she wore full makeup including turquoise fingernail polish that matched the Native American jewelry that circled her wrist. Diamond studs adorned her ears and the necklace around her neck matched the stones. She was smashing. Ari's grin only cracked when Frankie's gaze suggested she wanted to eat Ari up. "How do you do, Ms. Adams."

"Call me Ari, please."

"And I'm Frankie." She hesitated a beat and added, "Shall we?" She motioned to a rattan and wicker loveseat while she took the matching chair. As an afterthought she said, "Should I make some lemonade?"

"No, no," Ari said. "I believe Mina asked if I could see Dion's space?"

"She did. I should warn you, when the cops opened the door this morning..." Frankie gestured, her long nails extending like talons.

Ari frowned. "Is it that bad?"

"You'll have to judge for yourself."

"Did you know Dion well?"

Her playful gaze extinguished. "Only professionally as his landlady." Her hand went to her temple. "I can't believe this has happened. Is it true he died in the winemaking room?"

Ari nodded.

Frankie leaned forward in the chair, elbows resting on her knees. "Dion didn't tell me his deepest, darkest secrets and we didn't go out for brunch or anything like that, but we were cordial. Sometimes we'd chat if I was out in the garden or if I was unloading groceries, he'd always help." She leaned back. "An ideal tenant for sure, especially given the odd hours he kept."

"How odd?"

"Oh, you know. He'd get home at all hours after studying for that darn test. Sometimes he complained he was married to the study group. I guess in a way they were. Then there were the mornings he'd get up at three thirty or four..."

"Ms. Smith, do you know why he would get up so early, especially if he was staying out late?"

Frankie wagged a finger. "I told you to call me Frankie."

Ari couldn't stop the heat she felt in her cheeks. "You did."

Frankie waited until Ari looked up before she said, "It was only the last month or so, but a couple times a week he was driving up to Portland. He'd leave before sunrise and return here by noon or one p.m. before he went out to the vineyard for his shift and the study group meeting."

"Did he say why he was going up there?"

"He told me he'd met someone and mornings were the only time they could connect. I knew that was bullpucky."

"Why are you so sure?"

Frankie cocked her head to the side and grinned. "Because when people are in love, you can tell. Are you in love right now, Ari?"

Ari laughed and rubbed the back of her neck. "Very much so."

Frankie nodded, her grin still plastered on her face. "I can tell." She cleared her throat. "Dion was not. Everyone knew the thing he loved most was being a sommelier, and I'm guessing those trips to Portland were related to his professional goals."

"You're probably right," Ari said. "He'd accepted a job in Portland. He was most likely preparing for that."

Frankie pointed at her and winked. "There you go."

"When was the last time you saw him?"

"Two days ago." She looked away and shook her head. "There was something off. I could tell he was stressed. I wrote it off as testing nerves." She tapped the armrest, deep in thought and finally gasped, "It sucks to get older. He said something…weird. Now what was it?" She finally sighed and when she looked up, Ari saw a glimmer of despair in her otherwise confident, steel-gray eyes. "It'll come to me," she promised. "Now let me show you Dion's cottage. Or rather, Dion's battle camp."

She went inside her house to get the key and Ari strolled into the spacious and pristine backyard, the perimeter lined with a variety of rosebushes, an artistic border of wood chips meeting the grass. A vegetable garden covered much of the northern yard, and Ari imagined Frankie kept her incredible figure by tending to all of her plants. The cottage Dion rented sat to the south and looked like a mini-version of Frankie's house, complete with front porch.

She came out the back door, carrying a keyring with a few dozen keys, and they walked to Dion's place. "Dion's lived here for the past three years, so I haven't used a key in forever… well, until this morning." She sorted through them until she found the one. As she slipped it into the lock, she said, "I've never seen anyone cram more stuff into four hundred square feet. Welcome to a testament to a one-track mind." She glanced upward and added, "Sorry, Dion."

They could barely open the front door. Directly in front of them was a sofa piled high with books. A sea of yellow sticky notes that looked like tongues marked hundreds of pages. Ari glanced at several but couldn't discern Dion's organizational system of letters and numbers. Bookcases of varying heights were everywhere, and while the subject matter was the same—wine—the shelves were categorized: Geography, Table Etiquette, Varietals, etc. *There's an order to the chaos.*

"Would you like some help?" Frankie asked. "I've always fancied myself a sleuth."

"Well, yes, please. Can you tell me how long Deputy Lacaba was here and was she with anyone else?"

"She brought another officer. They were here fifteen minutes, tops." Frankie threw her chin toward the interior. "I think they found all of that…a little daunting."

"Did they say if they'd be back? They didn't tell you it was a crime scene?"

"No, and I asked William, the other officer, and he said they had what they came for and would contact someone about his personal things."

Ari glanced inside again and nodded. The left path led to the kitchen. Wineglasses of all shapes and sizes covered the counters. Many bore pink sticky notes with red scribbles. The path to the right led through an archway, probably to Dion's bedroom and bathroom. It was impossible to take it all in at once.

"Where should we begin?"

"It's overwhelming if you look at it like this, but most likely very little of this has anything to do with his death. Somewhere are his personal papers, his bills. Did you see what they took?"

Frankie looked away. "A red notebook, a photo, and a box. I have no idea what was in it."

"Did they find his computer?"

"No. And they asked me about it. I said he had a laptop."

"Probably it was in his car. In my experience as a real estate agent, a good place to start with houses that look like they belong to a hoarder is usually right inside the front door. Even collectors keep things like their car keys in a place where they can find them in a hurry."

Frankie pointed to a small table nearby. "Here's his mail and some other stuff."

Most of it was junk mail, but Ari also found a few credit card receipts—two for a grocery store in Cheshire and one for Carlotta's Diner in Phoenix, Oregon. Amid the magazines were two programs for the Laurelwood Wine Challenge. The competition had occurred two weeks prior, and when Ari scanned the names of participating vineyards and winemakers, she was surprised that Sisters Cellars wasn't listed—but Dion's name was, as a judge.

"Find anything?" Frankie asked.

"Just a program. Dion judged a wine contest recently."

Frankie looked at the cover and nodded. "The Laurelwood. Yeah, that's a big deal here."

"If it was a big deal, why didn't Mina enter any of her wine?"

"Good question. I don't know. Only thing I found was a dog-eared article in one of the magazines."

She showed Ari the page Dion had flagged. The bottom half was an ad for a jeweler in Roseburg, and the top half was a restaurant review of Racy's, a new wine bar in Eugene. Ari assumed the dreadlocked man in the photo that accompanied the article was Racy, who held a bottle of wine. She read the first paragraph and noticed the glowing words "trendy," and "upscale." The final paragraph was equally appreciative with a nod to the wines served there.

"Let's make a pile of things to take," Ari suggested, "starting with the article and program. Why don't you look around here and I'll head to the bedroom?"

"All right."

She took a quick photo of the receipts and set them back on the table. In the event the deputy intended to return, Ari wanted to leave any possible clues behind.

The narrow path paralleled the back wall, which was covered by a mural-size world map. At least a hundred pushpins, each with a colored flag, were clustered at the likely wine regions of the world—France, Australia, Argentina, Napa, Sonoma and Oregon—while smaller clusters covered the less likely locations such as Willcox, Arizona. Ari imagined each of the colors had a meaning most likely tied to the stack of three-inch blue binders that sat on a table beneath the map.

She went under an arch to a tiny foyer, flipped the light switch and saw a linen closet on one wall and entrances to the bedroom and bathroom. The closet contained no linens, just more blue notebooks and books on wine. These books were much older judging by the spines, and she guessed they were of less use in the study process.

She opened the bathroom door and blinked. "Okay, not expecting this."

The bathroom was charming and pristine. The vanity's blue and white ceramic tile looked new with clean grout and contained a pure white sink and a sparkling chrome faucet. Small gray hexagon tiles covered the floor and white bead board met a dark shade of blue paint halfway up the wall. The shower was as clean as the vanity and covered in the same ceramic tile. She was surprised to find a backpacking magazine on the toilet tank. *The one place where there's no wine, not a hint of it anywhere. In fact, the style is all Frankie.*

She crossed into the bedroom, unsurprised that yet again the door barely opened. A queen-size bed swallowed most of the room's square footage, neatly made with a manly brown comforter. A throw pillow sat in the middle of the bed proclaiming, *Life is Too Short to Drink Cheap Wine.*

A bank of windows provided a beautiful eastern view of the distant trees, and Ari knew if this were her bedroom, she'd lie in bed every morning and watch the sun come up. On the floor underneath the windows were stacks of wine magazines with the familiar yellow sticky notes protruding.

Ari muttered, "This guy must've bought them by the gross."

A small dresser sat across from the bed, its drawers rifled through. A few socks littered the floor, undoubtedly from Deputy Lacaba's search. Ari quickly scoured the contents, finding nothing of interest but impressed that she'd finally found a man who folded his underwear. His closet was equally tidy. Clothes neatly draped on wooden hangers. Shoes lined up on the floor. She felt inside the pockets of his pants and came up with a slip of paper in the back pocket of his jeans. Written in Comic Sans font was the message, *Tomorrow. After 8 PM.* She set it on the bed and took a photo before returning it to the pocket. On the top shelf was a black plastic file case.

"Yes," she said, pulling it down. But her excitement was short lived. While it did contain his personal papers, they were standard. His social security card. His birth certificate. High school diploma. She closed it up and after a momentary debate with herself, returned it to the closet.

The other side of the bed had more stacks of magazines, blue binders, a banker's box of office supplies including nine packs of sticky notes. At the bottom of the box was the 2019 Willamette Valley Vineyard Dog Calendar. Dexter's smile was contagious and Ari smiled as well.

"Hey, Ari," Frankie called. "I might've found something."

Ari threaded her way out to the kitchen. Frankie had cleared away several of the wineglasses and was studying a small notebook. "Look at this page and tell me what you make of it. I think the first column is dates, but most everything else is blank."

Dion had created a numerical grid. Down the side were what appeared to be five dates: *8-24, 9-1, 9-7, 9-26,* and *10-4.* The rest of the grid was blank, except for one date, *9-7,* where the entire row was completed. The second column had *179.5* filled in, and the third column read *101.5.* The fourth spot on that row had a checkmark.

Ari pointed to the last column. "Maybe because the number in the third column was smaller than the number in the second column, he put a checkmark."

"What do you make of it?" Frankie asked.

"It's almost like he's trying to prove something," Ari said. "But he hasn't gotten very far." She pulled out her phone and took a picture of the page. "Where did you find this?"

"Well," Frankie said, looking embarrassed, "I remembered something about when we built this cottage. My wife was insistent there be a secret place, a panel, a safe, something for valuables. She was a little paranoid." She laughed and said, "I did manage to talk her out of the panic room. Can you imagine that? Out here? In the middle of nowhere?" She waved a hand. "Anyway, let me show you this."

On the counter sat the plastic container holding silverware, the drawer where it belonged open. She reached into the back and Ari heard a click before she pulled out the false bottom.

"I told him about this drawer when he rented the place. He thought it was cool, and that's where I found this notebook." She held it out. "Want to take it?"

"No, I want you to put it back. I want you to call Deputy Lacaba and tell her you remembered something, which is somewhat true. She'll take it."

Frankie cracked a grin. "You're really quite the Girl Scout."

Ari blushed. "I'm not looking to best the deputy. I want her to succeed."

They left and Frankie locked the place up. "Might I offer you a lemonade and a piece of homemade banana bread before you go?"

She needed to get back to the vineyard, but her stomach was pleading for food. "That would be lovely. Thanks."

"Wonderful! You sit on the porch and I'll be back in a jiff."

While Ari waited, she studied the chart Dion had made and the note he'd stuck in his jeans. She had no idea what day was actually "tomorrow." It might not relate to his death at all, but her gut told her tomorrow had been yesterday.

Frankie returned with a tray. "I remembered what I wanted to tell you."

"Please," Ari encouraged, wasting no time biting into the heavenly banana bread.

"Dion asked me about Berto. Right out of the blue. Wanted to know if I still trusted him and if I thought he was losing it."

"Who is Berto?" Ari asked.

"Berto is my ex-husband and still a good friend. He's also a viticulturist at Sisters. I guess you could say he mentors both Cleo and Mina. He and I just weren't compatible." She cracked another of her seductive smiles and added, "Once he realized my interests were on both sides of the fence, he left. He couldn't deal with it."

"I'm sorry," Ari offered.

She waved it off. "Don't be. We're better friends," she said wistfully.

"What'd you say when he asked about Berto?"

"I said I trusted him with my life, but yes, unfortunately, I think he's losing it."

"Did Dion have many visitors out here?"

She held Ari's gaze while she pondered. "None that I recall. If I think of anything else, I'd be happy to call you. Can I reach you at the vineyard?"

"Until Sunday. We're just here while my best friend makes her wedding plans. I'm the maid of honor."

"And you're out here working on a murder investigation instead."

Ari shrugged. "Mina asked for my involvement." They stood and Ari said, "Thanks for your help and the banana bread. It was delicious."

Frankie walked Ari to the Range Rover. "It was a pleasure meeting you, Ari."

The sexual energy between them was obvious. "You as well," Ari said.

"Your girlfriend...or wife...is one lucky woman."

Ari reddened again. "I'm the lucky one."

Frankie boldly caught a strand of Ari's air and twirled it. "Some folks always say, 'if I were twenty years younger.' I completely disagree. Oh, no. I'd be happy to take a walk with you anytime, Ari, but I don't wander onto another woman's field, at least not without her permission."

"I don't think that would fly with Molly."

"I thought not. You strike me as a monogamous person."

"I think so."

"Then this has just been a delightful distraction during a rather depressing day."

"Agreed."

Ari slid into the car and Frankie shut the door. She pulled away and Frankie watched her go, hands in her back pockets, her one foot slightly turned as if she were posing for a picture.

Once she'd turned onto the highway Ari laughed and cried, "Oh, my God! That woman is...indescribable."

She knew she should be thinking about the case, but she couldn't get her mind off Frankie. She couldn't wait to tell Molly about her. She felt as though she knew her, but she couldn't quite figure out how—until she rolled into the parking lot and saw the Rover's reflection in a window. It was the only car Jane would ever rent on a trip. "Chick magnet," she had insisted.

Then it hit her and she burst out laughing. *Frankie is Jane in thirty years!*

CHAPTER SEVEN

Emily had apparently decided to open the tasting room, setting aside Mina's concerns. Ari wandered in. No sign of Jane amidst all of the visitors.

Despite enjoying a hunk of the best banana bread she had ever tasted, she was still hungry. She ambled over to a free space at the bar. There were no stools for good reason. People could do a tasting at the bar with the strong suggestion that the stay should be short and the turnover abundant. Anyone wanting a full glass of wine could drift to the indoor tables or out to the patio. She grabbed the menu and quickly settled on the fruit and nut tray with a glass of pinot noir.

Peri, the female bartender who'd come to Mina's aid that morning, smiled in her direction as she poured the next wine for the couple beside Ari. "This is our cab. Tell me what you smell."

The woman said, "I smell vanilla. Maybe some black currant?"

"Wow," Peri said. "I'm impressed. Those are both correct. Enjoy. I'll be back soon." She stepped over to Ari. "Hi. You're Ari, right? Mina's friend?"

"Close. Technically, I'm Mina's friend's friend, but I'm also Mina and Cleo's virtual friend. If that makes sense."

She reflected and said, "Yes, it does."

Ari placed her food and drink order and when Peri returned with Ari's pinot, she said, "I'm Peri. I don't think we've been officially introduced, although I saw you this morning with Mina."

Peri's spiky maroon hair stood at attention above the face of a model—angular with a strong chin. Her smooth skin was scrubbed clean and she wore no makeup. She glanced at the couple absorbed in their critique of the cabernet and whispered to Ari, "I once overheard Jane tell Mina that you solve murders."

"That's an overstatement. My partner says trouble finds me."

"Well, then you've quite a knack for that. I'd say you found a heap of it."

"Did you know Dion?"

"Oh, yeah. I'm the other somm, so I was like his work wife."

"I heard he was about to take a big test in a couple of weeks."

She nodded. "Several of us were—are. For the first time ever, the Willamette Valley has five people entered." She frowned. "I guess that's four now. It feels weird to say that."

"I get it. So four of you could become Master Sommeliers?"

She offered a little smile. "I wish. No, more than likely Dion would've been the only one to gain the title. He'd taken the test twice before so he knew what to expect. Usually you pass one or two parts and have to redo another. Dion had passed theory and service. He only had one more part—tasting. It's the hardest. You're given a set of wines and you have to name the vintner, the area, the year, the varietal. Everything."

"Really? Wow. Sounds ridiculously challenging."

"It is. But he was ready. Even though he could be a pompous ass, so could the rest of us. We'd all formed a study group to prepare."

"*We*, meaning the five of you?"

"Uh-huh. It's the only way to learn all of the information."

Ari hesitated and then said, "I heard that his cottage is nothing but test prep. Have you been there?"

Peri laughed. "Oh, no. Dion…controlled what he shared. If somebody asked for help with something, or asked to borrow something, he'd whip out one of his blue binders. But we never saw his system—and he never saw ours. Everyone works together, apart."

"Did everybody get along?"

She leaned against the bar and turned her back to the other customers. "If you're asking if one of us could've killed him, I suppose it's possible, but highly unlikely."

"But there were one or two in your group who didn't get along with him?"

"Yeah. At different times J.D. and Racy got into it with him." She added, "Racy actually threw a punch one time. But they made up quickly."

"How does that work?"

She laughed and looked away. "Wine is about passion, but it's also alcohol. All of us are very passionate about what we've learned and we fiercely defend our opinion when we think we're right, so it's not uncommon for a fight to break out after we've all tasted ten or fifteen different wines."

"I can't imagine drinking while I was studying."

"Yeah, and our drinking *is* the studying. Really, we don't drink all that much. Taste testing is more about spitting than swallowing. Sorry if that grosses you out."

"No, it doesn't. That must be hard, though, if you really like a wine."

"Those we drink," Peri said with a wink.

"What about J.D.?"

"His issue was financial." She leaned over the bar and whispered, "He'd told Dion those blue binders were a gold mine and could be sold as test prep for the exam, and he had connections with a publisher who might be interested. Dion promised him a percentage if he could hook him up."

"And instead he cut him out?"

"Yup. He got the name of the guy and called him. They were on their way to signing a contract, and J.D.'s not in the picture at all." She looked over her shoulder and scanned the patrons before she said, "I felt bad for him. He's older than the rest of us and I think he needed the money." She glanced at the couple beside Ari who were waiting patiently for their next wine. "Gotta work. Be back in a few."

After Peri served the couple she made a pass down the bar, answering questions, refilling glasses, retrieving purchased bottles of wine from a carton. While Ari waited for her food she tapped *Master Sommelier* into her phone and was surprised to see over eight million hits. She added the words *Willamette Valley* to the search and an article in Eugene's *Register-Guard* appeared first. In addition to explaining the upcoming test, a brief biography and interview presented the five candidates. In addition to Dion Demopolous and Peri Quinton, there was also J.D. Cormac, Emily Mills, and Racy Ryder. Peri, J.D., and Emily were native Oregonians while Dion and Racy hailed from California. *Racy. That has to be the same person from the wine competition.*

"Racy" was a surfing term, so Ari wasn't surprised he was from Cali. Growing up in her native Arizona, she longed for water and had spent many summers surfing in La Jolla. She pulled out the article and the program they'd taken from Dion's cottage. This time she thoroughly read the review, which praised the bar's industrial warehouse ambience and applauded Racy for believing in his wines and convincing some silent partners to help him get started. And he'd just gotten a boost when his malbec won the gold medal at the Laurelwood.

Hmm… So Dion judged a competition involving one of his friends—or at least one of his study partners. Was that kosher? She opened the program and skimmed through the participants. Racy had entered his malbec, named Respite, and a pinot gris named Pearly Mae.

She turned from the bar and studied the crowd at the tables. Some had brought their lunch while others enjoyed the food menu. Her gaze wandered back up to the hallway above the tasting room. Next door to her and Jane's room, the lights were on in the office belonging to Emily Mills, the general manager. Ari's angle only afforded her a limited view through the front glass wall, and it wasn't until Emily stood from behind her desk that Ari finally saw her. She was on her cell phone—and visibly anxious. She gestured with her free hand, and when she jabbed a finger in the air, Ari knew the recipient was getting an earful. Suddenly another person popped into the picture—Cleo, who had been sitting in one of the chairs across from Emily's desk. Cleo stood next to Emily, close enough to hear the conversation. Ari recalled what Mina told Deputy Lacaba, that Cleo was probably with Emily the night before. But was Cleo with her when Dion was killed?

Emily wrote something down, hung up, brought her hand to her forehead, clearly upset. Cleo leaned over the desk but didn't reach out to touch her. She didn't have to. Whatever words she said soothed Emily, who sat back down. Cleo departed quickly and came downstairs into the tasting room. She wasn't smiling, and it appeared she'd calmed Emily by taking on the burden herself. *That's something a lover would do.* Yet, when she saw Ari standing at the bar, she flashed a brilliant smile that, coupled with her dark brown eyes, projected an intense care. It was almost as if she could turn her charm on and off.

She waved and continued out the door as Peri returned with Ari's fruit and nut plate. Ari asked, "Would it be possible to meet with your study group?"

Peri offered a wary glance. "Why would you want to do that?"

"It sounds interesting and I like to learn about new things."

"Really? It wouldn't be because you want to question all of us, would it?"

Ari laughed. "No."

"Hmm. I don't believe you. Jane sings your praises too frequently during her FaceTime chats with Mina." She looked up, searching her memory. "I seem to remember a situation where Jane was being stalked? You caught the stalker."

Ari nodded. "Yes." She grinned and said, "So if you've already got me pigeonholed, can I ask you where you were last evening?"

"That's an easy one. I was with my mother in Salem. She has a little ranch there and one of the local plumbers and I spent the entire day and into the night replacing a pipe. I stayed over and didn't come back until early this morning when Mina called me after Denise found Dion."

Ari fussed with her fruit plate and asked, "I take it you and Mina are close?"

When Peri didn't answer, Ari looked up and met her gaze. "We are," she said simply. "We've known each other for a long time, since college."

"When was the last time you saw Dion?"

"Two days ago. We worked the same shift, and before someone else tells you, I'll mention we also had an argument a few days before that. I was still pissed." Ari raised an eyebrow and sipped her wine as Peri explained. "He owed me a favor. I'd covered for him a couple weeks ago so he could go judge a wine competition, and I wanted him to pay me back so I could go help my mom. He wouldn't do it. Said he had plans. I knew that was B.S."

"Why are you so sure?"

"This close to the test? The only thing he did besides work was study. He just didn't want his precious schedule interrupted."

"When was this?"

"Four days ago, Sunday. When I couldn't get up to my mom's, I had to reschedule the plumber." She adopted a sad smile. "Who would've known that inconvenience would be my alibi?" She shrugged and glanced down the bar at the other patrons. Some were definitely ready for another taste. "Our group meets at six thirty after everyone is off work. We're meeting tonight, if you're available."

"I can be there. Where is *there?*"

"Actually it's here. Right here at the bar." Peri backed up to return to work. "See you tonight for the interrogation."

CHAPTER EIGHT

Her phone pinged. Jane. *Where are you?*

In the tasting room enjoying some wine and a fruit plate.

Finish up and get out here. I want you to see the beautiful arbor where Rory will make an honest woman of me.

Impossible, Ari replied.

She glanced up again at Emily's office. The light was still on but she couldn't see Emily. *Probably actually sitting at her desk and working. People do that.*

Ari motioned to Peri to pay, but Peri shook her head. Ari left a generous tip before heading out back to the expansive patio. The view of the valley and the hundreds of grapevines was spectacular. As far as she could see in any direction, an array of perfectly straight plants extended to the horizon. She imagined that sunset would be spectacular as the sky greeted the land in a burst of color. How wonderful would it be to sit on the patio, enjoy a glass of wine and watch the day end? Perhaps she'd find time to do that tonight.

Over to her right was the arbor, and Jane, Mina, and Cleo were talking—rather, Jane was talking and they were listening and nodding. She waved Ari over.

"Well, this is truly lovely," Ari said.

"Thanks," Cleo replied. "We think of the entire facility as one being. Everything works in harmony, a sort of positive energy for the fruit."

"This is the spot where Rory and I will be married," Jane said. "Then the reception will be right there on the patio. What do you think?"

"I think it's perfect." There was a bark and Dexter stepped in front of Ari. She bent over to give him a scratch. "Good afternoon, boy." He wagged and offered his sweet eyes in greeting. "I think you should be in the wedding."

She glanced up at Jane who wore a look of panic. Jane was an animal "liker," not "lover," but here she was outnumbered. "That's one idea," she said with a forced smile.

Mina laughed and clapped her hands for Dexter. "Don't worry, Jane. Dexter can just sit on my lap."

A look of relief swept over Jane. "No offense, Dex," she said. "Damn it!"

They looked over their shoulder. Cleo had wandered into a nearby row of grapevines and was scanning a single plant.

"Mina look at this." She held a bunch of grapes in one hand and pruning shears in the other. When she turned over the grapes, Ari saw they were covered in mold.

"Yuck," Jane said. "Please don't make wine with those."

"I told Berto about this. I told him to harvest this area next, but instead, he harvests the east section."

"Who's Berto?" Jane asked.

Ari remembered Berto was Frankie's former husband—the man Dion had asked Frankie about.

"He's the production manager," Mina replied. "The professional middleman between Cleo's work out here in the vineyard and my work indoors." She took a breath and added, "He's getting older and battling some memory issues."

"Denise warned him about this too," Cleo added. "I'm sorry, Jane and Ari. I need to assess all of this right now. I'll join you again as soon as I can."

"No worries," Jane said. "This is your livelihood. I'm happy to help as long as I don't have to handle moldy grapes."

"Got it. Thanks. I needed a laugh. Mina can show you everything. She really could do her job *and* mine."

"That's not true," Mina said, shaking her head. "However, I can talk a good talk. Come this way and we'll leave Cleo to deal with this."

Mina led them across the path toward another area of the vineyard, one that bordered the production room. Ari didn't see any mold on these grapes. They looked plump and juicy with a rich skin color.

"These grapes are nearly perfect," Mina proclaimed. "Go ahead and pick a few. We don't use any toxic chemicals and most of these are old vines, meaning we—me and Cleo or my uncle—planted each and every one." She snagged a handful of grapes and popped one in her mouth. She closed her eyes and smiled. "They're ready."

"You know that just from eating it?" Jane mumbled through a mouthful of grapes. "I mean, I'm no expert, but yeah, these are awesome."

Mina laughed. "It's much more scientific than that. We tested this area yesterday. The acidity and sweetness need to be balanced. Usually that happens now in early fall. Of course, we use much more scientific methods to determine the exact moment to begin the harvest." She pointed to a bunch of grapes drooping from a vine. "These grapes are for pinot noir. You'll notice some are disintegrating at the top of the bunch. That's a sign they're ready or really close." She picked one and held it up. "The texture's good. If we peel back the skin, there isn't any green, not the meat or the seed. So at first glance it looks ripe, but we run other tests to be sure. Determining the harvest for each section is the most critical decision Cleo and Berto make all year. If we pick too soon or too late, the bottle of wine will be subpar."

"Well," Ari said, gesturing to the crowded patio, "you've obviously made the right call more often than not."

Mina smiled. "We've had some practice and a lot of learning through trial and error—mostly error. But more important is Cleo, and Berto too. They are both viticulturists."

Ari cocked her head to the side. "Say that again?"

"The viticulturists are the people in charge of the vines. At Sisters that's Cleo and Berto Parma. They spend their days walking up and down the rows of plants, checking for pests, pruning each vine to ensure the grape bunches are getting the most sunlight. They check weather patterns daily and adjust the irrigation schedule, and of course lead the harvest. They inspect every box of grapes that's picked and discard the bunches that aren't the best. They also inspect all the grapes we buy from other vineyards."

Ari glanced west again to the endless rows of grapevines. "That sounds like the most daunting task I can imagine."

"It is," Mina agreed, gesturing to the western field. "Think of the vines as children. They need to be loved, nurtured, and cared for when they're sick or hurt by birds or bugs. Each one of those plants is potentially worth tens of thousands of dollars since the lifespan of a grapevine is anywhere from fifty to a hundred years."

"Incredible," Ari said. "So if you grow all of these grapes, why do you need to buy others?"

"Because we're creating different wines. The Willamette Valley has a limiting climate because of the rain. The pinot grape grows fabulously here, but since I want to make other wines like cabernet, syrah, riesling, and several of my own designer blends, I need different grapes, usually from drier climates like the Rogue Valley which is further south. The malbec we're excited about? Traditionally Argentina and Australia are known for malbec, but we can get a decent grape here on the west coast, just not *right* here."

"So these grapes are just for pinot wines?" Jane clarified.

"Exactly. These vines will be harvested later today. Up for a little work?"

"Ha!" Jane exclaimed. "A *little* work? And the sinking of the Titanic was a boating accident."

"Picking is indeed strenuous," Mina said. "The largest vineyards use machines, but not us."

"Why not?" Ari asked. "Too expensive?"

"Yeah, that's part of it, but also a lot of the grape is wasted as it's separated from the stem. I want the whole grape, and to get it some extra work is required. It's the old adage, 'no pain, no gain.'"

"I remember the first time I worked harvest, which also turned out to be the last time I worked harvest," Jane said. She looked at Ari. "Mina invited me to come along and help some of her friends on the central coast of California."

"Paso Robles," Mina added.

"Yes. It was quite the weekend. I could barely walk for a week after I got home!"

Mina wagged a finger at her. "Oh, no. That's not what happened. Your injury had more to do with the evening activities and a certain foreign exchange student. It wasn't the grapes."

Jane smiled at the memory. "Ah, I'd forgotten about her. Still, I was much younger then."

"You're being dramatic," Mina scoffed. She looked at Ari. "No expectations. You're a guest. You don't have to help, and frankly, you're already helping."

"Well, I don't mind if there's time. Sounds interesting."

Mina ate another grape. "I have no doubt these will make some of the best pinot ever."

"Why?" Jane asked. "I get that a moldy grape isn't good at all, but in general what makes one grape superior to the other?"

"Basically three things, one of which is completely out of Cleo's control—the weather. Last month was particularly wet, and while the moist air can be a blessing to a grape, it can lead to mold. Another thing that's important is how the vine grows. Cleo watches each vine's progress and she shapes them to actually create a self-protective cover against the elements."

"That sounds incredibly tedious," Ari said.

"It is," Mina agreed. "It means Cleo—or Berto—lays hands on every single vine all winter, spring, and summer, helping them develop as they should. The third part is pruning. How far back the leaves are trimmed and which leaves are trimmed affects how the grapes will grow. How much sunlight will each bunch receive? Where is a single grape in relation to the other grapes in the bunch? On this vine? In this vineyard?" She made a sweeping gesture to illustrate the magnitude of her point. "And if that isn't enough, we can have a dry year! *Or,* Cleo can work her ass off and the birds eat practically everything. That happened last year with the pinot gris grapes."

Ari was gobsmacked. She shook her head. "I don't think I'll ever look the same way at another bottle of wine." They all laughed and Dexter barked. As they approached the production room, Ari gazed at Mina's little house down the hill. "Mina, can I ask a follow-up question to your interview?"

"Sure," Mina said, but Ari could hear the caution in her voice.

"You said you were home last night?"

"Uh-huh. We couldn't work in the building so I worked on my formulas and ideas for blends at home, and I watched the U of O's soccer team. I worked, then I came over here to check on the fermentation, and then I went home to bed."

"Did you check the security cam at the front gate?"

"We did. Everyone exited by eight thirty. Cleo was the last out," she said grimly. "And the first one back through around four a.m."

"Wait. What about Dion? Did he leave?"

"He did," Mina said, exasperated. "He left around eight. In fact, now that you mention it, that's really odd. All the other study group members were right behind him." She looked at Ari, confused. "And it doesn't show him returning, but he's on the production room cam at one a.m."

"Why would he avoid the front gate camera but not care that he was caught on the production room camera?"

Mina looked toward the exit. "The gate. It wasn't the camera he was avoiding." She pointed to the little cottage near the gate. "Berto lives there. Dion didn't want him to hear his car. He probably parked on the side of the road outside and walked up the hill."

"Hell of a walk," Jane said.

"In the dark," Mina added. She looked at Ari. "That must be how the killer did it as well."

"And you and Berto were the only people here?"

"I *thought* so."

Ari must've looked troubled because Mina asked, "What do you think that means?"

"I think Deputy Lacaba will be looking really hard at Berto."

Mina groaned. "That poor man."

"Did you notice Dexter barking at all?"

Mina thought about it. "Now that you mention it... When I came back from the production room around twelve-twenty, he scratched on the door, wanting to go out. Then I heard him barking outside just a little while later. I had to call for him to come inside so we could go to bed."

"Is there anyone on your staff who doesn't like Dexter or someone he'll bark at constantly?"

She shook her head. "Dexter gets along with everyone." She stopped herself and sighed. "Well, I take that back. He wasn't thrilled with John Graham, the guy who sells us our malbec grapes and had the problem about wanting his retriever instead of Dexter on the dog calendar."

Ari nodded. "But he doesn't come around anymore?"

Mina shook her head. "He never did. We go to him, but I don't make that run anymore to get the grapes. When I went alone or with Berto, I took Dexter. John would come out and Dexter barked at him. Oddest thing. He loves dogs but Dexter never took to him. But now it's Berto and Eddie, our CFO, who make the run." She sighed. "Dumbest fight ever."

"That is indeed a ridiculous reason to alter a business relationship," Ari agreed.

"Yeah, and I'll admit I didn't help the situation by telling him I thought it was a stupid reason to be upset. That's when he said he didn't want to talk to me anymore."

"Is it just malbec grapes you buy from him?" Ari asked.

"No, some other varietals as well. That's why they drive down to his place multiple times during harvest. But the lack of communication between us led to misunderstandings and misinformation. He hasn't provided as many grapes as he promised and last year we got the malbec grapes so late we just missed an important competition a couple weeks ago. Some up-and-coming malbec won. We should've been there *and* won."

"Was that the Laurelwood?"

"Uh, yeah," Mina said. "How did you know?"

"I found a program for it at Dion's house. Did you know he was one of the judges?"

She nodded. "Yeah, he filled in for somebody. We weren't entered, so there was no conflict of interest."

Jane scratched her head. "So wait, you got grapes late last year and you couldn't compete in a competition a few weeks ago? I'm confused."

"It's because of the aging process," Mina explained. "The wine business is at *least* twelve to eighteen months out. All the grapes we'll pick during this harvest won't make us a dime until next year."

"That's a hell of an investment," Ari said.

"No kidding. But I love it," she said, smiling.

"Sounds really competitive," Jane said.

"It is. For example, the grapes we use for our cabernet grow in a secret location. I've got an exclusive deal with a small vineyard in Sonoma and only a dozen people know where it is. That's part of the reason our cabernet has gained some buzz, and eventually it will win an award. Successful wine is partly the grape, partly the winemaker, partly luck with the weather, and a decent amount of business savvy. Marketing our wine correctly has become very important at a time when every other retiree is trying their hand at winemaking. It sounds so glamorous but as you'll see, it's backbreaking work."

"How many grapes do you pick in a day?" Ari asked.

"Depends on who's doing the picking. We ask people to come and help, like the ones arriving in a little while, but that's really more for publicity. It's a different way to get people out to the vineyard. But they know they can stop whenever they want and most do after two hours. By then backs are hurting, arthritis is flaring and the novelty has worn off. Our professional pickers can pick a ton in about eight hours."

Jane studied the bunch in her hand. "How much wine does a ton of grapes make?"

"Roughly sixty-three cases or seven hundred fifty-six bottles. Let's head to the production room. It's the nerve center of the operation."

As they cut across a few rows of vines, Mina continued to explain the difficulties nature could inflict on the grapes.

Jane stopped and touched her arm. "Mina, why is that man asleep over there?" She pointed to a man sitting in front of a grapevine, his back curved and his shoulders slowly rising and falling. He wore a wide-brimmed straw hat and he cradled a lime green water bottle in the crook of his right arm. The light breeze carried his loud snore across the vineyard.

"Shit," Mina murmured as they approached him. She knelt and shook him. "Berto? Berto, wake up."

His snore sputtered and he threw his head up. "What?"

"You were asleep again."

"Oh, no. I'm sorry, Mina," he said in a thick accent. He looked at Jane and Ari. "My apologies."

"Jane and Ari, this is Berto, my production manager. Berto has forgotten more about vineyards and winemaking than I'll ever know. He's the reason the malbec and the gris are so good."

"No," he disagreed. "That's you, Mina." He turned to Jane and Ari. "Again, I'm sorry you found me sleeping on the job during harvest."

"No need to apologize to us," Jane said. "I wish I could nap in a sitting position. It'd save me from a ton of boring meetings."

His white teeth glistened against his deep suntan when he smiled. "Gracías."

"You okay now?" Mina asked.

"Sí."

"You need to check the central section. Cleo found mold."

His face turned stony. "Shit." He scrambled to his feet, tipped his hat to the three of them and hurried away.

Mina watched him go, her jaw clenched in worry.

Jane touched her arm. "How old is he?"

"Seventy-four. I may have to retire him." She blinked away tears and led them to a dirt road that followed the southern perimeter of the vineyard.

"Does this path circle the property?" Ari asked.

"Yes, and several points of egress cut across the fields. It also leads to the main gate." She threw up her hands. "I just can't believe Dion died twenty yards from me and I didn't know it. I can't wrap my brain around it. If he'd had his stupid phone with him, I could've saved his life! I would've seen that the breaker was off in about five seconds. I could've saved him."

Ari stopped walking. She realized what she'd missed. She looked at Mina and said, "Yes, you could've."

"And I still can't believe he was going to quit."

"Are you serious?" Jane echoed.

Perhaps Mina was a terrific actress, but she'd appeared genuinely distraught when she'd learned the truth during the interview and now she looked like she might cry.

"That bastard. After everything I've done for him. I'm sorry for speaking ill of the dead. I know I sound selfish, but that's just a kick in the teeth."

CHAPTER NINE

Mina led them into a cavernous room with rows of oak barrels stacked four high on long shelves that spanned the length of the back wall. Opposite the oak barrels were two tall shiny tanks. Gauges were attached to the front, and Mina glanced at each one as they passed.

"These are the tanks for the white wine. Our red wines age in those barrels, and the process for making red wines is much more involved."

"And that's why reds are more expensive?" Ari concluded.

"Exactly."

She led them to the back and two towering machines. "Here's how it works. People pick the grapes and put them in those crates over there. We bring them inside and each crate is placed on that scale." She pointed to a metal pad with a display window on the side. It reminded Ari of a scale at a veterinarian's office.

"Scales? Why do you have to weigh the grapes?" Jane asked.

"It's the law. We have to account for how much wine we're making. It goes to how much we'll be taxed, how many bottles of wine we'll produce, what goes on the label. Our scale is small potatoes compared to some of the big places. We keep track of the weight tags and that's what we report."

She pointed to the large machine on the right. "This is the crusher-destemmer. All of the grapes are examined and the chosen grapes are put on a conveyor belt. They go through this machine and flow into these large containers. This is where my job gets fun. I make decisions about the fermentation process, which yeast to use, and later how to blend the various finished wines that result."

Jane looked puzzled. "Yeast? Like for bread?"

"Yeah but there's dozens and dozens to pick from. Yeast is the key to turning grapes into wine. I study all the yeasts and pick the one I want for each wine."

"Sounds like a lot of responsibility," Ari commented. "I mean, if you make the wrong decisions…"

Mina took a deep breath. "Yes, if I make the wrong decisions and the wine tastes terrible, or even mediocre, then Sisters Cellars takes an enormous hit, perhaps it goes under. Now, no one goes into winemaking to get rich and only the largest vineyards, those bottling a hundred thousand cases a year, will be wealthy. We're here to make memories. We want people who drink a bottle of Sisters Cellars wine to remember the occasion where they consumed it—their daughter's wedding, a son's bar mitzvah, celebrating the incredible job promotion." She suddenly stopped and blushed. "Sorry."

"No need to apologize," Jane said and gave Mina a one-arm hug. "Your passion is amazing."

Ari scanned the facility. She noticed a small group of people clustered around several tables and sinks, including Cleo and the red-haired woman who'd found Dion. Two were wearing white lab coats and held what appeared to be a stubby telescope to their respective eyes.

Jane pointed to them. "What's going on over there? It reminds me of my ill-fated experience in Ms. Cimino's Chem I class."

Mina laughed and turned to Ari. "Did Jane ever tell you about how she almost blew up the chem lab at school?"

Ari shook her head.

"There's nothing to tell," Jane protested. "Ms. Cimino rushed over and turned off the gas, saving me and the rest of the class." She sighed. "She was so beautiful."

Mina rolled her eyes. "In answer to your question, in addition to Cleo and Eddie, there's Denise who works with Cleo and me. The two people in the lab coats are students from the university. What they're holding are refractometers. They measure pH level, acidity, and sugar in the grapes. Basically, they're determining how developed the grapes are so we can make the next decisions about harvest."

"That *also* sounds like a lot of responsibility," Ari repeated.

"It is. Our entire livelihood depends on the weather and one of the most delicate fruits in the world. While we can't control the weather, we can control most everything else."

"It really is like raising a child," Jane said.

"It is. And the viticulturists are the nannies. They study the soil, the pests, pruning methods—everything and anything—about the grapes."

"I had no idea," Ari mused. "Is that why some wine is good and some wine tastes terrible?"

Mina looked away and considered her answer. "It depends on your palate. What one person likes, another doesn't. Some people think all whites are terrible. Some vintners play it safe, especially the big places. They know what their customers want and they deliver it. Rarely do they introduce a new wine. Here, we have some standards that we make every year, but I like to take risks too." She rubbed her hands together gleefully.

Denise glanced over, and after a word with the students, charged toward Mina, her clipboard clutched to her chest and purple pen in hand. Mina smiled and offered, "Ari and Jane, this is Denise Hemsen, a true Jill of all trades and the Queen of the Purple Pen."

Ari started to introduce herself, but Denise immediately showed her back to Ari and Jane and stared at Mina. "You have to do something," she said urgently.

"Denise, our guests—"

Denise whirled and forced a smile for a nanosecond. "Apologies. I'm Denise. And there's an emergency." She turned away again and said, "Mina, I don't care what Eddie told you. The science tells another story." She thrust the clipboard under her nose. "The north section isn't ready for picking. Not today. Maybe tomorrow. For sure next week. Look at these levels. And Cleo agrees with me now."

Mina scanned what Denise presented and shook her head. "No, you're right. But Eddie was so sure…"

Denise groaned. "Eddie knows next to nothing about raising grapes. You need to lock him in his office and tell him just to stick to his spreadsheets." She stopped herself and after swallowing whatever else she was going to say, glanced at the huddle continuing across the room without her. "And here's a heads-up. In about a minute they're gonna want to know what you want to do about the mold Cleo found in central section. The mold that Berto missed."

Mina nodded. "Thanks."

"And have you seen Berto?" She framed it as a question, but her face suggested she already knew the answer.

"We just saw him out in the vines. I'm sure he'll be back soon."

Denise seemed to understand what Mina was implying and let it go before she evaporated back into the group.

Jane squeezed Mina's shoulder. "Is everything okay?"

Mina raked a hand through her hair and looked over at the huddle. "We've had some problems lately. Nothing that compares to Dion's death, but issues. The group isn't working like a team. As you saw, Berto is struggling with his memory and his physical health. Eddie really wants to be more involved in the actual process of cultivating grapes and winemaking. So he sometimes inserts himself, which pisses off Denise because her job is to be both my and Cleo's right hand."

"She feels threatened?" Ari suggested.

"To some extent yes, but also…" She exhaled and said, "He's not very talented."

"Has anyone told him he should just stick to the 'F' part of his CFO title?" Jane asked.

Mina glared at her. "If you mean me, no, I haven't." Her face softened and she added, "But I know it's coming. I'm sorry to be abrupt with you." She pulled Jane into a hug. "I'm so glad you're here."

"It's okay. You look really stressed."

She nodded. "Dion's death just put me over the top. Employees keep telling me that Deputy Lacaba made them feel like criminals during their interviews with her. Plus three—well, I guess two now—of our employees are taking the Master Somm exam in just two weeks, and they're on edge. I can't wait for that to be over."

"Were you counting on harvesting those grapes Denise mentioned, the north section?" Ari asked.

"Yeah. There's a whole process, a checklist. If it's followed, and I *thought* it was, it maximizes the yield from the harvest, which creates greater profits. But any barriers or mistakes and it all backs up. Those groups that come and help us pick the grapes? It's vital we take advantage of their charity because they only come once."

"Those are some of the people arriving today," Jane said.

"Yes, assuming they don't cancel because of Dion's death." Mina squeezed Jane's arm. "I'm sorry I can't give you the attention you deserve…and so richly desire."

They all laughed and Jane kissed Mina on the cheek. "I appreciate your undivided attention, but this is your business so if there's stuff you need to attend to—"

"Don't worry. I've got this." She gave her a wide smile. "In fact, I think we ought to go punch some grapes. It's a great way to take out our frustration."

Jane put her hands on her hips. "I haven't punched anything for a long time. Point us toward the brutality."

They wandered through the rows of barrels. Ari stopped to peruse a card encased in a plastic sleeve, identifying the barrel behind it. She was standing in front of a malbec that had been made the year before. The card also listed other dates when various tests were performed to check its levels.

"You are a good detective," Mina commented. "That's one of the malbec barrels. It's almost ready, but not quite," she said wistfully.

"Will there be other competitions you can enter?"

"Sure, but from a marketing perspective, each one counts."

"Well, malbec is my favorite," Ari admitted. "Let me know when you bottle it. I'll be first in line to make a purchase."

"You've got a deal." Mina pointed to a sign above a different area of the room that read *Witches' Lair*. "It's a joke and you'll see why."

They paused in front of an enormous steel box. "This is the press. After the grapes are destemmed, if we're making white wine the grapes come straight to the press, which will separate the juice from the skin. The liquid is called the must. We add yeast to the must, put it in one of those enormous tanks you saw, and run tests on it until we think it's ready to bottle—or be part of a blend. Compared to red wine production, it's much simpler."

She headed to a large box filled with smashed grapes. Two men each raised and lowered a wooden pole into the mixture, pushing down the top, which seemed to have a different consistency than the mixture underneath. "So, here's your red wine."

Jane gazed into the vat and turned up her nose. "No offense, but it looks like oatmeal and it smells like stinky sneakers."

Mina laughed. "Yes, at this point it does. That's the CO_2. Today we only have a few wines fermenting, so the levels are containable. Still, try not to breathe too deeply while we're here." Jane's eyes widened and Mina said, "Really. It's okay. You *can* breathe, Jane."

She smiled. "Great."

Mina took one of the poles. "This is one of the most physically demanding parts of the fermentation process, the punch down. It's basically mixing things up to make sure the nutrients distribute evenly. So we keep punching down until the grape skins rise to the top and the temperature and our other tests tell us it's ready for pressing, which will finally separate the skin, and then the wine will be ready for barreling." She thrust the paddle toward Jane. "Give it a try."

Jane held up her hands and shook her head. "No, no. I'd be afraid to screw it up."

"You can't screw it up. Just up and down."

Jane did as she was told and Mina seized the other pole for Ari. After five punches, Ari understood why Mina's upper arms were toned. The resistance Ari felt each time she extracted the pole was significant, indicating the mixture was incredibly thick and still had a long journey before it found its way to her wine rack.

"How long is this process?" she asked.

"Usually two or three days," Mina said. "But they're three of the longest days for us. This stage is so critical. There's almost always someone here around the clock, except for last night," she added sadly.

While Jane punched away, Ari surveyed the space. She saw three points of exit. Two had been sabotaged from the inside… and the main door from the outside.

He should've had his phone. Mina could've saved him.

"Ari?" Jane called.

"Huh?"

"Having an important thought?"

Jane and Mina stared at her, but she wasn't ready to share. "Just maybe. I'll keep you posted."

Loud voices echoed from the other side of the room and a procession led by Cleo engulfed Mina. Joining Cleo were Denise and Berto, who had apparently just arrived. The quartet went straight to Mina and talked over each other, or rather, Eddie and Denise talked over each other while Cleo and Berto listened. Mina held up a hand until they stopped.

"I assume this is about the north section. Denise, you've made your position clear. You don't think it's ready. Eddie?"

He glanced at Cleo and Berto. When he gazed at Mina, he offered a smile of glimmering white teeth that could melt ice. "I'm the odd man out here. I say north section is ready to go. Let's get the troops out there to pick. Use the man—and woman—power while we have it."

Mina turned to Berto. "What do you think?" He fiddled with his hat and eventually said, "In this case, they're both right."

Mina frowned. "How so?"

He sighed. "We could wait a little longer like Denise wants. It might pay off, but like Eddie said, the workers are coming today." Both Denise and Eddie started to speak again but Mina's hand flew up and her gaze remained focused on Berto. "But, the most important factor is that we've had a wet September. We're not going to yield nearly as much fruit as we did last year. North section could wind up with mold just like central section."

Cleo jumped in. "How did we miss the mold in the first place?" She shot a harsh look at Eddie.

His jaw dropped. "Don't look at me! Berto missed it."

"What?" Berto cried. "You said you wanted to help and I told you to tend to that section."

Eddie shook his head. "You did not. You told me to watch east section, but you never said anything about central section."

Ari watched Eddie closely. If he was lying, he was good at it. Berto, however, shuffled his feet and scratched his head, clearly doubting himself.

"Look, none of it's good news," Eddie said gently. "The wet September is affecting everything. If you check the weights for the past few days, you'll see that we're light."

Berto looked puzzled. "Why? My team picked the west and south sections. I didn't see any mold. The waste was minimal."

Eddie rubbed his chin. "Huh. I'll have to look at the tags again. Maybe I'm wrong."

"I'd say so," Berto spat and huffed off.

When he was out of earshot, Eddie looked at Mina and then Cleo. "They were short. Don't know why, and I don't want to fight with a sick man." He paused before he said, "Did he tell you about his interview with Deputy Do Right?"

"No, what happened?" Cleo said.

"Lacaba hammered him. He doesn't have any alibi and other than Mina, he was the only one around. It would've been easy for him to lock Dion in here. It's not like he'd have to physically confront him."

"So you think she's going to try to make a case against Berto?" Mina asked.

Eddie shrugged. "I don't know. I mean of course he didn't do it...right?" He headed off toward the vineyard. All eyes turned to Denise who stood apart from them clearly fuming.

"Anything to add, Denise?" Mina asked.

"Nope. Pick it. Don't pick it. I really don't care." She leveled her gaze directly at Mina. "You got issues here and I don't need it. I thought I could wait until the end of harvest, but I can't. I'm giving you my two-week notice."

"Now?" Mina cried. "But we need you. We need everyone!"

Her expression softened but her gaze was cold. "I'm sorry, Mina. Really, I am."

She walked off and Mina covered her face with her hands. "How is all this happening? Everything is falling apart at the worst possible time."

Cleo took Mina in her strong arms. She kissed the side of her head and said, "It's going to be okay. Breathe, baby."

"I am."

Cleo laughed. "No, you're not." Mina's shoulders rose and fell. "Now you are." She stepped away. "Okay, decision time. When the picking group gets here, we send them to central section. I'll take Berto and we'll do a first pick. When the group gets here, we'll stay a row ahead of them. And for now we'll leave the north alone. Okay?"

Mina kissed her softly. "'Kay."

Cleo offered a kiss on the cheek and as she left she said to Ari and Jane, "I'll bet you thought you were getting away from drama."

Jane rubbed Mina's back. "Hey, we're here and we'll help. Ari will figure out who killed Dion and I'll keep punching those grapes down—for at least an hour."

Mina laughed and swiped at the tear that had slid down her cheek. "I know we'll be okay. Once Denise calms down I might be able to convince her to stay, at least through harvest."

"How bad is it with Berto?" Ari asked. "Does he have a diagnosis?"

"Not really. I mean, at seventy-four some forgetfulness is expected but over the past year it's gotten much worse. At first it was little things, like he couldn't find his pruning shears. That happens almost on a daily basis. We find him asleep in the vineyard. Then there were bigger things. He forgot to prune an entire two rows of grapes. He screwed up the yeast order. But the worst mistake was messing up the weight tags. We had an internal audit and realized we'd paid thousands of dollars in taxes we didn't need to pay. Try getting money *back* from the federal government. I've been deluged with paperwork about that for the last few months. Anyway, the doctor's using the word dementia."

"That's so sad," Jane said.

"Yeah. He's always been super sharp. We started producing malbec because he used to make it in Argentina. Like Cleo, that's where he's from originally."

"His ex-wife, Frankie, is concerned as well."

Mina offered a sad smile. "Well I hope the doctor is wrong." She sighed. "You didn't come here for any of this. You came to talk about your wedding, not my problems." She clapped her hands. "Let's get to work."

CHAPTER TEN

Jane left with Mina to prepare for the guest grape pickers and Ari headed to their room to call Apollo, Dion's brother. She had thirty minutes to kill and she also thought about calling Molly. More questions swirled and she needed a sounding board. As she walked she scrolled through the pictures she'd taken in Dion's cottage—of the note and the graph from the little notebook in the secret hiding place. She'd briefly shown it to Mina who promised to look at it more closely later. Ari sent it to Mina's phone as a gentle reminder.

Approaching her door, she heard raised voices in Emily Mills's office. She glanced through the front glass and saw Denise leaning over the desk and pointing her finger at Emily, who appeared the picture of calm.

"I won't accept this resignation."

"You don't have a choice."

"Tell me what it would take to keep you here."

"Deal with Eddie," Denise barked. "You need to keep him up here with you where he belongs and away from the wine. If he messes with my pinot gris one more time…"

Emily replied so quietly Ari couldn't hear what she said.

"Mina won't do it. She has zero objectivity when it comes to Eddie," Denise fired back.

"I understand and I agree," Emily said. "I thought having him pick up the grapes with Berto would keep him out of your hair."

"And he's even screwing that up, or rather, Berto's screwing it up and Eddie's letting him."

"I'm working on it. Please, please don't leave. I really am trying."

Denise sighed. "We can't have what happened to the malbec happen to the pinot gris."

"It won't," Emily stated confidently.

"It better not. We're not missing out on another competition or losing to some ridiculously named wine. *Respite*. Sounds like a rest area."

"Does that mean you'll stay? You won't quit?"

"Just keep that letter in case I change my mind," Denise growled and turned to the door.

Ari decided to take advantage of the opportunity. She stepped into the hallway and practically ran into her.

"Oh, my gosh," Ari said. "I'm so sorry."

Denise raised a hand. "It's okay."

"Um, can I make an observation?"

Denise squirmed and looked at her watch. "Uh, sure."

"As someone who has also opened a door and found a dead body, I think you're dealing with it incredibly well. Much better than I did, really."

For the first time since she and Jane had arrived, Denise really looked at her—not through her or past her. And Ari saw the most amazing green eyes—and the huge, tired bags below them. "Thank you. I can't tell you…I can't tell you how that's just wrecked me." She started to sway and Ari took her elbow.

"It's okay. Let me get you a glass of water."

Denise nodded and Ari led her to a chair in the guest room. She went to the adjoining bathroom for a glass just as Emily opened the outer door. Mina had told Jane that the staff often used the guest bathroom if they found the exterior door unlocked. Ari had forgotten to lock it.

"I'm so sorry," Emily said, backing out of the bathroom. "Just force of habit."

"It's okay," Ari said to her retreating form before the door closed.

"I think I'm going to be sick."

Denise rushed past her to the toilet. Ari stepped back into the bedroom and tried to block out the wretched sounds. Denise was clearly overwrought by Dion's death, and Ari had to wonder if there wasn't another emotion—like guilt—making her physically ill.

When she reappeared, she headed straight for the chair and put her head between her knees. Ari sat on the bed, waiting and watching.

Denise looked up, her red curls flopping everywhere. "I'm so sorry. This is absolutely the worst presentation I've ever made to any stranger I've ever met."

Ari narrowed her eyes. "I'm...honored?"

Denise threw her head back and laughed hysterically. Again, Ari watched and waited. *It's like she's having a breakdown.*

"Denise, by chance have you been interviewed by Deputy Lacaba yet?"

She nodded vigorously. "She knows I didn't do it. I was at a party last night with thirty people until about two a.m. We were at a club with security footage. The club manager sent her the security footage and I was cleared. I actually watched her make a red line through my name."

"A red line, huh? She just crossed you off?"

"Yup."

Ari raised an eyebrow. "That's an interesting way to solve a case."

"Is it? I wouldn't know."

"Did she happen to say who she suspected?"

"She didn't have to say. She suspects Berto. She must've asked me twenty questions about him."

"And what did you say?"

She shrugged. "Well, he certainly could do it. He knows more about wine than all of us put together. And more about the winery. He worked for Mina's uncle. He designed the entire production room. If anybody knows the ins and outs, it's him."

"I had no idea. Did he have a problem with Dion?"

Denise shook her head. "I don't think so. He just doesn't have an alibi." She looked around and bolted for the door. "Thanks for the water. I have to get out of here!"

"Denise, wait." She didn't turn around but she stopped in the doorway. "I'm here if you need to talk, okay?"

She nodded and slipped out the door.

"I know who killed my brother," Apollo announced.

They had barely exchanged greetings before he jumped on it. "You do?"

"Yeah. It was a man named Racy."

"You mean Racy Rider, one of Dion's study mates for the sommelier test?"

"That's the one."

"He threatened Dion?"

"Uh...well...I don't know for sure if that happened."

"What exactly did he say?"

He sighed. "Let's see. Dion called him a lying sack of shit who thought he could get away with stuff just 'cuz he came from money. And Dion was going to make sure Racy's sorry ass wound up in jail."

Ari massaged her temple. "Apollo, that sounds more like Dion threatening Racy."

"Oh. It does, doesn't it?"

"Why don't you tell me everything you know, and I'll just listen."

"Um, well, that's about it."

Ari tossed her pen on the table and shook her head.

"The thing is... I wasn't a great listener when it came to Dion. He was exhausting. Every story took twenty minutes to tell, and he'd stop and quiz me to make sure I was still paying attention, ya know? Usually that didn't go so well because I was in the middle of doing something for my family, like giving the baby a bath or watching my oldest boy doing his homework. But Dion thought he was the center of the universe—no, scratch that. He *was* the universe. We were all just actors in his little life play. I'm sorry for saying mean stuff now that he's gone, but half the time I just tuned him out. An 'uh-huh' every few minutes was really all the participation he needed from me during a conversation. I can't remember exactly what he said about Racy, but the guy was into something questionable, something that clearly hurt Dion directly or indirectly."

"Well, that's a start," Ari said. "When was the last time you spoke to him?"

"About three days ago."

"How did he sound?"

"Tired, but happy. The test was coming up and he was certain he'd pass. He said to me, "'Ap, this time I cross the finish line.' He was excited about his new job in Portland but felt guilty for leaving Mina after everything she'd done for him."

"Was the money the only reason he took the job?"

"Yeah. He, well…" Ari thought he might be getting choked up. "Geez, now I feel like a scumbag for what I just said. Forget all that, okay? That's just me being stupid. Can you forget it?"

"Yeah, already forgotten."

"Here's the thing. My daughter, his niece Victoria, isn't well. She has cancer. Dion helps with the bills."

"I see." Ari fought to control her emotions. She'd lost her mother to cancer, and a series of recent events had resurfaced many memories, some of them quite painful. "Did he mention Racy or anyone else specifically during that call?"

"He did… Now if I can only remember… I was washing the dog, which made the conversation difficult because we live near a fire station. Every time a siren goes off, Bodie, that's our beagle, bays like crazy. Dion would just keep talking through it. Hmm. What did he say?"

Mina had left a bottle of pinot noir as a welcome gift on the table, and Ari grabbed the corkscrew and popped the cork while she waited.

"I got it," he said as she poured a glass. "He mentioned that he felt like a real detective because he'd gone on a stakeout and gotten the goods on Racy. Then he made a joke. I just remembered it because I'm out here by our ginormous freezer."

Ari took a long sip. *If he says anything about pounding meat...* "So what was the joke Dion made about the stakeout?"

"He said it was a great trip because he got to have a great wine paired with the steak he'd had for dinner. Get it? Steak on the stakeout."

"Did he mention the name of the restaurant?" Ari asked.

"Hmm. I remember I wasn't impressed. It wasn't a flashy place or anything. Something like Charlie's....or Carly's."

Ari remembered the receipt she'd found in Dion's cottage. "Do you mean Carlotta's?"

"Uh, yeah, that could be it."

"Anything else, Apollo?"

"No, like I said, I've never counted listening as one of my greatest skills. Hey, have you talked to the deputy? I gave her the code to crack his phone and I was wondering if there was anything useful on it."

"Oh," Ari hedged, "I haven't spoken with her for a few hours. I'm sure it helped."

"Great! Dion dropped his last phone in the lake when he visited us, so we went to get a new one. My older son is a little tech genius and he picked the passcode: zero, four, one, four, zero, eight. That's his birthday. He didn't want Uncle Dion to ever forget it."

"Thanks, Apollo. If I think of anything else, I'll be in touch."

"Thanks. I really appreciate your efforts. He was really the only family I had left—other than the one I've made for myself." His voice broke and he sniffled. "Just...Just have this solved when you call again."

CHAPTER ELEVEN

Ari stretched, the tips of her fingers nearly touching the ceiling. She'd slipped off her loafers when she got back to the room, noting the sides were caked with mud. When she'd packed for the trip yesterday, she never envisioned being close to the winemaking *process*—only to the wine. She'd brought her work boots for the brief tour she'd imagined, and she put those on now and headed out.

She lingered in the open hallway, looking down at the tasting room bustling with late afternoon arrivals. Out on the patio Happy Birthday balloons surrounded a table of retirees enjoying wine with cake. Couples sat at the bistro tables basking in the stunning view of the vineyard. The indoor tables were just as crowded as the bar and the patio. While many visitors appeared to be tourists, there seemed to be as many locals. One table roared with laughter during a Trivial Pursuit game and another foursome played serious bridge. Movement below caught her eye. Emily led two butch women, one carrying white balloons and the other carrying a cake with two brides in the center, into the event room. *The place where Dion knocked over the centerpieces and left his phone.*

"Ms. Adams?" Ari jumped and Deputy Lacaba said, "My apologies if I scared you. You looked deep in thought."

She gestured toward the crowd below. "Oh, I was just people watching."

Lacaba leaned on the balcony and shook her head. "Don't these people work? It's Thursday afternoon."

"Well, many are probably tourists or retired. I'm on my way to see if I can help with the grape picking. See you later."

As she turned to go, the deputy said, "I need to thank you."

Ari blinked and turned back. "Come again?"

For the first time, the corners of Lacaba's lips turned up. It wasn't a smile, but it was close. "Yeah."

Ari took a step toward her and put her hand to her ear. "I didn't hear you."

Lacaba smirked. "Don't get crazy about it. I just got back from Frankie Smith's house—again. Only this time I went alone."

"Oh?"

"She told me about you helping her remember the false-bottom drawer her wife installed in the kitchen. And she made a point of telling me—twice—that you insisted on leaving the evidence and having her call me. So, thank you."

"You're welcome," Ari said with a nod.

"Can I assume you found the note in Dion's pocket as well?"

She raised an eyebrow and Ari felt her footing in the conversation shift. The line between Deputy Lacaba's usual serious tone blurred her slightly playful one.

"Yes. I didn't include that in my message because I don't know if it has anything to do with the case."

Lacaba pushed away from the railing and stuck her hands in her pockets. She cocked her head to the side. "You don't really believe that, do you?"

Tomorrow. After 8 P.M., the note had read. Ari matched her pose and hooked her thumbs in her belt loops. "I think a man who folds his underwear is probably too fastidious to absently leave things in his pockets. Either he kept it as a reminder, or he was so preoccupied with something terribly stressful that he forgot to remove it."

Lacaba nodded. "Agreed." Ari sensed she wanted to ask something but collaborating with a civilian was strictly against policy.

"Anything else?" Ari encouraged.

"I think it's a note from the person who left the tasting room door open for him. What do you think?"

Now the corners of Ari's mouth turned up. "If I answer that question for you, will you answer one for me?"

She shrugged. "Depends on the question."

"Fair," Ari said. "Yes, I think the note was written by Dion's... accomplice, for lack of a better word."

"Really, it wasn't *written*, as much as it was composed," Lacaba corrected.

"True. And maybe that's a clue to the identity of the *composer* in itself."

"Maybe we have two people trying to sabotage the winery."

"*We?*"

Lacaba shifted on her feet and cleared her throat. "I meant *me*. You know that."

"I do. And for the record, I don't believe Dion was attempting to harm the winery. I think he was trying to help in some way."

Lacaba's doubt was evident. "Not so sure I agree." Tensing, she asked, "What's your question?"

"I wanted to know if there was anything significant on his phone."

"Honestly, nothing of import so far." Lacaba exhaled, clearly breathing easier now that she was solidly on the legal and ethical side of protocol. "A few hundred files though, thousands of notes and pictures—something like six thousand pictures—so it's taking the tech people a while. And even then they don't really know what they're looking for. Fortunately, it's all in the cloud."

"Understood. Thank you," Ari said.

"Well, I'll be seeing you," Lacaba said with a cordial nod and headed back to the conference room.

Ari gazed down at the tasting room as Emily and the two butches crossed the tasting room again and went into the event room with a cart full of boxes. It was quiet on the second floor. No one in Eddie's office, or Cleo's…or Emily's. She peered through Emily's front window at her cluttered desk. When Ari had seen it that morning, nothing littered the surface but during the day the papers, folders and messages multiplied as she went from task to task. And there was certainly enough brewing at Sisters Cellars. A thought was percolating in Ari's brain. She wished she had Jane for a lookout, but she didn't want to lose the chance to snoop. Still, if Deputy Lacaba left the conference room…

She ducked into Emily's office and quickly scooted behind the desk. She pulled open the desk drawers, finding the usual collection of detritus and office supplies. Not surprising, Emily had one file drawer completely devoted to her Somm test—notes, a few books and her testing registration which included the invitation to test. Attached to the form was a personal check from the account of Cleo M. Vidal for fifteen hundred dollars. Ari wondered if Mina knew Cleo was paying for Emily to take the test. In the other file drawer she found the slimmest personnel files she'd ever seen. No one had any evaluations at all.

One folder was labeled RECOMMENDATIONS. Sitting atop the heap was a copy of the recommendation Emily had written on Sisters Cellars stationery to The Hearthstone Experience in Portland—for Dion Demopolous. In the letter Emily praised him for his fine work ethic and urged the upscale restaurant to hire him. Ari noted the date was August 10th. They must have hired him. This explained his constant trips to Portland that Frankie mentioned.

Ari glanced at the front glass. She needed to hurry. She scanned Emily's desk, finding nothing interesting except a folder from a major airline with two tickets to Spain for next March—one for Emily and the other for Cleo. *But Jane said Mina and Cleo didn't travel with the "third" person.* As she stood to leave, her gaze fell on the paper sitting squarely in the middle of the desk. She'd almost missed it because it was hiding in plain sight. Also written on Sisters Cellars stationery was Denise's brief letter of resignation, stating her intent, her grievance, and her diplomatic conclusion. What caught Ari's attention wasn't the content, it was the font. Comic Sans. The same font as the note in Dion's jeans.

She headed outside and thought about what she'd learned. First, Emily knew Dion was leaving and if Emily knew, did that mean Cleo knew? Pillow talk was powerful. Second, the relationship between Cleo and Emily was strong, perhaps stronger than Cleo's bond with Mina. Jane had said Mina was worried about Emily's involvement. She had good reason. Finally, Ari was now sure she knew who had let Dion into the tasting room. The only question was why.

Ari wandered onto the patio and scanned the vineyard. A cluster of people up the eastern slope moved left and then right as they snipped grapes and deposited the bunches in the plastic bins next to them. A bark got her attention and when she looked down, Dexter was jumping in front of her.

"You're sneaky. How ya doin', boy?"

His tiny tail wagged furiously and she smiled. He was just a bundle of joy. He pranced ahead but kept looking over his shoulder, making sure she was following him. She'd love to have a dog like Dexter. *If I can only convince Molly.*

She surveyed the picking layout and realized that all of the volunteers were on one side of a row while Berto and his small crew worked the other side. Whereas the volunteers clipped slowly and methodically with their pruning shears, the trained crew was in constant motion. It looked as if they were stabbing the vine, extracting the bunches of grapes and then tenderly—but efficiently—tossing them into their bins. The bins actually told the story. Whereas the volunteers had a taller stack of empty bins versus full bins, Berto's stack of empties was rapidly dwindling and his crew was starting a new row.

"Oh, what's this?" a volunteer called in a somewhat disgusted voice.

Cleo jogged over to her and inspected the problem. "Ah, yes, that's a little mold. Thanks for your eagle eyes, Wanda." Cleo stood up and announced, "Remember what we talked about earlier, gang. Wet September means there's going to be some moldy grapes. One of our natural challenges. If you see any, call it out like Wanda and I'll come over and take a look. We have a special bin for those grapes." She took the bunch from Wanda who continued picking with a smile on her face at being singled out for Cleo's praise.

Cleo saw Ari and stepped away from the volunteers. She looked stressed and Ari whispered, "Everything okay?"

"So far, not so bad. Berto's mind might be going but nobody picks as fast as he does." She pointed to the row where the volunteers worked. "This entire row, all the way up to the plateau, is basically free of mold. Berto hurried up here just as the bus was arriving and he got ahead of them. Of course he didn't pick every single moldy grape. That would actually be more suspicious. All vineyards deal with mold—and birds—and disease."

"So really, that row is getting picked twice."

"Yeah, but with a good PR spin." A wide grin spread across her face and in the fall sunlight she looked absolutely breathtaking.

"Getting back to Berto," Ari said, "Mina mentioned he might retire, or rather, the two of you might ask him to retire."

Cleo shrugged. "Mina and I don't agree. I know he falls asleep and sometimes he loses things. And yes, there was that huge mistake last year."

"Can you explain that to me?"

Cleo looked up the hill. Berto was waving at her. "Better than that. I'll show you."

A truck with a flatbed trailer sat on the adjacent dirt road. Two of Berto's crew acted as runners, lugging the full bins from the vines to the flatbed and returning to the pickers for the next full ones. It was obviously a long-practiced process and each worker knew his job. Cleo hopped into the driver's seat and motioned for Ari to join her in the cab as she started the truck.

"So after the grapes are picked, the very first step in the process is weighing them."

The truck chugged back down the hill and Ari looked for Jane amidst the volunteers but didn't see her. She imagined Jane had quickly tired of the activity and was probably back in the tasting room enjoying a beverage and playing *Words with Friends* with Rory.

They pulled up behind the production room next to the scale. Cleo parked the truck and pressed a call button on the side of the building. Ari noted the door was propped open, and Cleo said, "We're leaving it open until the locksmith can get here and change the lock. This time we're installing what *I* wanted, a keypad. Mina thought it was too much money, but if she'd listened to me, Dion would've had a way out."

Ari heard bitterness in Cleo's tone, and she wondered if Cleo and Mina's relationship was in trouble. "Did the killer plug all the locks?"

"Yeah…well, no, not all of them. Had the sense to leave the storage room lock alone. It doesn't go anywhere."

She hadn't noticed a storage room. "Where's it located?"

"Past Mina's office. It's a room of junk, really. I've been after her to organize it, but she always has a reason not to."

There's that tone again.

Two workers emerged and started pulling bins from the flatbed and setting them on the pad. When the platform was completely covered, Cleo pressed a button and 117.4 appeared on the LED screen.

"So, that's how much the grapes weigh including the weight of the containers. We know each bin weighs two pounds, and there are fourteen, so twenty-eight pounds of that weight is the containers." She tapped the calculator on her phone.

"That means we have 89.4 pounds of grapes. We record that on this weight tag and enter the information into our logbook. Eventually, the logbook is audited by our accountant and we're taxed for the number of grapes we use to make wine."

"Makes sense," Ari said.

"We also pay for the weight of the grapes we purchase from other vineyards, like the malbec grapes. That's where the error happened. Near as we can tell, Berto forgot to subtract the weight of the container in his numbers. Nobody caught it for a long time, well after we paid our quarterly taxes."

"Wouldn't Mina, or someone, have noticed there wasn't as much wine being made?"

Cleo let out a long sigh. She crafted a neutral expression. "Eventually she did notice, but she'd allowed Eddie to be in charge of the crushing and fermenting. Denise told Mina she thought there was a problem, but Mina listened to Eddie who said everything was fine. Turns out we were missing a third of the grapes we expected. Eddie talked to John Graham, the supplier, and he'd sold us fewer grapes than promised. He said it was because harvest was unpredictable, but the rumor was that he sold to a restauranteur. Mina was so angry, mainly at herself but also at Eddie for not giving her a heads-up." Her face softened. "It's kinda sad. He fashions himself a vintner, but he doesn't have what it takes. We're pushing to have him stay with the books and go with Berto to get the grapes. The only roadblock is Mina. She's dragging her feet because she doesn't want to tell one of her oldest friends—and an old flame—that he's not wanted out here."

Ari cocked her head to the side. "It seems to me he's still really involved. Denise was very upset with him earlier today."

Cleo looked down. "Yeah, I know. Some of this is on me too."

Before Ari could ask another question, Jane strolled out of the production room, Dexter leading the way. "There you are! Cleo, I think you might have the smartest dog in the world. I asked him to find Ari and he did." She rummaged through her purse and produced a dog treat. Dexter sat at attention until she held it out. "Good boy." He ran off with it in his mouth. She looked at Cleo and added, "Don't worry about the treat. Mina told me you only feed him the best ingredients and I got those from an organic store."

"It's fine, Jane," Cleo said. "Dexter enjoys having company and he's allowed to indulge a little on special occasions. I do agree with you. He's a very smart little dog. There've been several times where I thought he understood English."

"Mina says she heard him barking last night when he went out," Ari said.

"Really?" Cleo was clearly surprised. She dropped her gaze. "I wish I'd been there."

Ari touched her shoulder. "One of the more difficult aspects of a murder is that a lot of secrets are revealed, secrets that don't have anything to do with the victim. Still they come out because each person has to eliminate themselves from suspicion."

Cleo shrugged. "That makes sense. I just don't know much. I got home and crawled into bed. Next thing I know, Denise is pounding on the door."

Jane crossed her arms and gave Cleo a hard stare. "How serious is this thing with *Em-i-ly*."

"About as serious as Mina's fling with Eddie," Cleo snapped. "Or her fling with Peri."

"Peri?" Ari asked. "The somm?"

"Uh-huh." She pointed at Jane. "You might want to dial back your judgy voice, seein' as you ain't committed to anyone yet. I knew when I got together with Mina that she was a player, and she knew I'm one as well. We went in eyes wide open and we're still together." She stepped into Jane's personal space. "I'm thinkin' you and Rory should have the same conversation."

"I haven't cheated once on Rory!"

"Are you sure she hasn't cheated on you?"

"Stop!" Ari cried. "You're friends. Remember that."

Both of them turned away. Ari knew Jane was too stubborn to admit she was wrong, and Ari sensed Cleo was the same way. Jane turned on her heel and said, "I'm going back to the room to shower. Mina asked if I would help bartend at the bridal shower since Peri has a study group meeting and…" She stopped and bit her lip. "Well, since Dion is gone." She didn't wait for a response from Cleo or Ari before she walked away.

Cleo groaned. She reached for the bandana around her neck and dabbed at the sweat. "I've made a mess of things."

"Want to talk about it?"

"Not really. I'm rather ashamed I've let it get this far. Honestly, I know you've only been here a day, but are we that obvious, me and Emily?"

"You're not unprofessional, if that's what you're asking," Ari said, "but those glass fronts on the offices make it easy to read body language. I saw you in Emily's office earlier. She seemed really upset by her phone conversation. What was that about?"

Cleo smirked. "She was speaking to our bottle supplier who'd just informed us that he's raising his prices because the cost of glass has increased. Emily was lobbying to keep the old price since we're longstanding clients."

"Was she successful?"

Cleo cracked a smile. "The supplier said he'd think about it, but I think she won that round. She's very persuasive."

"What are your feelings about her?"

"It's different from any of my other flings."

"Have you and Mina always had an open relationship?"

"Not always, but I pushed for it. Look, I come from South America. We have a much different view of love and sexuality."

"How enthusiastic is Mina about this?"

"She's in for the most part. She's quite different from anyone else I've known since arriving in the states. And she's the love of my life. I want to be quite clear about that. Even though Emily is special, Mina is my person, *mi vida*, my forever."

The sincerity in her voice matched the look in her eyes. If nothing else, she believed what she was saying. Ari nodded. "Have you and Mina discussed your feelings for Emily?"

Cleo shifted in her chair and wouldn't meet Ari's gaze. "We have. It's nothing that's come between us, at least not yet. Sometimes it's much easier being with someone the second person knows, and sometimes it's much harder. In this case, the fact that Mina and Emily are old friends—and former lovers—makes it easier. Did you know Mina went to school with Emily, and Eddie and Peri as well?"

"Yes. Jane had mentioned that Mina had hired several of her old school buddies. Has that worked out okay?"

Cleo scratched her chin. "For the most part, but sometimes it makes it harder, like with Eddie. Mina needs to have one of those critical conversations with him, tell him to stay out of the winemaking aspect of the business. He needs to worry about the *business* end, specifically the finances."

"It has to happen," Ari reiterated.

"Yes, otherwise I'm pretty sure we'll lose Denise."

"I know you'll lose Denise. I happened to pass Emily's office earlier and Denise was submitting her resignation."

Cleo tensed. "Is she gone for good? I saw her and she just said she was going home for the rest of the day. I didn't think she meant she was done."

"No," Ari clarified. "Emily convinced her to stay for now."

Ari sensed Emily and Cleo talked about everything, which meant there were probably few actual secrets just between Mina and Cleo. "Does Eddie want Denise's job?"

"Oh, yeah."

"But what about Emily?" Ari pressed. "She's taking the Master Sommelier exam too, right?"

"She is but she's not sure what she wants to do. She's very good about handling the business, including dealing with the Department of Agriculture, all of that stuff. She removes a tremendous amount of pressure from Mina and me. Now that she's really seen my job and Mina's job, I don't think she'd want to do it."

"I can see why," Ari said. "In the last day, I've gained a tremendous respect for anyone in the wine business."

The comment earned a smile from Cleo and she seemed to relax.

"Has Deputy Lacaba spoken with you yet?" Ari asked.

"No, I've managed to duck her today. With everything that happened because of Dion's death, and the volunteers coming, she moved my interview to tomorrow."

"And you were with Emily when Dion was killed?"

"Yeah, I was," she said, although Ari thought she heard a break in her voice. "I was with Emily last night until about four this morning."

"Is there another way to verify that, other than just the two of you vouching for each other?"

Cleo thought before she shook her head. "Come with me to pick up another load."

They climbed into the truck's cab and headed back up the hill. Once the trailer was situated, the workers loaded the bins and Ari motioned for Cleo to step aside.

She leaned closer and whispered, "You said you and Mina don't share the same thoughts about Berto. We saw him asleep in the vineyard and others are concerned. Is he still capable of doing his job?"

"Yes," she said, offering a sympathetic smile. "I know he's become forgetful, but he teaches me new things every day. I'll take a million Bertos before I'd take one Eddie." She paused and then added, "And Denise feels the same way, for sure."

"I imagine so. Any idea why Dion would be in the production room?"

Cleo opened her mouth and then quickly closed it. She looked around before she finally said, "Maybe to give himself a leg up. You know he was leaving, right?"

"Yes," Ari said. "But I think you're one of the few people who knew that."

"True," Cleo conceded.

"And Mina didn't know."

Cleo looked away, ashamed. "I should've told her. I *will* tell her. It's just that Emily told me in confidence and I couldn't betray it." She looked at Ari for support, but Ari kept her expression neutral. "I wonder if he went into the production room to take something that didn't belong to him."

"Like what?"

Cleo shrugged and said, "Maybe he wanted to steal a sample of the pinot gris? It's going to be one of the best in the valley this year. Someone with fine taste buds might be able to discern how it was made."

Ari looked at her, puzzled. "But I thought most wine couldn't be replicated."

"No, it can't be replicated but it's possible to make a close imitation."

"Any idea who would want him dead?"

"Not really. But since I knew Dion was going to leave, that probably makes me a suspect, doesn't it?"

CHAPTER TWELVE

Another whoop and hoot, followed by thunderous applause, filtered onto the patio where Ari enjoyed some pinot noir. The bridal shower was in full swing and judging by the noise level, everyone was having a wonderful time. Ari imagined Jane's bartending skills might be partly to blame, as she was known for a generous pour at her own bar, The Pocket. Jane had opened the bar as a new adventure, something completely different from her day job as a real estate agent. While The Pocket was supposed to be an investment, Ari guessed most of the profits were literally guzzled away whenever Jane stepped behind the bar. Thus, Mina might regret asking her to work the bridal shower.

Ari heard footsteps. Deputy Lacaba was strolling across the flagstone steps toward her, a briefcase in one hand and a gym bag in the other. She'd changed into an Oregon Ducks T-shirt and sweatpants.

Ari motioned to her attire. "Are you a Duck?"

For the first time, Lacaba grinned. "I am. Through and through. Went to college in Eugene after the Marines. Got my degree in political science. You?"

"I never went to college," Ari admitted. "It just wasn't in the cards."

Lacaba shrugged. "It's not for everyone. It certainly wouldn't have been for me either if I'd started college right after high school."

"Would you like some?" Ari offered. "I'm sure I can scrounge up a glass."

"No need." She sat down opposite Ari and picked up the bottle. "Unless you're easily grossed out. But I promise I'm not sick."

"Be my guest," Ari said with a dismissive wave.

Lacaba took a healthy swig and nodded. "It's good but I like their cabernet best."

"Oh, I do like a good cabernet. I'll have to try that next."

"I can't wait for the malbec," Lacaba added.

Ari looked at her shrewdly. She was leaning back in the chair, legs crossed, staring out into the vineyard. Gone were the worry lines and the cold eyes. "Sounds like you really are up on the Sisters Cellars wines."

"Oh, yeah. I'm a member of the wine club."

"Great. Does Mina know that?"

Lacaba made a face and shook her head. "I wouldn't mention that while I was on the job."

"Understandable." Ari gestured at her and said, "But I'm liking the casual Deputy Lacaba look."

She raised a hand. "Nope, now I'm just Rosa."

Ari smiled. "And I'm Ari." She filled her glass and said, "Does this mean we can't discuss anything about the case?"

Lacaba narrowed her eyes. "Hmm. I don't think I should say much. I'm dressed for the gym, but my uniform is just a few feet away. You, though, are a civilian and we're sitting in a public place, so whatever."

Ari looked over her shoulder before she said, "I have a theory. What if Dion's death was...unplanned? It couldn't have been accidental, because whoever put him in that room wanted, at the very least, to scare him. But what if that was the person's intention? I'm thinking—"

"Wait," Lacaba said, sitting forward. "Please give me a moment to see if I can figure it out myself."

Ari watched her wheels turn. She thrummed fingers on the table and suddenly looked up.

"The phone. That's why you think it was unplanned. The killer couldn't have known Dion would accidentally leave his phone in the event room. He—or she—assumed Dion had it with him and could call Mina or Berto." Lacaba sighed and she seemed to deflate. "How did I not see that on my own?"

"Hey, don't be hard on yourself. I thought of it because Mina brought it up. She was so upset that she couldn't save him."

"But why would someone want to scare him?"

"Maybe it's somebody who wants him to fail the test. It definitely puts everything in a different light."

"I'd also wonder how that person is doing emotionally. He or she is responsible for the death of another person."

"Good point. We should scrutinize everyone's behavior. And there's one other thing to consider."

Lacaba leaned on the table. "You have my full attention and I'm apologizing for my previous rude behavior this morning."

Ari laughed. "Okay. I think we need to determine why Dion was there. He wasn't lured there. He sought someone out to help him, to leave that door open. Why?"

Lacaba nodded slowly. Ari had been thinking of the ramifications for a few hours, and it would take the deputy a while to catch up. Lacaba looked at her watch. "I need to get moving." She stood and extended her hand. "Thank you for a most insightful chat." Boisterous chatter from the tasting room cut through the quiet. "Are you going to the study session?"

"I thought I'd stop by."

"I would but I…have to be somewhere."

"The gym can't wait?"

Lacaba's mouth moved to form an answer and finally said, "The gym is after."

"I see. I'm sorry. I didn't mean to pry."

"Oh, no," she said quickly. "I wasn't offended."

"Well, I'll see you tomorrow."

"Yes. First thing in the morning." With a nod she left through the side gate of the patio.

Deputy Lacaba was clearly a complicated woman. Ari had seen none of the nearly palpable anger that had radiated off her for most of the day. Earlier, it was almost as if she resented the assignment or was overwrought with stress to solve the murder. She'd said Sheriff Jerome wanted her to be his successor. Ari wondered how many male deputies wanted that same role.

Molly's FaceTime rang just as she was about to go into the study session. "Hi, babe." Ari peered closely at the background. "Where are you?"

"Down at Celebrity Theater. Some nineties grunge band I never heard of. The good thing is most of the audience is in their late forties. Their days of drunk and disorderly behavior are behind them." They both laughed and Molly asked, "Did you solve the case?"

"No, but I met Jane's twin in about thirty years. She propositioned me."

Molly cracked a grin. "Oh, really? Was she stunning?"

"For someone in her seventies, oh yes."

"So, do I have competition?"

Ari laughed. "You know what?"

"What?"

"I'm just glad we can joke about other women now…without the jealousy."

"Yeah, me too."

They made googly eyes at each other, but Ari meant what she said. Their therapist, Dr. Yee, had helped them with every aspect of their relationship, a notable one being Molly's jealousy anytime a woman—or a man—flirted with Ari.

"So, what's going on with the case?"

"Well, several things." She summarized Denise's ultimatum and subsequent retraction, Berto's questionable behavior, and Mina's inability to stand up to Eddie.

"What's the deal with Eddie?" Molly asked.

"He's Mina's old flame and apparently her more recent flame."

"And Cleo is okay with that?"

"Not sure. It ended, so maybe not." She threw up her hands. "But what does any of this have to do with the guy who died?"

"If you answer that question, you'll probably solve the case."

"Probably."

"You know I lost a bet with Buster." Buster was Molly's right-hand man. "I told him there was no way you'd find trouble in a completely different state. I told him that your magnetic attraction to mayhem and murder ceased at the state line. Now I'm out fifty bucks."

"Fifty?" Ari feigned outrage. "You should've known better than to bet anything over twenty."

"Ah, probably true. So, seriously. What are your thoughts on the case?"

"I'm not so sure the guy was killed intentionally."

"Really?"

Ari shared her theory and Molly nodded. "That changes motive entirely. Either someone wanted to rattle him or he was out to prove something and someone didn't want him to succeed."

"That's what I'm thinking, although I can't believe this place. It's got all the makings of a soap opera—deception, passion, greed—and incredible intelligence and diligence. I had no idea."

She swirled her wine and watched the legs of the full-bodied pinot drizzle down the sides of the glass. "What about you?" Molly's face changed and she exhaled. Ari set down her glass. "Babe, are you okay?"

"Sort of. I found out today that Don and Jenna are talking about a divorce."

Don and Jenna were Molly's brother and sister-in-law. "Oh, no. That's terrible. I didn't see that coming. Did you?"

"No," Molly whispered. "Right now they're just separated, so maybe things will work out."

"What about the kids?"

"I don't think they've told them much, although Kenny suspects. He's old enough to read situations."

"I'm so sorry."

"Yeah, me too. Well, I gotta get inside."

"And I better get to my study group. Like you said there's probably at least one or two more motives to consider. I love you."

"I love you, too. And babe?"

"Yeah?"

"This is probably wasted breath on my part, but please try to stay out of trouble."

Ari took another ten minutes, until she'd drained the rest of her pinot, before going inside. She'd been listening to the bellicose discussion of the four remaining Master Sommelier candidates through the open patio door, learning a lot from eavesdropping during their practice tasting session.

While the two females—Peri and Emily—stated their opinions with vigor and then backed off, the two guys, J.D. and Racy, made the same point two or three times and routinely trash talked anyone who disagreed with them—even when they were wrong. *Men.* She recognized a fifth voice—Eddie, the CFO. He seemed to be serving as a moderator, asking questions, keeping the conversation somewhat on track, and most importantly, pouring the wine.

She found them sitting at the large table in the center of the room. Wineglasses surrounded a metal bucket where any leftover wine could be dumped before the next sample was poured. Ten bottles of wine stood in front of Eddie, five in a paper bag that came up to the top of the neck, masking all of the labels. The other five bottles had been revealed, so Ari assumed they were halfway through the session.

"Hi, Ari," Eddie said. "Peri told us you'd be dropping by. You're just in time for our next taste. I know you've met Emily and Peri, and this is J.D. Cormac and Racy Ryder."

Emily nodded and Peri offered a wink. Racy was easy to recognize from his photo in the Laurelwood program, although now his curly hair was untamed and flailed in several different directions. He offered Ari an appraising look as if she was an unwanted distraction from their work. The final member of the group, J.D. Cormac, was older than his counterparts, with a salt-and-pepper goatee and graying temples. He looked like a college professor wearing a plaid shirt and sweater vest, but Ari knew from the article in the newspaper that he'd been in the tech industry and moved to Oregon from Silicon Valley. He offered her a mock salute.

Eddie poured four tastes, noticed Ari standing off to the side and said, "Would you like to try it?"

"Um, sure."

He added one more glass and distributed the tastes. All Ari knew was that it was a white wine. The four immediately held their respective glass to the light, twirling and swirling the wine. Then they each brought the glass directly under their noses and inhaled deeply. They took notes on their iPads with a stylus, constantly sniffing the wine, then making a note. Then more sniffing. Finally, they tasted it in their own way—a tiny taste, an enormous mouthful swished about like Listerine, or a small sip rolled across the tongue. Eventually each one spit out the wine into his or her respective paper cup rather than swallowing it, and Ari's concern about meeting with a bunch of drunks who couldn't remember anything was quelled. They really weren't drinking at all.

"What they're doing, Ari," Eddie explained, "is studying for the third part of the Master Sommelier test, the tasting portion. They'll taste six wines and determine the varietal, the region from which it was produced, and the year."

"Wow," Ari said.

"It's considered the hardest test in the world. That's why there's only about two hundred Master Sommeliers."

"Would've been two hundred and one," J.D. grumbled.

"Are you also studying for the test?" Ari asked Eddie innocently.

He cracked a grin. "No, I'm just helping them out. I'd rather do what Mina or Cleo does. That's why I'm a pest and keep wandering down to the vineyard or the production room. I'm trying to soak up as much knowledge as possible. They've been very gracious." His face sobered and he said, "Denise, not so much."

"Were you friends with Dion?"

Eddie shrugged. "As much as anyone was. We had a cordial relationship."

"Have you been interviewed by Deputy Lacaba yet?"

"No, I think that's tomorrow." As an afterthought he said, "I was in Eugene out to dinner at Racy's restaurant."

He pointed at Racy, who said, "I'll vouch for him. He helps me with the restaurant and I feed him for free."

"Sounds like a plan," Ari agreed.

"Yeah, he was there last night. All the way till closing."

"What about you, J.D.? Where were you when Dion died?"

"I was home—alone. I didn't kill him but I don't have anyone to vouch for me," he said plainly.

"Emily, I think it's your turn to start," Eddie encouraged.

She again picked up the glass and glanced at her notes. "Wine is clear and bright, like the color of pale straw."

"Other impressions on appearance?"

"No hint of gas or sediment," Peri added.

Racy held up his glass to the light. "Medium concentration of color."

Eddie looked at J.D. "Anything to add?"

All eyes turned to him. He shrugged and said, "It's all been mentioned."

"Okay, J.D.," Eddie said, "why don't you lead off with aroma?"

He bent his nose over the lip of the glass and took a deep whiff. "Definitely smelling apple. Medium intensity."

"I don't smell the apple," Racy disagreed. "I smell underripe mango."

"I smell the mango," Peri said, "but I also smell the apple." She offered a collegial smile to J.D., who sat up straighter.

They all looked at Emily. Apparently not participating wasn't an option. "Yes on the mango and the apple, but I also detect..."

She stopped and took another deep whiff. "…something waxy, a bad oak. Reminds me of dog poop."

They burst out laughing and Peri sprayed her current mouthful of wine across the table, causing shouts of disgust from Racy and J.D.

Peri, embarrassed, said to Emily, "Dude, you gotta tell me when you're gonna say that shit."

Eddie whispered to Ari, "Emily is known for her graphic, colorful, and sometimes vicious figurative language." He added loudly, "We're not sure if the judges will appreciate Emily's metaphors and similes, but I guess she'll find out in a few weeks."

Emily turned up her nose. "I believe they will."

Eddie clapped his hands. "Okay, taste and conclusion."

Everyone took another taste and spit into their cup.

"Fresh," Peri said. "Structure has medium acidity, complexity is medium plus. My conclusion is temperate climate, possibly Australia. I'd say sauvignon blanc, 2012."

"Agree with fresh," Racy said. "Also dry. Medium body, high acidity; moderate plus in finish. I'd say this is new world. Aged for one to three years. Definitely sauv blanc. I say New Zealand. 2010."

"Others?" Eddie asked. "Who agrees with New Zealand?" When no one raised a hand he said, "Australia?" The two other hands went up.

Emily took another sip and spit. "Moss Wood, from Margaret River, Australia, 2010."

J.D. nodded.

They all looked expectantly at Eddie. He pulled off the paper bag with a flourish to reveal the Moss Wood sauvignon blanc label—bottled in 2010. Everyone groaned and ribbed Emily.

"Hey, I agreed with her," J.D. interjected.

"You always agree, J.D.," Racy muttered. "That's all you do."

"Hey, lay off, Racy," Peri said. "Leave him alone."

Racy reached for the sauvignon blanc and poured himself a glass. "Should we leave you alone, J.D.? Is that what you want? Is that why you killed Dion?"

"What?" J.D. cried. "I would never do such a thing! Unlike you, Racy, Dion was actually helping me study."

"Of course he was," Racy said before he took another slug of the wine.

"You're a jackass," J.D. hissed.

"Hey," Eddie said calmly, "let's not resort to name calling. Everyone's a little tense. The test is really close now."

"What do you care, Eddie?" J.D. retorted. "It's not like you have anything to gain or lose. You just sit on the sidelines and pour the wine. You're such a wannabe."

Eddie set his jaw and Ari saw his fingers clench around the lip of the table. "Shut up, J.D. I'd do just fine on this test."

"Then take it," he countered.

"I will," Eddie said.

"Uh, Racy, can I ask you a question?" Ari's voice broke the tension.

He looked at her, surprised. "Um, sure. Okay."

"I spoke with Dion's brother today. He said that Dion believed you were doing something underhanded."

"What?"

She shrugged dramatically. "I have no idea what he's talking about, but Apollo told me Dion was going to investigate. Any idea what he's talking about?"

Ari scanned the group. No one gave anything away. They'd all been together for so long they probably knew each other's tells, and when it was an outsider making the waves, they stuck together. Only Peri met her gaze and Ari imagined that was more to do with the obvious crush Peri seemed to have on her.

Racy took a deep breath. "I don't have a clue."

Emily seemed to cough the word, "Laurelwood," drawing everyone's attention. She looked away as if she'd done nothing.

He stared at her. "Implying something, Emily? I won that fair and square. It's not my fault Mina couldn't enter her wine. She doesn't hold it against me, so why do you?"

Emily shook her head. "I don't. But I think Dion did."

J.D. reached for the bottle of sauvignon blanc. "If we've answered your questions, Ari, I'd like to go back to the conversation. Eddie, I'd like to see you try and pass the somm test. What a score that would be." He took a sip and watched Eddie fume over the top of his glass.

Eddie leaned over the table. "Fuck you, J.D." He slammed a fist down and huffed out of the room.

The four of them looked at each other but no one called for Eddie to come back.

"Does this happen often?" Ari asked.

"Sometimes," Peri said. "Eddie thinks he's part of the group, but he's not."

"Hey, he knows a lot about wine," Racy countered. "Even if he hasn't taken the test."

"Like what?" Emily pressed. "Each day I am more and more convinced that what Eddie knows about wine wouldn't even fill a bottle."

Racy took another sip of wine. He'd been ready to say something but chose to swallow it instead. "He's helped me a lot with my restaurant. I don't mean to disparage the dead, and Dion might've been the only one of us who became an MS in Dallas, but he wasn't gonna be as successful as me."

Emily rolled her eyes. "Here we go again. Yes, Racy, *Respite* is a great wine, but you and I both know that if Mina had gotten that shipment on time last year, your wine would've been second at the competition—at best."

"You don't know if that's true," Racy said, but his tone suggested he did.

Peri raised her hands in submission. "Hey, just stop. There's no point. What's done is done." She looked up at Ari, her lips quirked into a grin. "So, Ari, how would you like to help us wrap up here. We still have four wines to go. Wanna take over for Eddie?"

Racy smiled. "Yeah, please do that. We like you, for the most part."

"Speak for yourself," Emily said. When Ari glanced at her she said, "Just kidding," with a smirk on her face.

But Ari wasn't so sure she was.

Two hours later the other four bottles were revealed. Ari was severely buzzed because unlike the Master Sommelier candidates, she hadn't spit out her wine—and she'd enjoyed that large glass of pinot noir on the patio before her stint as wine pourer. The time had been enlightening, although what she'd learned seemed to have little bearing on the case.

Without a doubt, the person most prepared for the exam was Emily. She'd correctly named the varietal, region, and year produced three times. The other three candidates had each gotten one right, but none of them knew as much as Emily. And apparently she hadn't known as much as Dion. The multitude of blue binders was most likely the key to his success. *Maybe he shared those with her?*

As the group packed up to leave, Ari glanced at the wineglasses, used paper cups and spit bucket, feeling obligated to do something with all of it. Peri was the closest and had been the most hospitable, so she touched her arm and asked, "Where does all this go?"

Peri scowled. "I'll take care of it." She set her messenger bag aside and scooped up the glasses with one hand.

"Impressive," Ari said, retrieving the bucket.

"Years of practice."

She followed Peri into the back kitchen and a large commercial dishwasher. They quickly stacked the glasses, and Ari felt Peri's eyes on her. "That's a very interesting group," she said.

Peri sighed. "That's one word for it. I'd call it friendship by necessity." She leaned against the wall and crossed her arms. "None of us would be friends under any other circumstance. But for this, we need each other. I've never heard of anyone passing this test alone."

"What was the deal with Eddie? Why isn't he taking the test? He says he doesn't want to but he seemed quite invested in the process."

"Oh, he is. But like he said, he's more interested in running a winery than being a somm."

"Well, I've never known a successful businessman who storms out of a room."

She rolled her eyes. "Eddie and his damn temper tantrums. It was bad enough when he and Mina were carrying on. Thought he was in charge of the whole place."

"Who ended it?"

"Cleo," Peri said with a laugh.

Ari said innocently, "So Mina and Cleo have an open relationship?"

"Only to a point. If things get too serious with the third party, either one of them has the right to call it off." She looked over her shoulder to make sure they were alone. "Frankly, I think Mina's about had it with Cleo and Emily. She's going to pull the plug on that one." Peri shrugged. "Everyone, including myself, has understood that eventually Mina returns to Cleo or Cleo returns to Mina. Eddie struggled with that. That's about the time he started hanging out with Racy."

"Who just won the malbec award?"

"Yes, for *Respite*."

Ari glanced over her shoulder before she said, "I don't want to be a traitor, but as someone who loves malbec, is it any good?"

Peri put a hand over her smile. She also looked around before she said, "Yeah. It is." She leaned in and whispered, "It's a lot like Sabrosa, Mina's malbec. Weird, huh?"

"Well, maybe that's because Mina taught Eddie and he's shared what he knows?"

"Possibly," Peri replied, but Ari saw doubt in her eyes. She smiled and said, "You should go taste it at Racy's restaurant. I could take you there if you like."

"Um, that's okay. Jane'll go with me."

She nodded. "I understand. Clearly."

"Thanks."

"And I won't keep hitting on you. I imagine your girlfriend is pretty tough. Mina says she's a former police detective."

"She's both—a detective and tough."

CHAPTER THIRTEEN

Ari felt a wet tongue on her cheek. When her eyes fluttered open, Dexter's little furry face was in front of her and his tail thumped in excitement.

"Good morning, Dexter."

Louder thumping as she scratched him behind the ears. She looked over at the other bed in the guest room and saw that Jane was already up—or had never come to bed. The guest room door was shut and the bed was still perfectly made. Ari knew for a fact Jane wasn't one to spend time fluffing pillows and straightening sheets.

Dexter barked for Ari to get up, and she glanced again at the closed door. "How did you get in here, boy?"

Ari rose and checked the door. Locked. The pocket door to the bathroom, however, was slightly ajar. She turned on the bathroom light and saw that the door leading to the hallway was open. A cold shiver ran through her. After the incident with Emily yesterday she'd meant to lock the door, but Denise had run in to vomit and she'd become distracted. So it was unlocked all night. The door wasn't heavy and there was a lever, not a doorknob, so she was certain Dexter had jumped up and pressed down the lever, opening the outer door. Then he'd nudged the pocket door open.

Had someone gone through their things? Nothing in the bathroom looked as if it had been moved. She returned to the bedroom and checked her suitcase. Everything was how she'd left it. She scanned the room, looking for something missing or out of place. Her gaze settled on a dark gray lump on the closet floor: Jane's treasured cashmere sweater. An earthquake could occur and Jane would still take the time to properly hang her Brunello Cucinelli V-neck.

Someone has searched our room.

After rehanging Jane's sweater, she returned to her suitcase and took a harder look. While she wasn't an anal packer like Jane, she had her own preferences. This time she checked the side pockets and found her rolled up socks had been shoddily and hastily stuffed back inside. She hugged herself, suddenly cold. Bad enough that their things had been ransacked, but *when* had it occurred? Last night she was definitely buzzed. Would she have noticed a dark sweater on the floor? Maybe. Maybe not. Could it be that someone had come in last night—while she slept?

She knew they wouldn't have found anything for there was nothing to find. She had no notes or evidence. Only the program, article and the pics on her phone, which was still charging on the nightstand. She dressed quickly, relocked the bathroom door, and decided to check in with Deputy Lacaba. She took a step into the hallway and heard loud voices.

"I'm not blaming you." *Cleo.*

"It sure the hell sounds like you are!" *Mina.*

"He's still in your head. You've got to at least acknowledge that."

When Mina didn't immediately reply, Ari took a few more steps toward Cleo's office. Any closer and they would see her through the glass front. She looked over the balcony into the tasting room. No one else was around to hear this argument and she was grateful that the quiet allowed her to hear it alone.

"I'll admit that Eddie was different," Mina said. "And you need to admit that Emily is different."

Now it was Cleo's turn to be silent. Ari debated whether she should interrupt them or not. Since they were both still suspects, she decided to hear how this ended—and hopefully not get caught.

"I can't explain Emily, Mina. You are my other half, but Emily…fills holes."

"You know she'll dump you in a minute if the right person comes along, someone who'll pay for her next round of testing."

Ari couldn't hear Cleo's reply.

"What!" Mina cried. "You paid for her testing this time?"

"You paid for Dion."

"You *know* that's different. We owed him. And he would've passed! Everybody knows that."

"First off, I never fully agreed to using Dion as our sperm donor. I'm sorry he's dead, but it saves us from another knock-down-drag-out argument. And second, I think Emily will pass. She did brilliantly at the tasting last night."

Mina laughed. "That doesn't mean anything." She groaned. "I can't believe you did that. We can't afford it, Cle."

"What's done is done. If we want to save money that badly, I'll agree to retiring Berto, okay? That'll help."

"Oh, god. Don't go there. Not now. We've got enough on our plates with the harvest and Dion's murder." Mina cleared her throat. "About that. I know you didn't want to pick Dion to be the father of our children, but can you look me in the eye and tell me you didn't kill him?"

"I didn't kill him." Cleo paused. "What about you? I heard he was leaving us even after agreeing to be the donor, even after you paid for his test. We weren't getting a Master Sommelier. Can you look me in the eye and say you didn't kill him?"

"I didn't kill him."

"Well, someone did. Why the hell was he even in there? He knew it was a deathtrap. None of this makes sense."

"We agree on something. Hopefully, Deputy Lacaba and Ari can figure it out."

That's my cue.

Ari sprinted around the corner, past the glass front of Cleo's office, hoping they would think she'd just stepped out of the guest room.

"Knock, knock."

They both turned toward her with brilliant smiles.

"Good morning," Mina said. "Did you sleep well?"

"I did," she said cautiously.

"Anything wrong?" Cleo asked.

"Have you seen Deputy Lacaba this morning?"

They both shook their heads and Mina said, "Is something wrong?"

"Can one of you let me into the conference room? I don't want to say anything until I check something."

"Sure," Mina said.

They followed her, and in a second Ari could tell someone had searched the deputy's materials which were scattered about.

"What happened?" Cleo asked. "Who did this?"

"Yes, who did this?" Deputy Lacaba boomed, appearing in the doorway. Her hostility had returned.

"The same person who went through my things," Ari answered calmly.

"What?" Mina cried. "Seriously?"

"Yes, and I have the feeling they did it while I was sleeping in the room."

"No," Cleo said, shocked.

Lacaba rolled through the room, checking the records, restacking files, gathering the upended piles, whirling about the room like a dervish.

"Dexter woke me up this morning," Ari said. "That's how I figured it out."

Mina looked perplexed. "Dexter? How would he get in your room?"

"Not through the front door," Ari explained. "I'm assuming he pushed down the lever to the bathroom door, the one I forgot to lock. I meant to…but I got distracted."

Mina looked around. "Where's Jane?"

"I haven't seen her. Did she bartend last night?"

Mina rolled her eyes. "Yeah. Emily's going to flip when she sees how much wine was actually consumed. Anyway, I stopped by and Jane was having a great time with all the guests. Most of them were from California, and she knew a couple people." She waved a hand. "Not important right now. Let's focus on your room. Was anything missing?"

"Near as I can tell, no."

"Are you sure?" Cleo pressed.

Mina rubbed her wife's back. "Babe, calm down. It's okay."

"No, it's not okay. We've got serious shit happening here, Mina. I don't know about you, but I'm feeling completely out of control." She turned back to Ari. "Don't you think it's telling that whoever did this didn't care if we found out? That's why they didn't lock the bathroom and go out the front instead, that's why they didn't pick up all the files they messed up here. They don't care if we know. They're saying, 'Fuck you.'"

Ari nodded. "That's what it says to me."

Mina pinched the bridge of her nose. "I'm so sorry, Ari. You'll probably never want to come back. And when Jane finds out, whenever the hell that might be, she'll probably not want to have her wedding here."

"Mina, it's okay."

"I just don't understand. Why would anyone want to kill Dion? This murder has completely jeopardized our PR efforts, our entire harvest, the future of the business." She dropped into a chair as if for the first time the enormity of the situation weighed on her. She looked at Cleo. "We could lose everything."

Cleo knelt in front of her and stroked her face. "It'll be okay. I promise." She raised Mina's hand to her lips and kissed it. The tenderness between them was genuine and Ari understood why their other lovers had never destroyed their bond. She instantly thought of Molly. *It's that way with us.*

"Damn it!" Lacaba roared.

"What's wrong?" Mina asked.

"I can't find it," she said, panicked, and dropped to the floor to scurry around on all fours. She popped back up, sank into a chair, and held her head up with her fists. When she looked at them, her eyes blazed and her lips were curled. "None of you better be playing games."

"What the hell?" Cleo barked.

Ari knew better than to reach out and touch her, but she extended her hand across the table to get her attention. "What's missing?"

"His phone," she whispered. "I can't believe I left it here. I thought I put it in my briefcase with…the other stuff."

"I thought the tech had it."

Lacaba exhaled a groan. "No. They're so backed up that once they pulled everything to the cloud they gave it back to me so I could work on it too. Shit."

"It's got to be here."

She shoved herself out of the conference room chair, sending it spinning against the wall. She stormed about the place, cursing continuously.

"Um, we need to get to work. Is that okay?" Cleo asked quietly.

"Go ahead and go," Ari said, offering a wave goodbye.

Mina squeezed Ari's shoulder and offered a concerned look, as if she wondered whether Ari should be left alone with the exploding deputy. Ari nodded and Mina wisely shut the door behind them.

Ari sat and waited for Lacaba to run out of gas. Three minutes later she dropped into a different chair. "So much for being sheriff. I'll be lucky to be dogcatcher."

"Let's analyze this a moment. I left my bathroom door unlocked so that explains how someone could get in. But you locked this room, right?"

"Of course!" She closed her eyes. "I apologize. Yes, I locked it. Whoever got in here had a key. And if I find out who that was, they'll be sending me to jail for what I'll do to him—or her. And if I don't find that phone quick and I have to tell Sheriff Jerome, call the funeral home. He's going to kill me."

Ari searched the conference room once more, but the phone was definitely gone and not misplaced. Her own phone pinged with a text from Jane. *Over at Mina's making toast. Want some breakfast?* Ari knew the translation was, "Do you want to come over to Mina's and cook?" Jane rarely used her kitchen and owned only a single frying pan.

Sure.

Deputy Lacaba shooed her away as she gathered herself and prepared to interview some of the field workers. Ari felt a little guilty leaving her when she was so upset, but it was clear she wanted her to go. As she crossed the tasting room, Peri emerged from the back and smiled when she saw Ari. "Hey, thanks for filling in last night as wine pourer."

"No problem. It was interesting."

Peri leaned over the bar and whispered, "Did you learn anything useful other than Eddie's a grade-A prick, Racy's full of himself, and J.D. has absolutely no confidence?"

"What about you and Emily? What should I have learned from the two of you?"

Peri grinned...and yawned. "Sorry. Up late." She poured herself a coffee and offered a cup to Ari.

"Thanks. I'm on my way to Mina's to make breakfast for Jane, but she can wait another ten minutes."

At the mention of Jane, Peri offered a dreamy smile. "She doesn't strike me as someone who cooks."

"Not even a little." Ari sipped the magic elixir before asking, "So, what should I have learned from watching you and Emily last night, other than Emily really knows her wine?"

Peri nearly spewed her coffee. "Sorry, I've done that twice now in front of you."

"What's so funny?"

"She cheats."

Ari blinked. "What?"

Peri glanced around the room. "No one is supposed to know, and it started out as a joke against Dion, but before we practice the tasting test, Eddie shows her the bottles. It used to infuriate Dion when she'd *guess* a wine that he missed. I think she paid Eddie to let her do it."

"Why would she do it in the first place?"

"Dion never took her seriously. I don't think she feels anyone takes her seriously." Peri's gaze drifted upstairs toward the offices. "She's stuck up there, completely removed from the real action. Once in a while she comes down to help, but her job is intense. I think she's jealous that Eddie gets into the mix and doesn't get in trouble even when his real job suffers."

She bit her lip, and Ari could tell she was holding something back. Ari sipped her coffee and waited. Her phone pinged. She knew she didn't have much more time. When Jane was hungry, she wanted her food ASAP. Hungry turned to *hangry* on a dime. Texts would most likely arrive every thirty seconds until she got there.

"Three things…"

"What?"

Peri rubbed the rim of the cup, definitely conflicted. When she looked up, it was as if she'd made a decision. "Dion could be a real prick, but he was helping me." She sighed. "But…he could be a real prick."

"Who was he a prick to?"

"J.D."

"How?"

"You know the blue binders he created, right?"

"Uh-huh."

"So, J.D. knows people. He told Dion he could introduce him to a publisher who makes study aides if Dion would give him a percentage. I mean, those binders are unbelievable. Dion designed a method of study like no other. So anyway, the publisher meets Dion, and I don't know how or why it happened, but they cut J.D. out. J.D. has never forgiven him. So last night he said, 'Good riddance.' Not that that makes him the killer, but there's no love there."

Ari knew this. "Okay, what's number two?"

Peri finished her coffee and set the cup on the counter. "You know Emily and Cleo are a thing, right?"

"Yeah. I do. And Mina knows."

"Yup. That's how they do it." She leaned against the counter and crossed her arms. "Here's the thing, though. Emily wants out of the office. She doesn't want to do what Mina or Cleo does, but she did want Dion's job."

"She wanted to work with you."

"Exactly. And she thought she was right in line to do that with him leaving. I mean, she's Mina's high school friend, she's sleeping with Cleo, and Eddie, who makes everyone crazy, has no desire to be a somm. Emily was the logical choice."

Ari's phone pinged again. She didn't bother to read the message. "I don't see why this is important. Dion was leaving. I think that's the worst kept secret ever."

Peri leaned a little closer. "Listen, I know for a fact that he changed his mind. He was staying. And since Emily is in charge of HR, the first person who found out was her."

"When did he change his mind?"

"When he found out the publisher's timeline—three days ago. He told me at work, just off the cuff. He knew Emily was going to throw a fit so he wasn't going to tell her until after the test. But when he told the restaurant in Portland, the manager called Emily. She was in a huff because Emily had written such a glowing recommendation and said how wonderful and reliable Dion was."

"Understandable. The manager was counting on him moving there."

"And," Peri added, "it ruined Emily's plans."

"What's the third thing?"

Peri glanced at her and her face turned red. "Promise you won't get mad?"

"No, I can't promise that until I hear what it is."

She closed her eyes and with a shotgun delivery said, "Jane seduced me and we spent last night together." Ari's look of surprise pushed Peri to add, "I didn't initiate it. In fact, I could probably scream, 'Me Too.'"

Ari's stomach was doing somersaults. *Oh, Jane.* "What happened. Exactly."

"Well, you left me in the kitchen, right?"

"Yes."

"So I'm cleaning up and I hear heels. I turn around and she's there. I say hello, ask if she needs anything and when she shakes her head, I go back to cleaning the sink. I'm just the hired help.

She's the owner's best friend. Hell, if she wants to roam around the kitchen, I'm not gonna say anything."

Ari turned her hand in a circle. "Got it. Keep going."

"All of a sudden she's pressed against my back and she's whispering in my ear about how hot I am. Then she gropes my breasts and asks if she should stop."

"And?"

Peri cringed. "I didn't make the right choice."

Ari buried her head in her hands. "Oh, shit."

Ari used most of the three-minute walk to Mina's house thinking about Jane's imploded relationship with Rory. But before she rang the bell, she thought about what Peri said about Dion. He wasn't leaving, which could be part of the reason he was killed—by Emily—whose alibi was a night of passion with Cleo.

But it didn't explain why he was in the production room. He might have wanted to be there alone, but, as Mina had stated, harvest was a 24-7 job. Someone was always there—except on that one day.

Most likely whatever Dion was searching for was in Mina's office, and Mina was still a suspect, a somewhat unlikely suspect, but Ari couldn't rule her out entirely. She needed to get in there but that would be impossible during harvest, especially if eagle-eye Denise was around. She pictured Denise storming into the office and shouting, "What the hell are you doing in here? Are you a spy for one of our competitors?"

There had to be a way, but she was running out of time. It was early Friday morning and she and Jane would leave Monday. That gave her a little more than forty-eight hours. Not a lot of time to catch a killer.

Her phone pinged again. *I'm eating a cushion right now. Needs syrup. Nom. Nom. Nom.*

She adopted a pleasant expression, one that said she knew nothing about the fling with Peri, knocked on Mina's front door and stuck her head inside. "Jane, I'm here!"

"Well, it's about time."

Ari's first impression of Mina's home was that it fit her. A hodgepodge of comfy furniture greeted Ari, including a worn caramel-colored leather sofa, two navy blue wingback chairs—and a retro pink settee. All faced a sixty-inch television mounted above the fireplace.

The open floor plan flowed into the kitchen where Jane was a flurry of activity, pulling out pans, plates and silverware. Mina's compact kitchen was functional and included high-end appliances. This was a kitchen for someone who knew how to cook. *And if she were here right now and could see the mess Jane was making...* They would need to do a good job on the cleanup effort.

"Hey," Ari said.

Jane looked up from a cutting board. Tears streamed down her face.

"What's wrong?"

"Oh, onion." She wiped her eyes and Ari noticed the onion sitting on the cutting board.

"Jane, all you've done is slice it in half."

"Can't help it. Maybe I'm allergic."

Ari wasn't buying it, but there was no point in pushing the issue. Jane would reveal whatever was bothering her when she was ready. "Why don't you let me do that and you pour me a cup of coffee?"

"Gladly."

Jane surrendered the knife, wiped her eyes once more, and found another coffee cup. Ari shared Peri's gossip about Dion and asked, "Do you think there's any chance that Mina killed Dion?"

Jane gave her a hard stare. "None. Absolutely none. It wouldn't make any sense on any level. This is her life. Whether Dion was a part of it or not didn't matter. Mina's a survivor and fiercely independent. She can survive anything—even Cleo's betrayal."

"Okay, if you believe in Mina that much, then we need to search her office. Dion was in that production room for a reason. I just hope it wasn't to find something incriminating on Mina."

"It wasn't," Jane said confidently. "I just know it. Let's call her now. I guarantee you she won't mind anyone rummaging through her stuff. She's such a good person and she has nothing to hide." Tears streamed down Jane's face, the onion nowhere near her. "I probably should've snatched her up when I had the chance."

Ari offered her a sympathetic smile. "So when are you going to tell me the real reason you're crying?"

CHAPTER FOURTEEN

Ari's efforts to pry the truth from Jane failed miserably. Every time she mentioned anything except the murder case, Jane replied with a question about Dion. She especially didn't want to talk about the bridal shower from the evening before. She said she slept on Mina's couch, which Ari knew was a lie, since earlier Mina had been just as puzzled by Jane's sleeping arrangements. The most troubling piece was Jane's attention to their conversation. She actually listened and participated. Normally Ari couldn't string together three sentences before Jane's phone pinged and it was her turn to play *Words with Friends* with Rory. But not a ping sounded.

As they were cleaning up, Ari got a text from J.D. Cromer. *Ms. Adams, I'd like to speak with you privately. Can you meet me in an hour at Carlotta's Diner off I-5?*

During the drive she recounted some of the comments J.D. had made during the study session. He'd not played well with others and the gap in age between him and the other members also seemed to cause friction. She definitely needed to speak with him about the publishing deal—and his whereabouts at the time of Dion's death.

Carlotta's proved easy to find because of the enormous neon yellow "C" that engulfed the rest of the letters that spelled out its name. It reminded Ari of a Pacman eating the little dots. At night, she imagined, truckers would see that sign from a mile away. Directly underneath the enormous name was another sign that read, *I-5's Best Steak and Eggs!* This was probably the place where Dion had eaten his "steak during the stakeout."

An effective sign was critical to a business open twenty-four hours a day, as was ample parking. The recently restriped paved lot was three times larger than the restaurant, an additional dirt lot extending past the pavement for the gargantuan semis that needed more elbow room.

The building was obviously vintage with large picture windows, a wooden and glass front door and a decorative red and white border that wrapped the building. All had been recently painted. Judging by the number of vehicles and customers she saw through the large windows, this was the hot spot for this stretch of I-5. She counted three security cameras as she circled the building. A fourth was definitely needed as most of the eastern side seemed to be unmonitored.

When she entered, a tiny bell jingled above her and an Amazonian woman came out from the back. Tall as Ari was, this woman bested her by five inches. She wore heavy makeup and false eyelashes that looked like spiders sat on her eyes. Her bouffant hairstyle, which Ari was nearly positive was a wig, complemented her uniform, a pink polyester dress with a white apron. She looked right out of the fifties, just like her building.

"Well, hello. Welcome to Carlotta's," she proclaimed in a deep baritone voice. Carlotta was trans, Ari guessed, and her personality was as big as her physique. She put her hand over her heart and said, "I'm Carlotta, and I'm so glad you've come to visit today. Will you be dining alone?"

"Actually, I'm here to meet J.D. Do you know him?"

"Know him? Pfft. Of course. You must be Ari. He called and asked me to hold his regular table."

They walked through a retro dining area complete with aqua blue booths, black and white checked tiles and gleaming chrome stools capped with bright red seats. The building may have been older, but everything sparkled and shone. It was also filled with customers—locals, tourists, and truckers. At the counter, patrons talked to their elbow neighbors, all enjoying the food and the company. It was amusing to think that if she shouted, "Make America Great Again!" half of the room would applaud, and the other half would boo.

"Your place is terrific," Ari said.

Carlotta grinned. "Aren't you sweet? Thank you. We've enjoyed the top spot on Yelp for over a year and we're very proud of that."

Ari sat down at the only available two-seater table and Carlotta presented her with an abundant menu wrapped in clear plastic that also smelled as if it had recently been sanitized with a wet wipe.

"We serve everything all the time except for alcohol. Then it's only after three p.m. Can I get you some coffee?"

"That would be great. Could I ask you a couple questions?"

Carlotta raised a disapproving eyebrow. "Maybe," she said flatly.

Ari guessed she was asked constantly about her sexuality, so she seemed to relax when Ari said, "I'm a friend of Mina and Cleo's over at Sisters."

"Oh, yes." Then her face fell. "I can't believe it about Dion." She shook her head and fanned her face, most likely to keep her eyeliner from running. "Most horrible thing. I hope Sheriff J and Deputy Do Right catch whoever did this."

"I do too. Mina asked me to poke around a little, kinda like a P.I."

Her baby blue eyes went wide. "Like Stephanie Plum or Jane Lawless?" she whispered.

"Yes. So here's my question. I heard Dion came in recently."

She nodded. "He did."

"I'm not sure you'd notice seeing how busy you are, but did you see anyone else from Sisters Cellars or from John Graham's place here at the same time?"

She winced. "Oh, geez. I don't know. Maybe?" She pointed to the kitchen. "Gary would know. I'll go ask him and bring you some water."

Ari's phone pinged with a text from J.D. *I'm parking.*

Carlotta returned almost immediately with the water. "Gary says a week or so ago, Dion came in and ordered his steak and eggs to go. A while later Eddie and Berto came in for lunch but they weren't here at the same time. Does that help?"

Ari nodded. "Yes. Thank you."

Carlotta touched her arm. "I'm happy to help catch whoever did this. It's just awful and Mina and Cleo certainly don't need this stuff during harvest."

"True."

J.D. approached. He gave a hug to Carlotta and joined Ari at the table. He brushed back his salt-and-pepper hair and nodded at Carlotta's offer of coffee. He said to Ari, "Thanks for meeting me on such short notice."

"Of course. What did you want to discuss?"

"Two things. I wanted to make sure you knew what I told Deputy Lacaba, and I wanted to give you some more information."

Ari looked at him warily. "This isn't a competition, Mr. Cormac. I'm not trying to beat the deputy. I'll most likely share with her whatever you tell me."

He shrugged and Carlotta appeared with coffee. When she asked to take their order, J.D. said, "Order the steak and eggs. You won't regret it. Even vegetarians leave their principles at the door for Carlotta's menu."

Carlotta laughed heartily and waved him off. Once she'd retreated, he said, "I assume you will share this information. But I'm telling you because I think it will go farther than if I'd just told Lacaba. She means well but she doesn't make connections. She can't reach people."

Ari sipped her coffee and peered at him over the cup. His sincerity was obvious, and she was starting to think he manipulated the opinions people formed of him. "Go on," she said.

"First, I have no one to vouch for me the night Dion was killed. I went to the study group, which let out early, then I went home to watch *Stranger Things.*"

Ari remembered the security camera footage showed the group's respective vehicles leaving around eight o'clock. "Why did the group break up so early?"

He cracked a smile and wagged a finger at her. "See? You know how to ask the right questions. It was odd we broke up early because usually we have marathon sessions, but the tasting portion fell apart."

"How did that happen?"

"Well, Dion was supposed to bring the wine, but when he arrived he gave us some story about the supplier in Salem not having the three whites he wanted us to sample."

"You thought it was a ruse?"

"Well, given what happened to him, I'm guessing he already had plans for later in the evening and needed a reason to excuse himself. None of us would've believed he'd want to stop studying."

"Why would he deliberately end the session early?"

J.D. shrugged. "He obviously had something more important to do. I can't imagine what that would be, though. The test was everything to him. To use the time to enter a restricted dangerous area might imply he was looking for something." His gaze flicked from his coffee to her, assessing her reaction. "But you already know that. The question then is what was he looking for? Have you figured that out?"

"Have you?" she replied.

"I *know* he was definitely looking for something."

"He told you that."

"Yes." Carlotta appeared with several plates, prompting him to say, "Eat first, talk later."

Even though she'd eaten with Jane just a while before, her mouth watered. Everything smelled wonderful and the presentation, complete with garnish, rivaled five-star restaurants. No wonder the place was packed.

They ate in companionable silence, Ari enjoying every bite.

J.D. smiled and said, "Good, yes?"

"Very much."

She couldn't finish everything, her stomach unwilling to hold two breakfasts. She left for the women's room while he finished eating. A small hallway led to the restrooms, a back door at the end. It was marked as a fire exit, but Carlotta came breezing through it, slightly embarrassed to see Ari.

"You caught me. We tell customers not to use it, but a lot of our regulars do anyway."

"So somebody could literally sneak out the back?"

"And they have," she said airily. "Some without paying. Still, it's the fastest way to the trash, and that's worth it to me." She pointed at her and winked. "Just don't tell anybody, especially that fire marshal." She laughed and headed back to the dining room.

Ari stepped outside, noticing that it opened up on the fourth side of the parking lot, the side without a camera. If Dion was conducting a stakeout, was it here? In the parking lot?

A semi rumbled to life and slowly chugged around the back of the restaurant, kicking up a storm of dust behind it.

She headed back to the table just as Carlotta retrieved their plates. "Everything satisfactory?" she asked.

"Oh, much more than satisfactory," Ari replied. J.D. nodded his agreement.

Carlotta grinned. "I like you."

She left and Ari sipped her coffee, waiting. He took a breath and folded his hands on the table.

"Okay, everything above board. I'm a freelance investigative journalist. My real name is Walter Pembroke. J.D. Cormac is a fictitious name."

"For J.D. Salinger and Cormac McCarthy?"

Walter smiled. "Yeah. My favorite writers."

She held up a hand. "Wait, wait. I just saw your name… when I was surfing articles on the exam." He offered a knowing grin but said nothing. Then it came to her. "You're the guy who exposed the cheating on the sommelier exam a few years ago."

He nodded, seemingly pleased that she made the connection. "I wrote the story but it was the anonymous whistleblower who really deserves the credit."

"Did that person ever step forward?"

"No," he said. "He wanted complete anonymity. He was worried about his position, potential threats…"

"Excuse my ignorance. Threats from wine tasters? I would've thought something as highbrow as sommeliers would be above threats."

"Ah, no. The wine industry, actually the entire food and beverage industry, is extraordinarily competitive. It's huge in reach but it's actually quite small. A bad reputation sinks you. The whistleblower in that case wasn't willing to sacrifice his career to do the right thing…and Dion wasn't going to either."

"So he knew you as Walter Pembroke?"

He laughed and looked up as if he were reliving the memory. "I came here for a tasting about eight months ago and started talking to Peri. When she heard I was interested in taking the master somm test, she invited me to the study group. I thought Dion was acting weird around me for the first few months, and then about two months ago, when we were all walking to our cars late one night, he sidled up to me and said, 'Mr. Pembroke, if you want to remain anonymous, you'll meet me at the Denny's on I-5 just outside of Eugene in half an hour.' I was stunned but I went. We'd barely taken two sips of the crappy coffee when he said he might have uncovered something illegal, not as big as the testing scandal, but it would definitely rock the Oregon wine community if it were true."

"What was it?"

"He wouldn't say. He wanted to be very sure before he told me. Then a couple weeks ago, as we were walking to the parking lot, again he breezes by me and says, 'I'll need to talk to you soon.' That was the last time he ever mentioned it."

He paused and dropped his head. When he brought his hand to his face, Ari saw he was crying. "The night he died, I knew something was off when he didn't show up with the wine for the tasting practice. I think everyone knew it. This was Dion. He wasn't a flake, and his drive and enthusiasm for success motivated all of us. He wasn't allowed to be subpar. He didn't allow *himself* to be below average. Of course, we all acted like it wasn't a big deal but the looks going around the table… Eddie was the one who actually called him on it."

"What did Eddie say?"

"Something like, 'Turning into a slacker, huh?' Dion laughed it off, even agreed with him." Pembroke winced. "If I'd followed my gut, done what I'm supposed to do as a journalist, I'd have stayed with him that night. He'd said he was close to finding the answers he wanted, and I was right there to help. But I didn't. I left and went home. My back was killing me and I was getting a migraine, so I headed home and laid on my couch while Dion was dying."

He stopped. Dion's death ended his story. The hum of conversation and the business of eating was the reminder that life moved forward.

"Walter—"

"My friends call me Walt."

"Walt, what about the publishing story that you connected Dion with a publisher and he cut you out?"

Walt shook his head. "Only half of that story is true. The publisher is going to take possession of the blue binders Dion left me in his will. The nonsense about us fighting over the money is just that—nonsense. Ms. Adams, part of my cover story is true. Before I went into journalism I made a fortune in the tech business. I have no need for more money."

"So that was a ruse to make everyone think you and Dion were at odds."

"Exactly. The money generated from the publication of Dion's testing materials will go into a trust for the care of his niece, and the trust will be overseen by myself and my attorney. Do you know his niece has cancer?"

"Yes, Apollo explained that was one reason he was moving to Portland—to take a high-paying job."

"Well, he *was* moving to Portland, until he found out about the publishing deal. And Apollo…" He rolled his eyes and sipped his coffee. "Did Apollo mention his gambling habit?"

"Uh, no, of course not."

"Yes, of course not. That's why I'm overseeing the trust. Dion wanted to be kept out of it. He wanted to help his niece, but he was unable to stand up to Apollo."

"Apollo told me his name meant he was the boss."

"So true. I'm not looking forward to the conversation he and I will have in the near future when he learns the conditions of the trust."

"But how lucky for Dion's niece." She sighed. "So who killed Dion?"

"I have no idea." He checked his watch. "Do you have any questions? I have an appointment, but I feel bad for calling you on such short notice."

"No worries. Just one more question. Think back to the conversation at the Denny's. Did Dion make any random comments, a cryptic remark or retort that made your journalistic antennae go up? Something you normally might've followed up on but didn't, maybe because you didn't want to spook him."

He shrugged. "I've thought about it a hundred times." He pointed to her and said, "Here's one thing. Dion's heart led to Mina. If someone was hurting Mina, cheating Mina, doing *anything* to harm her or Sisters Cellars, then Dion would've done everything in his power to help her. I think that's what he was doing when he died."

CHAPTER FIFTEEN

As Jane predicted, Mina was willing to let Ari rummage through her office, but she asked to be present to answer questions or provide support. When Ari returned from her breakfast with Walt, she headed toward the production room. From this angle the building seemed to be split in two—like a Jekyll and Hyde. The functional, practical, winemaking production side was steel and concrete, and the lovely French chateau that charmed visitors daily was stone and wood. Somewhere in the middle the two parts connected seamlessly.

Ari found Mina and Denise facing an array of six wineglasses—two whites, three reds, and one rosé. Mina picked up one of the whites and swirled it in the glass. She sniffed it and took a sip. "Close, very close."

"The color is perfect," Denise commented.

"It is," Mina agreed. She smiled at Ari. "Good morning. We're just checking up on some of our aging wines. A few are very close to being bottled." She pointed at Ari. "Including that barrel of malbec." She picked up the middle glass and handed it to her. "Give this a try."

Ari knew enough to swirl the wine and inhale the unique aroma of berries before she brought it to her lips. Distinctly cherry and blackberry, it was bold and dry, just the way she liked it. "Oh, my. This is marvelous," she said.

Mina narrowed her eyes. "Hmm, I think you're overstating, but it's almost ready."

"Well, that's why you're the winemaker," Ari said. She looked at Denise, standing straight, ever the professional. "Good morning, Denise."

"Good morning," she said, her voice barely a whisper.

Their gazes met for an extra beat and Ari hoped she conveyed openness. She hoped Denise would come speak with her since they weren't done with their conversation. The only clue to her breakdown yesterday were the bags under her eyes, the dark circles as prominent as when Ari pulled her into the guest room.

"Okay, let's head into my office," Mina suggested. She turned to Denise who was writing furiously on her ever-present clipboard with her purple pen. "Can you finish the notes here?"

Without looking up Denise said, "Of course."

Mina touched her shoulder. "Are you okay? Do you need to take some more time off?"

It took a moment, but Denise slowly raised her head. "Of course not. We have a huge job to do."

"I would understand, Denise. I can't imagine—"

"I'm fine." Her terse reply bordered on shouting and she bit her lip. "Anything else?"

"No," Mina said quietly. "I'll be right back." When they were out of earshot, she added, "I can't imagine what that must've been like for her, finding Dion."

Mina's office was small and cramped. Bookshelves lined two walls; another held a corkboard with papers tacked messily over most of the surface. The wall that faced Mina when she sat at her desk was a brag wall of accolades, pictures of Opening Day and framed articles. She plunked herself down in front of the computer and Ari took a moment to scan the articles. Most were from different magazines, some of which were national publications, but the largest article was from the local newspaper and titled, "Sisters Cellars Rises from the Ashes."

Mina was watching her. "That was written in 2018 after our pinot noir, Phoenix, won a gold medal at the Willamette Valley Wine Classic. It really boosted sales."

Ari glanced at the three photos featured with the article, one of Mina and Dexter near the red wine barrels, one of Cleo and Mina in front of the enormous Sisters Cellars logo, and the third shot of Mina, Cleo, Berto, and Denise out on the patio, the grapevines behind them. Someone else was in the background, but blurred, and Ari couldn't make out who it was.

"How can I help?" Mina asked, obviously anxious.

Ari bit her lip. "I know you're horribly busy, but first, do you know any more than you did a little while ago…about Jane?"

Mina's face tightened and she met Ari's gaze. "Yes."

Ari leaned against the wall. "Can you tell me?"

Mina shook her head. "Ari, we can't do that. I like you too much. I like Jane too much. If we're all going to be friends, we have to respect boundaries. I'm certain she will tell you in her own way and in her own time."

Ari wiped away sudden tears. "I'm worried. And yeah, it may be childish, but I'm mad she told you before she told me."

Mina reached up and squeezed her hand. "I know. And to be clear, this isn't about you. It isn't even really about Jane," she muttered.

Ari snorted. "Sure." She glanced at Mina, who looked away. "Sorry," she said, reaching for a stool in the corner. "Down to business. We still haven't determined why Dion was in the production room when he knew it was so dangerous, and we're not sure whether his intent was to help or harm you."

Mina nodded. "I'd like to think positively, but after the last few days I can't be sure of anything." She gestured to her desk. "What did you want to see?"

On her phone Ari pulled up the picture she'd taken of the chart Dion had hidden in his cottage. "Has Deputy Lacaba shown you this?"

"Yes, and she was rather pushy about it. I told her I'd think about it."

"And have you?"

"Yes. I agree that the numbers on the left are dates, but the numbers and the checkmark for that one date… It's like he's keeping track of something. Of what, I don't know. But let's look at the calendar program I have. It's incredibly detailed and helps me track the production schedule. Let's work with the one row he's filled in entirely and see what we get if we enter in a date."

Ari leaned over Mina's shoulder as she typed 9-7. "Okay, so here's what happened on September seventh. A lot of maintenance work was scheduled in preparation for the harvest. We were still cleaning out the steel tanks, checking all the hoses and valves, finalizing the label design for the new pinot gris, which is awesome in my opinion. We continued testing on the southern section, had a visit from the Department of Agriculture, and we celebrated Denise's birthday."

"Sounds like a busy day."

"Not really," Mina mused. "Just a day in the life of a vineyard." She tapped on the keyboard and scrolled down. "Oh, and there was a shipment of grapes that arrived from John Graham." She leaned back and sighed. "I remember that. Turned into a bit of a clusterfuck. The Ag guy wasn't done with his inspection, and Eddie was in a hurry because he had an appointment in Eugene. He needed to get those grapes weighed and in the crusher-destemmer before he left. Fortunately, the Ag guy was nice and helped him out."

"How?"

Mina shook her head. "I can't remember, honestly. I may have heard this story secondhand. Denise or Emily may have been handling him by then. I always greet the Ag guy, of course, but usually I'm super busy so someone else babysits him. He goes around and checks that our machines are in working order, we're properly implementing approved sanitization and sterilization requirements, the accuracy of our scale, stuff like that. What I remember is that he made a concession and helped us out."

Ari looked around the room. There were piles of papers on her desk and in the corner was a small table that held three open magazines. "Those are my notes on blends," Mina explained.

"By reading about other winemakers and the combinations they've tried, I can get an idea of what might work or not work based on their experiences."

"So you don't keep any records in here? I don't see a filing cabinet."

"I keep the immediate stuff in this single filing drawer at the bottom of my desk. The stuff I need to look through and approve is in the inbox. Everything else is in the storage room."

Ari's gaze settled on the inbox. "Do you mind?"

"No," Mina said, handing her the stack. "I can't imagine any of this stuff being the reason Dion died. Are you looking for something specific?"

"No, but with everyone so surprised by his death. I think whatever was the catalyst is rooted in something recent."

The inbox contained a mishmash of magazines, purchase orders, expense account reimbursements, and a few weight tags. Every document had a place for Mina's signature, often in addition to Eddie's signature. He may have been the CFO, but Mina was the CEO and nothing got paid without her signature.

One reimbursement form stood out: a receipt from Carlotta's Diner. Ari had found a receipt from Carlotta's Diner at Dion's place and Apollo had mentioned his visit.

"Did you find something?" Mina asked.

"Dion had a receipt from Carlotta's Diner." She pulled the picture up on her phone.

Mina cracked a smile. "That Carlotta is a character. It's a great little diner off I-5. A lot of times I'd stop there on grape runs out to John Graham's place either to grab a meal or a cup of coffee. It's sort of the halfway point. Fabulous food."

"I agree. I just met someone there."

"Really? Who?"

"J.D. Cromer."

Mina slowly turned her head. "How did that go?"

"Fine," she said casually. "He was really broken up over Dion's death."

"Do you think he's a suspect?"

"I don't."

"Okay, good. So, back to Carlotta's. Eddie and Berto have kept up the tradition and stop there, but I don't know why Dion would go there. Seems really out of the way for him unless he was hiking or antiquing, but I can't see him doing any of that stuff this close to the test. What date was that?"

"Less than a week ago. Sunday."

Mina tapped the date into her program. "Well, Eddie and Berto were picking up grapes, but I don't have a receipt from them on that date."

Ari had a thought. She looked at the time stamp of Dion's receipt from Carlotta's: 11:52 a.m. "Could you look up staff schedules?"

"Of course." Mina clicked the mouse and tapped open a new screen. "Who do you want?"

"Peri's schedule for last Sunday."

Mina groaned. "I don't even have to pull it up. I already know she worked. Something came up with her mother's plumbing and she needed to be in Salem, but we were short staffed. I couldn't let her go without stepping behind the counter myself and pouring wine for the customers. And I've done that," she said quickly, "but not during harvest. She tried every staff member but no one would take her shift. She was especially pissed that Dion wouldn't fill in since she'd already covered for him and he wasn't working that day. She'd be really pissed to know he was off eating at Carlotta's and not studying."

At the bottom of the inbox Ari found a receipt for Racy's—for Denise. "And look at this."

Mina grinned. "That one's on me."

"What do you mean?"

"I asked her to stop by on her way home and sample his malbec. I wanted to see if it was worth the fuss."

"And is it all that great?" Ari asked.

"She said it wasn't any better than ours, which proves to me that we could've won that contest." She slapped the desk. "And next year we will."

Ari nodded and Mina forced a smile. "Anything else?" She needed to get back to work.

"The phone that was taken this morning. Who has a key to the conference room?"

"Emily keeps the key in her desk."

Ari frowned. "So anyone could've taken it."

"Yes, all of the senior staff know about that key and have used it. Sorry."

Ari looked at the graph once more. "I hate to ask, but could you run through these other four dates on your program just to see if there might be any patterns?"

"Sure," Mina said, her fingers flying across the keyboard.

Ari squatted next to her and she pulled a screen shot of each day and lined the four entries side by side. What became immediately apparent was that a smoking gun didn't exist. Grape pickups happened on only two of the dates and the Ag inspector didn't appear on any other dates. The only other calendar notation worthy of any attention was that Emily was absent on two of the four dates.

"You know," Mina said, pointing to the *10-4* date, "I should mention that the calendar is only about sixty percent accurate. For example, there's no pickup here, but I know one happened."

"It did?"

"Yes, and I'd have to go through all the weight tags to say which vineyard was visited, but I remember the date." She looked at Ari and said, "I'm sorry my recordkeeping isn't so great. We work with a bare bones admin staff and stuff happens as the day progresses."

"Hey, I get it. I'm in real estate. Clients call all the time and shift my day for me."

Mina laughed. "Exactly."

"Could you email me those screen shots?" Ari asked.

"Of course." She offered a smile with gritted teeth. "Anything else?"

Ari could see the storeroom door from where she stood. "Did you say you keep records in that storeroom?"

"Yeah, the older stuff. It's really my junk place. Nobody but me goes in there."

Ari followed her back through the production room. She unlocked the door and turned on the light. "It's self-explanatory, so if you don't mind I really need to get back to Denise."

"No, of course not," Ari said. "Thanks."

"Just holler if you have more questions."

The bare overhead lightbulb left much of the room in shadows but Ari could make out a large Sisters Cellars cutout against the back wall. A collapsed red canopy leaned into a corner; stacks of boxes had been shoved out of the way to retrieve it. All of the important and regularly used items like promotional materials and swag lived near the front. As she meandered between furniture—some broken, some not—stacks of tables, signs and poles, she realized that much of this stuff had been shoved to the back for safe keeping, probably for a day that would never come, but Mina didn't want to discard any of it—just in case.

She read the sides of a stack of boxes. GOOD WINE MAGS, ORIGINAL PROMO, OPENING DAY, OLD CORRESPONDENCE and UNCLE DICK. Mina was clearly a pack rat. The filing cabinet was near the door, most likely for easy access. Ari imagined that at times they needed to review information from the past and they needed to do so quickly. Near as she could tell, the wine business moved at a lightning pace, and Mina adeptly kept up. Ari read the labels on the drawers: Taxes, Weight Tags/Ag Stuff, More Ag Stuff, and Miscellaneous.

She eliminated the top drawer merely on practicality. If Dion was killed over a tax issue, only an auditor or an accountant would be able to autopsy the records and find the reason. She perused the miscellaneous drawer, finding articles on Mina and the vineyard, a plaque awarding Sisters Cellars as "The Best Vineyard of 2018," according to Eugene's *Register-Guard* newspaper.

Buried in the back was a stack of photos. She moved directly under the light and flipped through them. One showed Mina and Cleo out at the front gate, helium balloons all around them. The next picture told the story: opening day for Sisters Cellars.

The only people Ari recognized were Cleo, Eddie, Emily, and Berto. Denise wasn't yet on the scene, and it would be another year before Dion arrived. They were all laughing and smiling. In most photos they each held a glass of wine. The last four photos made Ari smile: Dexter. He wore a bowtie and a look of sheer happiness.

Ari switched to the second drawer, Weight Tags/Dept. Of Ag. The files bulged and Ari fought to remove one from the front. The tab read, *19-20 Weight Tags.* Nested inside the large manila folder was a second folder with *Dept. Of Ag* on the label. She went back to the file cabinet drawer to inspect the other folders. All were labeled in a similar way, the years in chronological order—backward.

She thrust open the third file drawer and wasn't surprised to find a multitude of binders whose spines held placards with riveting titles like *Understanding Your Department of Agriculture.* Ari imagined Mina had sat through countless seminars and webinars learning how to navigate vineyard ownership. She was about to shut the drawer when a white envelope caught her attention. It was unmarked and seemed to have been thrown into the cabinet haphazardly.

She stepped under the light and was shocked to see the top photo was of Jane, a much younger Jane in a skimpy bikini straining to contain her ample cleavage, holding a cigarette in one hand and a beer in the other. The wind blew her trademark blond hair behind her shoulders, and her mouth was open as if she were chastising the photographer for taking the photo in the first place. Ari chuckled. "Ah, Jane." The other photos featured Mina, Eddie, Jane and others Ari didn't know. One was quite suggestive. A topless Jane relaxed against a beautiful brunette, the brunette's arm across her bare chest. They looked at each other adoringly. "I wonder who that is?" Ari mused. Jane couldn't have been more than sixteen.

The rest of the photos were typical beach photos, but she had to gently pull them apart as their backs were sticky. She guessed that for whatever reason, Mina had removed them from an old photo album.

The last picture was of a much younger Mina, cigarette between her lips, wearing very short shorts and a bikini top. Eddie was wrapped around her in a possessive pose, cigarette dangling from his lips as well. The fingers of his right hand dipped under the waistband of her shorts and his left hand cupped her left breast. What Ari found most interesting were the placement of Mina's hands—over each of his wrists, either encouraging him to touch her or attempting to remove his touch. Her expression gave nothing away.

She took the photos, the *19-20* file and just to be on the safe side, she withdrew the thick *18-19* file. "I adore light reading," she muttered.

CHAPTER SIXTEEN

Ari headed back to Mina's cottage, hoping the photos might drive Jane from her funk. She scanned the area looking for Deputy Lacaba. If she saw Ari with the files, she wouldn't be happy. Ari had every intention of sharing them with her if she found something significant, but she doubted she would. Still, they might give her a better sense of the big picture.

She found Jane on Mina's back deck, pacing and talking on her cell phone to a real estate client. She was giving the woman the "Talking Off the Ledge" speech which was often necessary with first-time home buyers, once they realized the behemoth of debt they had just shouldered. Ari waved at her from inside the kitchen and made some tea. When Jane finally disconnected and returned inside, she wore a smile on her face. She'd taken a shower, donned a smart yellow blouse and white jeans.

Ari pointed at them. "Seriously, you're wearing white?"

Jane groaned. "I know it's after Labor Day—"

"That's not my point. We're visiting a vineyard in a state where it rains constantly. Those pants have little to no chance of remaining white."

"Ha! I'm not going outside again. I don't need to worry."

Ari swallowed her next question. Jane was inferring she'd seen enough because there was no need to make further wedding plans. *She has to tell you in her own time.*

"Why are you here making tea?" Jane asked. "You're supposed to be out solving a murder."

Ari poured chamomile in each mug and brought Jane up to date with the conjecture that Dion's death was probably unintentional. "I want to show you some photos and see what you remember."

Ari held out the envelope and Jane pulled out the pictures, her hand immediately covering a gasp. "Oh, my God."

"This was when Eddie and Mina were a thing the first time, right?"

Jane chuckled. "Yeah. In fact, I think I took this picture."

"Seriously?"

Jane touched her forehead. "God, this was so long ago."

"I can't tell if Mina is happy or angry with Eddie."

"Well, that's a usual question. At least it was then. Mina wasn't very good at communicating with people or sending the right signals."

Ari remembered the picture in Dion's house of him with Mina. He had it bad for her.

Jane tapped the photo. "I remember this summer. I think this is when I came out."

"I imagine so, judging by that picture of you and the brunette."

Jane sighed. "That was Lacy. She was my first...or second. She was nearly nineteen... Anyway, I came out to Mina, and if I'm remembering correctly, twenty seconds later she told me she was bi, and ten seconds after that she kissed me. And a few days later, we were lovers."

"Wow. That day wasn't the same day you took the picture of her with Eddie, was it?"

"Maybe...I don't think so." She shrugged. "I can't remember. We were so young." The light reflected Jane's eyes, and Ari thought she saw tears. *Jane never cries.*

"Are you all right?"

Jane took a deep breath. "Of course. Aren't I always all right?"

Ari turned a photo over. "Why would Mina hide these pictures?"

"You really think she hid them?"

"Well, they obviously were in a photo album. They got stuck in an envelope and tossed in a file drawer reserved for binders from boring seminars Mina attended. I don't think she wanted someone, probably Cleo, finding them."

"Well, Cleo can be the jealous type. She struggles a lot more when Mina has a girlfriend than the other way around."

"I don't think that's true when it comes to Emily."

Jane raised an eyebrow. "Why do you say that?"

"I was snooping in Emily's office—"

"Good for you!"

Ari laughed. Old Jane was back. "I found two tickets to Spain for Emily and Cleo."

Jane's jaw dropped. Then she shook her head and set her mug down. She reached for her phone. "I'm going to have it out with Cleo."

Ari took her arm. "No, don't say anything. I have no idea if Cleo knows. What if this is all in Emily's head?"

"Fine. You could be right." Jane tossed her phone down. "Okay, I'm ready to be your Watson."

"My what?"

"C'mon, Sherlock." She picked up the huge weight tag folder. "What are we analyzing next? Who do we need to talk to? The game's afoot!"

They spent an hour sifting through the bulging weight tag files from the current and previous year. While Jane's attention span frequently waned with most tasks, she was a whiz with paperwork which was part of the reason the real estate game suited her. She loved to pore over contracts, make sense of ridiculously worded demands from buyers, and help her clients calculate profit margins and interest rates. For once Jane was the model of patience, and Ari was not.

"We don't even know if the weight tags are related to this graph Dion made. It could be something completely different."

Jane peered over her new neon pink reading glasses. "Like what?"

Ari stifled a laugh. Jane had never worn glasses and she'd worn black for a week when she learned from the ophthalmologist that she needed them. Ari found her choice of frames hilarious.

"Focus," Jane chided. "I know what you're thinking. So, once again, if this table doesn't have anything to do with the weight tags, what else could it be?"

"A ton of things!" Ari cried. "Winemaking is all about chemistry, so it's all about numbers. This could be about pH levels or amounts of yeast…or brix scores."

"What the hell is that?"

"I have no idea," Ari said. "I just heard Mina talk about it using a bunch of numbers."

"Okay, take a deep breath," Jane ordered. When Ari just sat there, she said, "Do it!"

Ari joined her in a deep, cleansing breath and slumped back in the chair.

Jane whipped off the glasses and tapped the earpiece against her chin. "This move right here," she said, waiting for Ari to look at her. "This is the only great thing about glasses. I know I'm so hot right now."

Ari burst out laughing and Jane joined her. When the giggles subsided, Ari said. "I love you, you know that, right?"

"I know."

Ari hoped Jane would share the Rory story but instead she returned the glasses to her face and picked up a weight tag. "Let's use some logic here. Make a case that Dion's chart *is* about weight tag numbers."

Ari looked at the tags that matched the dates on Dion's graph. "Okay, first is that a weight tag exists for each date. Most are for grapes that Eddie and Berto picked up, but one is from a day's picking here at Sisters."

"Yes, good point. Even though one tag was generated by John Graham's place, the other ones were created by Sisters Cellars."

"Okay, and here's another argument that these numbers represent weights—the amount of numbers is the same, meaning the weight tags have three whole digits and a digit to the tenth place and so do the few numbers Dion wrote."

"Like 179.5," Ari said.

"Yes. All the numbers look like that."

"It's just that there aren't enough tags. I feel like we're playing bingo. There's five dates and we have five tags, but there are ten spaces for numbers."

"We're missing pieces of the puzzle," Jane said.

"The most important part." Ari stood and stretched. "And of course, this table might be completely unrelated to his death."

"True," Jane conceded. She pulled the weight tags into a pile in front of her. "I don't understand how they screwed this up. How do you have less than what you expected?"

"Well, from everything Mina and Cleo said, the weather and the pests affect the fruit so differently each year. I suppose Mina could expect the same yield as the year before and be completely wrong. I'd also imagine that her fight with John Graham doesn't help."

"What do you mean?"

"Well, if they were talking and communicating, I'd assume he might alert her to the issues. Give her a heads-up. But if he's that mad, then not only does he not communicate important facts, it's very likely he's enjoying her pain over the whole thing."

"Schadenfreude," Jane said.

"Exactly."

Jane scratched her head. "I still don't understand how this fits with Dion's murder."

Ari leaned back in her chair and looked up at the ceiling. "Me either. Maybe I need to go talk with John Graham. I'll just steer clear of discussing calendars."

"What if Dion's death was a really bad practical joke?" Jane asked. "From what you said about last night's study group, Racy has a short fuse. If Dion did something to piss him off, then this might've been retaliation." She shrugged. "What do you think?"

Ari grimaced. "Of course you could be right, but I think this graph is critical. I think that's why he was hiding it."

"So somebody else knew what he was doing and wanted to stop him."

"I think so."

"You said Dion told his brother that Racy was doing something underhanded?"

"Yeah, but he didn't say what. I'm wondering if it had something to do with the Laurelwood wine competition he judged."

"But if Racy is the accidental killer, he'd need a partner. He doesn't have access to keys here. How would he—or Dion—get in the building?"

Ari saw movement and glanced out Mina's front picture window. "I think we're going to get an answer to your question right now."

CHAPTER SEVENTEEN

Ari met Denise at the door. She looked horrible and her eyes were glassy as if she hadn't slept in days.

"Can we get you something to drink?" Jane asked.

"Honestly, I need a shot of bourbon, whiskey, whatever."

"On it," Jane said.

While Jane went in search of a drink, Ari led Denise to the couch. She perched on the edge, her hands covering her knees. When her left leg began bobbing up and down, she squeezed her knees harder. She looked straight ahead through Mina's front window as if she were sitting in a car watching a movie at a drive-in.

"Here you go," Jane said, presenting her with a crystal shot glass. She'd brought a glass of water as well. "I went ahead and gave you a double because—"

Denise threw back her head and downed the shot in a single gulp.

"Okay, then," Jane said. "I thought maybe you'd sip it. My mistake."

She took the empty glass and Denise sat back on the couch. The effect of the bourbon was nearly immediate. It was as if her bones had liquified. "I don't have a lot of time. I'm on my lunch break," she said in a velvety voice.

"That's okay. If you get back late I'll be happy to vouch for you with Mina," Ari said.

"First, I didn't kill Dion, at least not directly."

"What exactly did you do?"

"You already know, I think. The way you looked at me this morning in the production room."

"Well, *I* don't know," Jane said.

"I left the tasting room door open for Dion."

Jane raised her eyebrows and looked at Ari for confirmation. When Denise dropped her chin, Ari nodded.

"Why did you do that?" Ari asked.

"Because he asked me to."

"And why was that?"

"He said he needed to get something and he didn't want anyone to know. When the production shut down for the day, he thought that would be the perfect opportunity. I asked him repeatedly what he was doing, but he refused to tell me. He said it was best if I didn't know and that I needed to trust him. I told him I wasn't sure that was a good idea, but he said he was righting a wrong."

"You don't have any idea what that might've been?"

"No." She touched her temple and closed her eyes. "I've thought of nothing else since yesterday morning. I haven't eaten. I haven't slept. As you've both personally experienced, I've been rather bitchy." She looked at Jane and then Ari. "I apologize."

"It's okay," Ari reassured her. She rose and took the seat next to her. "I imagine it was horrible, finding his body."

"It was."

"I shared with you that I've also discovered a body, but at least I didn't know the person. This was your friend."

"Well, I wouldn't really say we were friends," she corrected. "We worked together."

"But he obviously felt comfortable enough to ask for your help."

Denise drank some water and said, "I suppose."

"Can you tell us more about how this happened?"

She nodded and carefully set the glass down, her hands still slightly shaking. "It was Wednesday, midday. I was working in the lab area. It was lunchtime, no one around, about an hour before we quarantined the production room." She looked at Ari and added, "I usually take a late lunch. I like the quiet time with everyone else gone."

"Given what you do, that's understandable," Ari encouraged. "I imagine you enjoy some silence."

"I do."

"Is that where Dion found you?"

"Yes. He was…agitated. At first I thought he was excited, but the more he talked, the more I realized he was upset. And when I didn't immediately agree to help him, he became hostile."

"Were you afraid?" Jane asked.

"Not for myself. But I was worried for him. His test was in a few weeks and he seemed completely distracted."

Ari leaned closer. "Is that why you eventually agreed to help him?"

"Yes. I told him I'd think about it, and I'd leave a note for him on the employee communication board in the lounge by four o'clock."

"What's that?"

"It's a place where people can leave messages for other employees, make general requests for ride sharing, sell items, ask for recommendations."

"But there's nothing secure about it?" Ari clarified. "Anyone could read a message left for a different person."

Denise looked panicked. "Yes, I guess that's true. I typed out the message because everyone knows my trademark purple pen. It's what I use all the time. I was worried that after Dion picked up the message, he might just drop it into the trash or leave it on a table for anyone to find." She knotted her fingers together in her lap. "I never thought anyone would read a note that wasn't for them. Pretty naive on my part, huh?"

Ari squeezed her hand. "You're just assuming the good in people. Personally, I think that's a great quality." They exchanged a smile before she said, "So you left the typewritten note on the board."

"Yes. I made it cryptic so if he dropped it and someone found it, they wouldn't know what was going on. They wouldn't know I'd broken a rule," she whispered.

"Did you see or speak with Dion at all the rest of Wednesday?"

"Well, yeah, I saw him. We all had to move out of the production room, so everyone was trying to work in other places like the vineyard, the tasting room, the patio... It was cramped quarters."

"Did he say anything to you?"

"No, he just nodded at me once."

"Do you think someone noticed you put it on the board?"

"I don't know," she said, exasperated.

Ari touched her arm. "Here's the thing, Denise. Whoever locked Dion in that room knew he was going to be there. The easy guess would be that his killer read your note after you put it on the board and before Dion retrieved it. But that's just a guess. So when you think back to that day, do you remember anything odd or strange?"

She stared at the table for a long while before she shook her head. "Nothing's coming to me."

"I know you said you were alone when Dion approached you in the production room, but are you absolutely certain? Think back to that meeting. Did you hear anything unusual? See something in your peripheral vision that at the time didn't seem important?"

She closed her eyes and Ari could tell she was really trying. Her eyes flew open. "I saw Berto. He has that lime green water bottle attached to his belt loop so he sometimes makes noise when he walks. About three minutes before Dion approached me, Berto came by and dropped off two more glasses of the pinot gris for Mina to sample before we shut the room down. I watched him walk away, but I can't say for sure that he actually left the production room." She looked at Ari and then Jane. "Could it be that Berto killed Dion?"

Ari held up her hands. "Don't think like that right now, Denise. We're just trying to put events together. Tell us about that night and when you left the tasting room door unlocked."

"The tasting room closes at six. Emily's job is to come by and lock everything up. The tasting room has French doors, so there's a double-sided deadbolt and she's one of the few people with a key—"

"Who else has a key?"

"Other than me and Emily? Just Mina and Cleo." Ari nodded. "At 7:55 everyone was gone, so I slipped back down to the tasting room and unlocked the deadbolt. Then I left and went to my party." She shrugged. "That's really all I know." She lowered her gaze. "Except for the next morning..."

Ari patted her shoulder and the three of them sat in silence. Denise seemed so distraught and guilty. Ari knew from experience that while she would carry many memories of Dion, the moment she found him and the expression on his face would most likely be the image that smothered the others and compelled her attention.

"May I go now?"

"Of course. But I think you need to share this information with someone else."

"Deputy Lacaba." She grabbed the edge of the table. "Will I be in trouble?"

"I don't know, Denise. I can talk to the deputy."

"She doesn't like people who break rules—at all."

"What if I came with you?"

Denise exhaled and started to cry. "Thank you." She grabbed Ari's hand. "What about Mina and Cleo? They're going to hate me."

"No way, Denise," Jane said. "They're not going to hate you. I've known them a long time. You'll be fine."

She nodded and looked up at the ceiling. Ari wasn't sure if she was praying or just trying to regain control.

"Why don't we head over to the conference room and talk with Deputy Lacaba first?"

"Okay."

The three of them left Mina's and started up the path to the patio. Jane pointed at Denise's necklace. "What's that?"

"Oh, this is a tastevin. It's a tiny spoon that sommeliers used when they tasted wine like centuries ago."

"I've never seen anything like it."

"Mina and Cleo gave it to me for my birthday."

Jane smiled. "Well, it's beautiful."

"Thanks," she said, and for the first time, she seemed to relax.

"Denise, I don't know if you can answer this or not," Ari said, thinking back to her conversation with Mina in her office. "Do you remember a day during the last harvest when the Department of Agriculture inspector showed up right as some grapes were being delivered? Berto and Eddie had gone to get them from John Graham? Does that ring any bells?"

Denise looked away and then she chuckled. "Uh, yeah. I remember that. When Leonard the Ag inspector arrived, Mina was in the middle of a crisis, so I met him. He started doing his thing, reviewing the weight tags, checking the scales, and then Berto and Eddie showed up. Eddie was in a rush because he was going to be late for a tux fitting with his brother who was getting married the next weekend. Leonard had just started checking the scale, but he was nice enough to let Eddie weigh the grapes and get them into the crusher-destemmer so he wouldn't be late. When Mina heard about it later, she was ticked off that Leonard had been inconvenienced." She paused and said, "In general, winemakers have hot and cold relationships with the Ag guys. Some of them can be real pricks and they're always looking for stuff to catch us on, so Mina wants us to be completely transparent and accommodating when he drops by. But I told her it was fine. Leonard's a nice guy."

"Glad it all worked out," Ari said. "Going back to Dion... Do you have any idea why he would risk his life and enter an area that was off limits?"

"No," she said. "But..."

"But what?"

Denise fingered the tastevin. "This is entirely speculative, but whatever reason he had for going in there, I don't think it was for himself."

"Then who was it for?" Ari asked.

"The only person Dion would risk his life for, especially right now when so many things were going his way, is Mina."

CHAPTER EIGHTEEN

Accompanying Denise to meet Deputy Lacaba proved to be an excellent idea, since it was apparent when they arrived that she was still in a foul mood. Ari had hoped she might get over losing the phone but they could hear the deputy and another woman shouting through the closed door.

Ari heard the second woman say, "If you think I'm gonna let you roll over our employees like some Nazi, you are sorely mistaken!"

Denise looked at Ari with wide eyes. "That's Emily."

Jane put a hand around Denise's waist. "It's gonna be okay."

Denise nodded and leaned into Jane, and Ari glanced down at the tasting room, which fortunately was so noisy that the exchange went unnoticed. The conference room door flew open and Emily, bright red in the face, stopped suddenly, surprised at the audience in the hallway. "Sorry," she managed before she stormed back to her office.

"Maybe now's not such a good time," Denise whispered.

"It'll be fine," Ari assured her. "Why don't the two of you wait here and I'll go in first?"

"That's a great idea," Jane said.

Ari took a deep breath and prepared for whatever she would find inside. Given Lacaba's foul mood, she wondered if the place was trashed and Mina and Cleo would need to redecorate.

She found Deputy Lacaba standing at the head of table, palms flat on the maple top, eyes downcast. When Ari shut the door, she jerked up and away from the table. "What?"

"I know you're not having a great day—"

"And you're gonna make it worse, right?"

"No, I don't think so. Denise is outside. She came and shared with me that she was the one who left the door unlocked for Dion."

Lacaba's face clouded over. She stuffed her hands in her pockets and paced. "That's just rich."

"What is?"

"She came to you rather than me."

"So what?"

Lacaba whirled and faced her. "I'm running this investigation." She stabbed her chest with her finger. "It's my ass on the line. I can't be telling Sheriff Jerome that a real estate agent is solving the case."

Ari glared at her. She bit her tongue and didn't utter the caustic comment ready to burst out of her. Her fingers had wrapped themselves around the top of one of the chairs in a strangulation hold. She let go and headed for the door.

"And to be clear, you're not sitting in for *moral* support," Lacaba spat.

One remark too many.

Ari stopped and turned slowly to face her. She could only imagine how angry she looked because Lacaba's eye twitched. They stared for a long moment and finally Ari said, "If you believe you don't need anyone for anything, I doubt you'll make dog catcher," and stormed out.

When she slammed the conference room door behind her, Jane, Denise, and Eddie, who was apparently waiting for his interview, jumped.

"Whoa!" he said. "What happened?"

Denise wrung her hands. "She thinks I murdered him."

"Seriously?" he asked.

"No," Ari said flatly and turned to Denise. "Unfortunately, Deputy Lacaba isn't allowing me into your interview."

Denise paled. "But you said—"

"I know what I said, and it was my intent to go with you."

"I'm giving her a piece of my mind," Jane announced.

Ari grabbed her arm. "Don't. Jane, I'm not defending her, but she's had a horrible day and I wouldn't be surprised if she put the cuffs on you and took you in."

Jane backed up and whispered with Eddie. Ari turned to Denise, "Just tell her the truth. Stick to your story and don't let her bully you. All you did was help a friend, who told you he was helping another friend. You didn't murder anyone and you didn't cause anyone to be murdered."

Denise was trying to believe Ari but she winced when someone dropped a bottle of wine on the floor in the tasting room. "You can be a badass, Denise," Ari told her. "I've seen it. When you thought the harvest was threatened, you took control. You're not afraid to tell it like it is, right?"

Denise's face shifted. "No, I'm not."

"You're not afraid to confront people in authority."

"I'm not," she said, her voice growing stronger.

"You get in there and set things right."

"I will."

Denise marched to the door, nodded at Ari and Jane and went inside. Jane patted Ari's shoulder. "Let's hear it for the life coach."

Ari rolled her eyes.

"Jane said Denise is the one who let Dion into the tasting room," Eddie said. "Wow."

Ari frowned at Jane. "Jane shouldn't be telling stories."

Eddie put his hands up. "Hey, it's all good. I got no beef with anyone. I don't know if Jane told you, but we were all friends back in the day. I was a year older and Mina's brother was my best friend."

"I didn't know Mina has a brother."

"Well, she *had* a brother," Jane clarified. "Mick died from injuries in a car crash the winter before we graduated from high school."

"God, I'm so sorry."

"It sucked," Eddie said. "He'd bought a new car... All set to start his new life. Slid on a curve and went over the barrier." He sniffled and added, "Held on for a week, coming in and out of consciousness."

"Sounds like you were very close."

Eddie gazed at her stoically. His blue eyes were cobalt, and Ari imagined many women were drawn to him. "We were. He made me promise that I'd look after Mina." He chuckled reminiscently and said, "He didn't believe in the whole bisexuality thing and told me that once she got it out of her system, she'd be mine. I believed him for a while..."

"Yes, I heard you and Mina were together at one point."

"More than one point," Eddie corrected. "There was the ancient past of our youth, but we also connected about a year ago... It was a fling. Nothing more."

"I'm not sure I believe you," Ari said softly.

He blinked, clearly surprised by her reply, but in a split second the cockiness returned and he shrugged. "Believe what you want."

"Tell me about your relationship with Dion."

"It was fine."

"What does that mean?"

"We weren't best friends but we were professionally courteous."

"Where were you Wednesday night?"

"Right where Racy told you I was—at his restaurant."

"What were you doing there?"

"Just helping at the bar, retrieving liquor, busing tables, doing whatever I could. He's my buddy and I want him to be a success."

"But isn't he the competition?"

"Well, sort of, but Mina's not running a restaurant."

"But she is creating malbec."

"True. But I think there's room for two good red wines in the valley, don't you?"

"Sure. What did Dion think?"

"He obviously thought it was okay since he was one of the judges who helped Racy win the Laurelwood."

"Hmm. Good point." She paused as a way of ending that part of the conversation. "So, I've heard that you want Denise's job."

"Whoa," Eddie said, holding up his hands. "Not sure where you got those facts."

"Well, is it true? I mean, look at the way you're dressed. Obviously you spend more time outside than indoors."

"I do both," he said. "Right now Mina and Cleo really need my help, especially with Berto fading." His face turned serious; he seemed genuinely sad for Berto.

Jane asked, "What are your goals, Eddie?"

His expression shifted and Ari saw some of the façade crumble. He cleared his throat and sat up straight as if he were preparing to give a speech. He pointed a finger at them. "I want to make wine. I want to create wines so smooth, so bold, that even after the bottle is empty the experience remains. I want my wine to be so effervescent and so perfect for the palate that it becomes the standard by which critics judge other wines. I don't—I won't—make mediocre wines."

"Sounds admirable," Jane said. "It really does. I've often believed that winemaking was a cruel industry for creators. You make something wonderful, but once it's drunk, it might never be replicated again."

His eyes grew large. He threw his arms out and Ari thought he might hug Jane. "You get it! You really get it." He took a breath and refocused himself. "Thank you."

"Forgive my thick headedness," Ari interjected, "but if you want to be a winemaker, and you work at Sisters Cellars, how are you *not* aspiring for Denise's job?"

He glanced at the door to the conference room. "I don't know if you've heard, but Denise is quitting."

"No," Ari said. "Really? When is she leaving?"

"Yes," Jane echoed, looking completely surprised—perhaps a bit too surprised. "When?"

"I think she would've left the moment she found Dion but Emily convinced her to stay through harvest. But after it's over…" He shrugged. "So you see, I wouldn't be taking anyone's job. It's open."

"That would be true if Denise actually leaves," Ari said. "Who do you think had a reason to kill Dion?"

"Anybody in the study group," he retorted. "They are the most arrogant pricks I've ever met. All of them were jealous of Dion, especially J.D. and Emily."

"We've heard there was jealousy, but there was also a lot of camaraderie as well."

"Don't believe that."

"So you think one of them killed him for revenge?" Ari asked.

"Possibly, but there's another reason, a political one."

Jane made a face and glanced at Ari before she asked, "What do you mean?"

He leaned closer. "You know about the exam, right? You've heard how hard it is, how prestigious it is, all that stuff, right?" They nodded. "There's only two hundred master somms in the world, and that's after decades of giving the test. How would it look if more than one person from the same area passed the test in the same year?"

"But we'd heard that Dion was the only one likely to gain the title since he'd already passed two sections of the test," Ari said.

"True, but J.D. and Emily really know their stuff. I should know. I'm the one facilitating the practice tastings."

Ari leaned against the railing, trying not to look smug. "Actually, Eddie, we heard that you and Emily conspired during the tastings as a way to get back at Dion. You know, telling her which wines were being tasted before the practice started?"

His bravado deflated and the cobalt eyes lost some luster. "That was only a couple times," he mumbled. "We were just messing with Dion. Such an arrogant bastard."

"You mentioned J.D. Why would he want Dion dead?"

Eddie didn't answer immediately. Finally he said, "I overheard Dion tell Emily that something wasn't right with J.D. He wasn't who he said he was, and Dion was going to investigate."

"Investigate J.D.," Ari confirmed.

"Uh-huh. My money's on him."

Apparently, before Walt and Dion got on the same page, Dion had confided in Emily.

The door flung open and Lacaba barreled through it. Denise followed and Jane wrapped her in a hug and started down the hallway, Ari following.

Lacaba said to Eddie, "I'm sorry I'm late, Mr. Navarro." Then she added, much louder, "Unannounced visitors who just cut the line are so rude."

"It's fine. Just please, call me Eddie."

The charm had returned and Ari imagined his cobalt eyes and white teeth decorated a façade of goodness. There was something about him…

CHAPTER NINETEEN

"What's your gut telling you?" Jane asked Ari after Denise had headed back to the production room and they had slipped into the guest room.

"I think Eddie's hiding something. There's definitely a lot of anger."

"No kidding. He sure didn't hold back about the study group." She propped her chin on her upturned palm. "Do you really think jealousy is enough of a motive? I mean, a man died."

"Because of his phone, I think we need to assume Dion's death was an accident. I think the intent was to rattle him so badly that he failed, but the perpetrator couldn't have known that he'd lose his phone in the event room."

Jane nodded. "I'm with you on that. So could Eddie be our perpetrator?"

"Absolutely. It's obvious he has a huge jealousy streak. I think he covets several of the positions here—Mina's, Cleo's, Denise's, Peri's and Dion's. But I also think he's worried that he's not up to par with them."

"Egotism mixed with self-doubt," Jane said.

"Exactly."

"He says he was with Racy."

"And Racy backed him up when I visited the study group."

"But restaurants are busy places. Perhaps Racy lost sight of him?"

"Quite possibly. I'd like to see that place." Ari hesitated, and asked, "Want to go with me to Racy's restaurant?"

Ari could tell Jane wanted to say yes, but spending the evening together would mean talking. Jane didn't look as though she was ready. "Hey," Ari said. "Never mind. I'll find somebody else to join me or I'll go by myself."

She turned to go and Jane blurted, "Rory cheated on me."

Ari whirled around. "What? Are you sure?"

Jane dropped on the bed and tears streamed down her face, taking her eyeliner with it. "Oh, I'm sure."

Ari rushed to the bed and pulled Jane into a hug. "Oh, honey."

Jane sobbed and Ari held her. She bit her lip, realizing her mistake in asking Jane that question. She'd always assumed if Jane and Rory broke up, it would be on Jane, because it had always been Jane's fault in the past. But this time she was really trying. She was determined... *And look what it got her.*

"Did Rory just call and tell you out of guilt?"

"Oh, no," Jane snorted. She pulled away and retrieved some tissues from the nightstand. She wiped her face and blew her nose. "I found out completely by accident. Last night at the bridal shower. Most of the women were from California and the bride knew Mina way back when. I spent the evening chatting them up just like I do at my bar, so by ten o'clock they were telling me all kinds of shit. The youngest woman there is sitting at the bar tapping on her phone. I'd listened to bits and pieces of her conversations all night. The other women had been giving her shit about her older lover. She kept defending the woman, saying she was learning a lot of new positions, and they were..." Jane choked up and closed her eyes for a moment. She took a deep breath and said, "They were planning a trip to Greece."

Ari sighed. Rory and Jane had planned to honeymoon in Greece. Ari thought the tickets were bought and the arrangements made, but apparently Rory had swapped traveling buddies.

"So, it's around ten and I'm starting to gather up the dirty glasses and she's sitting at the bar, sipping her wine. She blurts, 'I hate it when she plays that word!' I ask her innocently, 'What word?' She said, 'zaftig.'"

Ari's breath caught. Rory often used zaftig to describe Jane's voluptuous figure.

"I didn't connect it at first. I just said to her, 'My fiancée loves that word and loves to use it about me.' Then, I swear, Ari, she looked up and recognized me. All she said was, 'Oh.'"

Ari squeezed Jane's hand as the tears began again. "She gulped her last sip of pinot and rocketed out of that room. I have no idea where she went. It was like she disappeared. For all I know, she was hiding in the vines until the rented limo returned for them."

"What did you do?"

Jane scraped a hand through her hair and rubbed her neck. "What I do best. I reacted."

"You called Rory."

"No, first I texted her. I wrote something like, 'Your new young squeeze certainly isn't zaftig. She's flat as a board. What will you do with your hands?'"

Ari laughed and immediately recoiled. "I'm so sorry, but that's like the greatest line I've ever heard."

Jane sat up and shook her hair. "Thanks. I thought so too." She kissed Ari's cheek and said, "It only took twenty seconds for my phone to ring."

"And how did that go?"

"It went quick. She said, 'So I guess you met Flame.'"

"The woman's name is Flame?"

Jane nodded. "God, what are the parents of the Millennials thinking? How will they grow old with some of these names?"

"No clue."

"Anyway, after I said something snarky about her name, Rory had the audacity to defend her. After that, I just couldn't. I didn't even care. I said nothing and Rory plowed on, talker that she is. Pick a platitude and she probably said it. 'She hadn't planned it. Flame pursued her. She had second thoughts about moving to such a conservative state as Arizona.' Blah, blah, blah."

"And did she say she would end the affair?"

Jane looked down and picked some nonexistent lint from her pants. "That was the one thing she didn't say. I let her run out of gas and there was this gaping hole in the conversation. Then she tried to bait me because she was getting pissed off. She said, 'Aren't you going to say anything? Don't you want to yell at me?' And I did. I *really* wanted to give her...something. But instead, I just said, 'no,' and I hung up."

She leaned against Ari and cried again. Eventually she looked up and said, "I'm done telling this story now. Saying it to you and Mina is all I'm doing. I made her tell Cleo and you'll have to tell Molly. And a couple more ground rules..." Ari nodded. "I never want to hear anyone utter her name again but I may talk about her, probably in the worst possible terms. Y'all just have to let that go."

"And we will." Ari kissed her head. "I love you." She took Jane's cheeks between her hands and said, "So, since it really is about me, why couldn't you tell me first? Why was it so hard?"

"I didn't want you to be disappointed in me."

"What?"

Jane batted her eyelashes to ward off more tears. "Mina and I are alike. We're so much alike. That's why we're friends."

Ari pulled away. "We're not alike? I thought we were alike. If we're not alike, why are *we* friends?"

Jane pulled up the corners of her mouth into a broken smile. "Because you're who I want to be."

Ari was too stunned to speak.

Jane patted Ari's knee, stood, lifted her arms above her head and took a deep cleansing breath and released. "I'm going for a walk."

"Want some company?"

"No, that's okay. Later I'm going to meet up with Peri, so no, I cannot join you for dinner at Racy's."

"About Peri—"

Jane put a finger to Ari's lips. "No, no judgment." Ari nodded and Jane removed her finger. She grabbed her purse and added, "Hell, maybe Rory sees what I don't, maybe—"

"No. Shut the fuck up!" Jane took a step back. Ari rarely swore, and now it was Ari's turn to raise a finger. "You're not doing that. I won't go off on Peri, but you're not minimizing yourself nor are you dismissing what you wanted—and almost had—with Rory. You put yourself out there, honey. Yeah, this one didn't work out, but for the first time in your life you saw the other side. It's still there, waiting for you."

Jane smiled and threw her arms around Ari. "I love you."

"Yeah, back at ya."

"And there was a positive to last night."

"What was it?"

"I made two hundred bucks in tips. And what's really ironic is that Flame left me the biggest one."

Jane might not have wanted company, but Ari felt restless and needed to move. She decided to walk the perimeter of the vineyard or as far as she could go. At least that was her intention, until she reached the back staircase and heard Emily say, "Well, she grilled me really hard. Thank God I didn't have that thing on me. She probably would've shot me."

Ari guessed Emily was directly under her, hiding in the small alcove underneath the stairs. Ari stayed perfectly still, well aware that if someone came around the west corner they would probably acknowledge her or Emily, and Ari would have some serious explaining to do.

"You just need to work your end," Emily said. "No... No, you can't let it go. Listen, that asshole Dion is responsible for all of this."

There was a long pause and Ari slowly brought her gaze over the top railing. Emily was still on the phone, waving her free hand. Although she wasn't speaking, her gestures implied whatever the other person was saying didn't please her.

"It's hidden where nobody will look. I'll go back in the conference room tonight before I leave. She had to have written down the password. Once I know that, I'll erase those photos and it will magically appear again. No one'll know except us."

They said their goodbyes and Ari slowly returned inside. She counted to five, swung the door open and nearly ran into Emily. "Oh, sorry."

"You're fine," she said as they passed, her gaze glued to her phone.

"Hey, Emily. Can I ask you a question?"

She slowly turned and Ari imagined an eye roll preceded the smile she offered. Today her red lipstick matched a blood-red suit. "Of course."

"What do you think Dion meant when he told his brother that Racy was up to no good?"

The question took her by surprise and the glacier covering her face cracked. "I really have no idea."

"Do you think he'd be doing something to harm Mina?"

"I'm not sure. He's deliberately competing against us with this malbec he's making. But it's not like we don't know about it."

"True."

She offered a closed-lip customer service smile. "Anything else?"

"No, except that you and Cleo were together the night Dion was killed, right?"

Her smile evaporated. "Yes, that's true and that's what I told Sheriff Jerome and the deputy. Cleo left around four a.m." She pointed to the upstairs. "You'll excuse me?"

"Of course."

Ari refrained from sticking out her tongue. She was really starting to hope that Emily was behind Dion's death just so she could see Deputy Lacaba click the cuffs around her bony wrists. "So much for my walk," she grumbled.

She headed back around to the production side of the building almost certain she knew where she'd find Dion's phone.

CHAPTER TWENTY

Ari wondered what Dion could possibly have on his phone that Emily wanted—or didn't want anyone else to see. She found Mina and Denise in Mina's office discussing the blending of some of the finished wines.

"Good news?" Mina asked. Translation: have you solved Dion's murder?

"No, not yet," Ari hedged. "Could I borrow your key to the storage room again?"

"Sure," Mina said hesitantly, handing her the individual key she kept in her top drawer. "Please tell me this doesn't have anything to do with our taxes."

"As far as I know, it does not."

She waved as she left and headed for the corner of the building. She wasn't certain Emily had hidden the stolen phone here, but the storeroom was certainly somewhere no one would look—for anything.

She stood in the doorway, trying to think like a busy office manager with a packed schedule—and wearing an expensive suit. She wouldn't want to come very far into the room. The dust in the air was enough to choke anyone. Ari quickly threw open the file drawers, doubting any of them would be chosen. Just not hidden enough. She scanned the odds and ends and her gaze settled on the stack of boxes. She read the sides again and chuckled at UNCLE DICK. That would certainly be symbolic of what Emily thought of Dion. She unstacked the boxes as the one she wanted was second from the bottom, removed the lid, and smiled. There was the phone.

She reached for it—and froze. She pondered her options. Deputy Lacaba was in no mood for games, that was for certain. However, she would be overjoyed to learn the phone had been found. Of course, Emily might not live through the day if the deputy knew why Ari had found it. She drummed her fingers on her knee.

She decided to take a peek. She checked her own phone, finding the password Apollo had given her. Once past the home screen, she opened the photos and grouped them by year. She groaned. He'd taken over three thousand photos since the beginning of the year. She grabbed a chair that appeared to have four good legs and carefully sat down. Then she looked at the locations of the year's photos—Cheshire, Oregon; Eugene, Oregon; Phoenix, Oregon; Cheshire, Oregon, again and again. She focused on all of those and worked backward from this week. She couldn't imagine Dion having anything on Emily outside of the vineyard and she guessed whatever he had was more recent.

Many were photos of wine bottles, notes from the study sessions, pages from books about countries and varietals—pictures of harvest, unloading the flatbed. On and on she scrolled, seeing absolutely nothing Emily would care about, unless it was the entire process of Dion's preparation. She wouldn't know what was important that Emily might want, so she didn't give that topic another thought.

She tapped on the summer months and a dust bunny flew into her mouth. She coughed and sneezed, deciding if she didn't find something in this batch of pics she was giving up and handing the task to Deputy Lacaba. More bottles, more pages…

And then a photo of a desk—Emily's desk. She could tell because of the calendar. She stopped and maximized the photo. Why would Dion have a picture of Emily's desk? And then she saw the tickets. The two airline tickets to Spain for Emily and Cleo. He'd taken the photo in the middle of summer. Ari couldn't remember if Jane had mentioned how long Emily and Cleo had been together, but it couldn't have been very long into the relationship. Wow. To make those kind of travel arrangements with a woman who already had a wife…pretty gutsy.

This must be what Dion had on Emily but she doubted anyone in the sheriff's department would look twice at the picture. She only knew it was important because she knew the ground rules: *no kids, no traveling. No traveling.* And she remembered what Denise said. *If Dion was doing something for anyone else, it would be Mina.* Was he blackmailing Emily? Threatening to tell Mina?

She glanced at her watch. She wanted to get to Racy's restaurant and she had to decide what to do with the phone. She wasn't going to leave it and go tell Deputy Lacaba. That would just be an opportunity for Emily to take it. She also wasn't sure if she wanted Emily out of the picture, which she most certainly would be if Lacaba learned she'd taken the phone. And who was Emily speaking with on the phone earlier? "You just keep working your end," she'd said.

Ari decided for a half-truth and texted the deputy. *Good news! I found Dion's phone here in the storage room! Do you want me to bring it to you?*

Her reply came nearly instantaneously. *Stay right there with it! Don't let it out of your sight! I can be there after my next interview. DO NOT MOVE.*

Ari sighed. "Terrific."

She didn't take the deputy at her literal word and stepped out of the storage room for some fresh air, the phone securely in her pocket. She'd returned it to the locked home screen and practiced her answers in the event the deputy asked if she'd unlocked it. She decided the answer was no.

While she waited for her, she strolled about the production room, still amazed at the process. She carefully stepped over the maze of hoses that ran across the room like arteries of a freeway. All carried various wines to their final step, barreling or bottling. In the opposite corner of the room two women worked with the bottling machine. One set the bottle and filled it up, while the other removed it after it was corked and set it in a case. It was white wine, and Ari wondered if it was finally time to bottle the pinot gris that so excited everyone.

She stepped through the enormous bay doors and looked out into the vineyard. Cleo and the team were finally harvesting the upper noir. A sense of calm came over her. Perhaps it was proximity to nature or the security of a process—the hum of the machines, the efforts of competent people, and the final product that would bring joy to a celebration. All were qualities she associated with the act of focused work and all were qualities she admired.

"It's something, isn't it?"

She turned and smiled at Berto. "It is. That's exactly what I was just thinking. And you've been doing it for a long time."

"Yes," he nodded. "Most of my life."

He fidgeted and squeezed his University of Oregon baseball cap between his two strong hands. Ari recalled how deftly he'd picked grape bunches out in the vineyards. In a single motion he lifted the chosen bunch from the vine with the left hand and snipped it with the shears in his right. They were dark brown hands, calloused and sun stained. *And now he seems nervous.*

"How long have you worked for Sisters Cellars?"

"Since it opened. I met Mina when she was an assistant winemaker for a competitor down in the Rogue Valley. We got along really well, so when she finally bought this place from the bank I came up here. Did you know her relatives owned it?"

"I did. How well did you know Dion?" she asked casually.

"Pretty well since we both worked here. Sometimes during the off-season he'd follow me around the vineyard. He wanted to know everything there was to know about winemaking, not just from the production side. He wanted to know about the fruit and everything we did to nurture it."

"Sounds as though he was as passionate as you about the art of winemaking."

"He was." He looked down and gave the hat a hard squeeze. "Such a tragedy."

He frowned, and for the first time he looked his age. His jowls hung low, his ruddy complexion highlighted all the creases on his forehead, the bags under his eyes were pronounced in the sun. He pulled his water bottle from its holster and took a long swig.

"Can you think of anyone who would want to hurt him?"

"Not really. People were jealous of what he knew, his devotion, how hard he worked, but that shouldn't get anybody killed."

"Well, I was thinking it might've been an accident."

He looked very surprised. "Really?"

"Well," Ari explained, "whoever did this had to think he'd had his cell phone with him. Before he passed out, he'd call someone for help. That person who locked him in the production room couldn't have known he'd accidentally leave his phone in the event room."

Ari could see the wheels turning. Berto's eyes, hooded before by his dark lids, looked lively as his gaze flitted around the production room.

"What are you thinking, Berto?"

He shrugged. "So maybe it wasn't about him at all."

"Why would you say that?"

"I just don't get it. I don't understand what happened to him."

The pain in his voice was obvious and the ball cap took the brunt of his anger. She pulled out her phone and tapped on her photos. She showed him one of the weight tags from the voluminous file she and Jane had reviewed. "Berto, can you help me understand this? What do the numbers mean?"

He squinted and brought the phone closer to his face. "It's pretty simple. It's just the date and the weight of the grapes. And the price. We also keep track of the yeast, everything we add to the grapes to make the wine…it's a lot. But we have to do it for the state and the Feds."

"But this is just the initial weight for the grapes, right?"

"Yes. This is the tag we fill out each time."

"Is it just for the grapes at Sisters Cellars?"

"No." He pointed. "So, this is one that Mina personally filled out. You'll see it's from Seller X in Sonoma, County, California."

"What's the X for?"

"It's a code. The only person who knows where Mina gets those grapes is Mina. Now if the Feds ever asked, she'd have to tell them the exact address but just for the weight tag, this is okay."

"Really?" Ari challenged. "No one else knows who the seller in Sonoma is?"

He sighed. "Well, probably Emily."

"Why would the location of the grapes be a big secret?"

He smiled and his white teeth gleamed against a backdrop of sundrenched skin. "So no one else approaches that seller." He handed her back the phone and pointed to the vineyard. "Every winemaker wants the same things from the fruit: a viticulturist who nurtures the grapes for longevity of the vines and a seller who is honest and fair with the price. If Mina has the finest fruit she can find, her work is half done. More importantly, it allows her to be creative with the blends, push the envelope of new designs. It's really very exciting."

Ari nodded. "Thank you." She flipped to the next picture. "Now, this one is for grapes you and Eddie got from John Graham, right? You and Eddie are the ones who go down and pick them up, correct?"

His eyes narrowed and his face, which had seemed so open, now started to close. "Yeah, Mina and I used to do it. Then Mina got busy and she had that stupid fight with John about the dumb calendar, and I went alone." He looked down and Ari sensed he was ashamed.

"When did Eddie start going with you?"

"Before the harvest last year." He sighed. "I had some issues remembering how to get to Graham's place. So Eddie came along."

"Did it help?"

He looked up, an odd expression on his face. "Not really. There were even more mistakes. I didn't record the weight correctly a few times. Mina thought she was getting more grapes than she did. That's when we came up short and got behind. We didn't have the malbec ready in time for the competition. That's on me."

"It sounds to me that it would be on Eddie too," Ari observed. "If he'd been sent to go with you, shouldn't he also be responsible?"

"I suppose," Berto said, but Ari could tell he didn't really believe his words. For some reason he was giving Eddie a pass.

"Where were you the night Dion was killed?"

"Home, watching TV. I live in the casita at the far end of the property. Mina's grandparents used it as temporary worker housing and then it fell into disrepair. Eddie helped me fix it up."

"Berto, your house is so close to the entrance that I was wondering if you saw anyone come through the gates the night Dion was killed."

"No. I fell asleep in my chair like I always do."

"When did you wake up?"

"Oh, on and off all night, but I didn't see or hear anything."

"Are you sure?"

He scratched his nose again. "I think so." He sighed. "Maybe."

He put the ball cap on his head and hid his eyes. Ari thought if he were a turtle he'd have crawled back into his shell. "I need to get back to work."

"Berto, before you go, could you send me John Graham's phone number?"

He looked puzzled but said, "Sure," got out his phone and sent it.

"Thank you." Ari touched his shoulder. "And thank you for everything you've done here. I've been so impressed."

All she saw were his white teeth gleaming under the ball cap. A sure sign that he was smiling.

CHAPTER TWENTY-ONE

An hour had passed and Deputy Lacaba still had not arrived at the storeroom. Ari texted and asked if she'd just like her to bring the phone up, assuring her there wasn't anything else to see. Ari took her affirmative reply as progress: at least the deputy trusted her to transport a phone.

On the way she tried to call John Graham's cell number, but when the call dropped three times she Googled his business number and finally spoke with the receptionist. He was out camping off the grid, which explained the dropped calls, but he'd be returning later that evening. Ari left a message and decided to keep the exchange to herself for now.

"So who do you think stole the phone?" Deputy Lacaba demanded the second Ari crossed the conference room threshold.

She lowered herself into a conference room chair. "Well, there are only four people with keys. Mina, Cleo, Emily and Denise."

"Not Mina. Not Denise," Lacaba fired. "Gotta be Cleo or Emily." She shook her finger at Ari. "There's something going on there." She paused and her face reddened. "I mean, I know there's something going *on*, but there's something fishy."

"Maybe," Ari agreed. "But why would one of them take the phone?"

"Do you think one of them killed Dion?"

Ari exhaled. "I think it's interesting that they are each other's alibi. I think Emily is more likely than Cleo because Cleo's an owner. This is her and Mina's life."

"Yes," Lacaba said, "but Dion was betraying them by leaving."

"Well..." Ari hedged.

Lacaba's face turned dark. "What do you know?"

"I've heard people say today that Dion was staying. And he'd told other people."

"Why did he change his mind?"

"Not sure on that part, really. Maybe guilt? Loyalty to Mina?"

"Maybe he thought he had a chance with Mina if Cleo and Emily became a permanent thing."

"I don't know," Ari admitted. "I'm going out to dinner," she said. "Did you need anything else?"

Lacaba tapped her fingers on the conference table. Her warm brown eyes slowly met Ari's gaze. "Before you go, if you have a few minutes, will you meet me outside on the patio for a drink?"

"Would you like a glass this time?"

Lacaba laughed, and Ari thought she had a great smile.

Fifteen minutes turned into thirty. By the time Lacaba arrived, Ari was halfway through a glass of the heralded pinot gris. She'd found Mina in her office and told her about her "conspiratorial cocktail hour" with the deputy, and Mina insisted on providing something that would please Deputy Lacaba.

When Lacaba arrived, her jaw dropped and she pointed at the bottle. "How did you..."

"Mina said we would be the first."

"With pleasure," Lacaba said, and Ari thought she might clap her hands in glee.

Ari poured her a glass and watched as Deputy Lacaba studied, sniffed, swirled, and finally took a sip.

"This is amazing, don't you think?"

"It's the best white wine I've ever tasted."

Deputy Lacaba—now Rosa—leaned back and stared at the vineyard. "Just give me a moment to enjoy this."

Ari closed her eyes, listening to the sounds of birds—and machines. She marveled that she and Rosa could become friends. *Maybe.*

Eventually Rosa turned slowly and said, "Wanna tell me what you found on the phone?" Ari stared at her in surprise. "I had to call Apollo about coming down here and getting his things out of the cottage. He mentioned that he'd given you the password."

"Well, I—"

Lacaba held up a hand. "We're on day two of a homicide. I need to move as quickly as I can. I'm not going to broadcast your assistance to the world, especially to the sheriff, but the fact is, you're not in my way and you're not impeding my investigation, true?" Ari nodded. "You're using what's at your disposal, which is just having conversations with people under the guise of being a visitor. People have their guard down. You have no real authority so they relax. On the other hand, I'm employing my own tactics of a formal interview with the hope that suspects and witnesses will tell the truth in a serious setting while I'm wearing my badge. I'll acknowledge that to solve this case, I need both." She took a breath and added, "I don't have time to review ten thousand photos, nor do I want to."

"Okay, then," Ari said. "Hand me the phone."

She showed Rosa the photos and explained her theory about Dion blackmailing Emily. The deputy decided to re-interview Emily the next day and hit her with the photos.

"Do you think Cleo knows about the trip?"

"I don't know. Emily wasn't hiding these tickets, but they were buried on her desk."

Rosa swirled her wine. "I don't want to know how you know that, right?"

"Not even a little."

In a sign of quid pro quo, Rosa explained her interviews with employees at Racy's restaurant.

"Racy was there that night, but there's a lot of time no one can account for. I spoke with a bartender, the maître d', and the shift manager on duty that night. They all have similar stories. They saw Racy making the rounds, shaking customers' hands, but then he headed up to his office."

"Alone?"

"Far as they knew. Apparently that's really how he rolls. He's a glad-hander, and he's not interested in doing any work. Nobody has ever seen him serve a plate of food, wash a dish, escort diners to a table—even answer the phone. He's there to be the face, and once he's satisfied he disappears until someone needs him, which they rarely do."

"Does he have a private door off his office?"

Rosa smiled. "Of course."

Ari stroked her chin and asked, "What about anybody outside? Taking out the trash or having a smoke break? Did they notice him or his car?"

She shook her head. "I checked myself. The service door and the dumpster are around the corner from Racy's private exit. No one has a reason to go there. It would be like wanting to run into the boss. And before you ask, nobody saw Racy's car leave. That doesn't mean he didn't."

Ari sighed. "So his alibi is very shaky. And he definitely wanted Dion to fail. He knew about the job offer in Portland, which meant that if Dion became a Master Sommelier and left, he'd make a splash into the restaurant world."

"But their restaurants are in two different places," Rosa countered.

"I don't think Racy's motive is rooted in a restaurant competition. If Dion became a Master Sommelier and Racy didn't…"

"Dion's success would greatly eclipse the success of Racy's wines," Rosa replied.

"So, since Racy vouched for Eddie, he's not cleared either."

"Yup. People remember seeing him, but it wasn't like anyone was watching him. He's not even an employee. And the restaurant closes at one, so if he left just after twelve, he could've easily arrived back here before one a.m."

A half hour later, Ari asked Jane again if she wanted to go to Racy's. She rarely skipped a chance to try a new restaurant, maintaining that her status as a "cooking minimalist," her term for someone who only passed through a kitchen to get a bottle of wine and a wineglass, meant she had to be a restaurant expert as a matter of survival. Missing a chance to have dinner out at Racy's high-end trattoria was unusual, but Ari understood when she again declined.

"Can't the deputy go with you?" she asked.

"No. The sheriff has decided that he and the deputy will have dinner every night until this is solved."

"Ah."

"Are you okay? Where are you?"

"I'm fine, I'm at Mina's. We're looking through old albums and drinking wine. She's taking a break from harvest to indulge my whim to walk down memory lane. She did confirm what I suspected about that picture we found. You know, the one of her and Eddie? I was the photographer and that was the day I came out to her."

"Interesting. Did you ask her about the context of that photo? Remember? Her hands were on his wrists."

"I did, and she said she couldn't remember."

"Do you believe her?"

There was a long pause. "I'll just be another sec," Jane said, and Ari realized Mina was standing there. "No, go on and start the sauce."

"I'm back."

"Did you hear my other question?"

"I did. And I'm not sure."

"Oh."

"Look, this is just a weird convo she and I are having. Many of the people we're discussing from our misspent youth are dead."

They soon signed off and Ari dropped onto the guest bed and stared at the light gray walls. She'd been so looking forward to this trip, for weeks. She'd never been to Oregon, and she'd hoped to do some hiking, drink some fabulous wine and bask in happiness with her best friend. Nothing had gone as planned.

She headed to the bathroom and splashed cold water on her face. She didn't relish going to a restaurant alone, but there didn't seem to be any options for companionship. She could sit and ponder the case some more…

Before Rosa finished her wine and left for dinner with Sheriff Jerome, she shared that most everything on Dion's computer was test prep and a few personal folders for things like correspondence and Christmas card lists. She sighed. "I guess I'm done pondering."

She grabbed her bag and headed down the back steps. The whir and whine of winemaking machines as well as the lights in the production room meant harvest was in full swing. In the twilight she recognized Eddie operating the crusher-destemmer, Denise weighing a box of grapes and Berto hauling several hoses back inside. He might've been struggling with his memory, but there was nothing wrong with his physical strength.

She smiled. She knew who she could invite for dinner.

"You can't imagine how delighted I was to receive your call, Ari," Frankie Smith said as she climbed into the Range Rover. "I'm so glad we get to spend some more time together."

Ari felt her cheeks burn. *What is it about her?* She cleared her throat and said, "I'm grateful you were available, Frankie."

She smiled and glanced at the older and very fine-looking woman sitting beside her. Although Ari had only called her forty-five minutes ago while Frankie was gardening, she'd quickly changed into black pants and a lovely white silk shirt. A tasteful gold braided necklace and matching earrings completed her ensemble. She was the definition of classy.

"So tell me what we're investigating tonight."

"Well, I don't know if this is part of the investigation—"

"Bullshit." Frankie shook a deep blue fingernail at her. "You told me you're deeply in love with your girlfriend, a statement I believe is true. Therefore, as much as I wish this were a date, it is not. So tell me what you're up to and how I can help."

Ari sighed. "Okay. Someone suggested I pay a visit to Racy Rider's restaurant."

"Try saying that three times fast."

"No thanks. I know that Racy and Dion didn't always get along, and Racy is definitely a suspect."

"I can see why," Frankie said flatly. "His restaurant is nothing special, really. The offerings are basic. There's no real flair or signature dishes."

"I read some good reviews. I think they might've been some blurbs as part of an ad."

"No doubt, and I wouldn't be surprised if they lifted phrases out of context." She held up a hand. "You be the judge and tell me what you think. If you disagree with me, well… There's no accounting for taste."

They both laughed and Ari said, "So you think Racy's won't make it?"

"Oh, no, he'll stay in business because of the wine and his charisma. His reds, especially the malbec, are good."

"Well, I do appreciate a fine malbec."

"As do I, but people have expectations when they go out for dinner. If he ever asked me for advice, which of course, he wouldn't, I'd tell him to rebrand his company and call it a wine bar. Less expectation on the food side."

"Rebrand? Were you in marketing?"

"I was. Thirty-seven years with a winery in Junction City. That's where I met Marj."

"Was she your wife?"

"Well, we couldn't call it that, but yes, we were closer than most straight married couples I know." She sighed. "Had twenty wonderful years together before pancreatic cancer took her. Blessedly, it was fast."

"I'm sorry. I don't know you well, but I'd guess the two of you were a hell of a couple."

Frankie smiled. "We were." She squeezed Ari's shoulder and said, "So tell me about your woman."

Ari related the story of how she met Molly during an investigation involving one of Ari's best friends. The conversation quickly branched off to other topics and before she knew it, the navigation system announced they'd arrived at Racy's.

Ari gazed at the old brick building in what was clearly an industrial area of Eugene. Gooseneck lights protruded from the front and illuminated the white sign with black letters—*Racy's*. Judging from the row of cars that lined the street, business was doing well.

Inside, the old brick had been sandblasted to its former glory. The place looked antiquated but not old. Vintage but not dreary. And whenever possible, modern technology like LED lights and hidden speakers ensured it was retro and retrofitted. It reminded her of her own office building back on Grand Avenue in Phoenix.

They were greeted by a very pale young man with completely white hair. Ari wondered if he suffered from a pigment issue or if he was just being chic with a bleach bottle. Dressed in black pants, shirt and tie, his appearance was certainly memorable, and for a second Ari had déjà vu and thought she had seen him before. He seemed very pleasant as he assured them the wait would only be a few minutes.

Ari pointed at the banner that hung over the bar area: 2019 Winner Laurelwood Challenge-Best Malbec. "Berto was very upset that Sisters missed the chance to be in the competition."

She nodded. "He told me, and he feels very guilty about it. We may not be married anymore, but we still talk." Ari bit her lip, and Frankie gazed at her with a knowing smile. "I can see there's something you want to ask."

"Does he talk with you about his…curious behavior?"

"He has, and I know he's frustrated. I have no idea why these things are happening to him." She pressed her lips together, embarrassed.

"What?" Ari asked.

"I did something I shouldn't have. After the third or fourth time he fell asleep in the vineyard, I went to Cleo. I was worried. I wanted someone else to confirm these things were actually happening. I wanted to see if there was another explanation—something, anything—that wasn't the onset of dementia."

Her eyes filled with tears and Ari gently squeezed her hand. "Like I said earlier, I don't know anyone here very well. But from what I gather, a whole lot of people like Berto and will look out for him, Mina included."

"I know she and Cleo look out for him, and Eddie too. I've just never seen these behaviors that keep happening, and we spend a decent amount of time together." Ari could only shrug. "But it just sucks to get old in so many ways," Frankie continued. "People talk about all the wisdom you've gained and the good deeds you've done. What I wouldn't give to have my dexterity back in my hands. Damn arthritis."

They were called to the table and presented with menus. Ari opened hers. "There must be thirty different dishes," she commented.

"Part of the problem, I think," Frankie said. "Racy is trying to do too much at once. A piece of friendly advice: stay away from the fish."

"Got it. Well, I'll definitely be ordering the malbec."

The server appeared and took their drink and dinner orders. Ari had the pork chops and Frankie had spaghetti. "One of the few dishes most restaurants don't screw up," Frankie said.

"Ms. Adams."

Ari turned as Racy arrived at their table. His long, kinky hair was pulled back into a stylish ponytail. He wore a pink dress shirt and black pants. If anyone wanted to find the owner of the restaurant, they'd have no trouble spotting him. "I'm honored that you're joining us tonight." He pointed at Frankie. "And you look familiar."

"I've been here a time or two. I'm Berto's ex-wife."

"Of course." He extended his hand. "Frankie, correct?"

"Yes."

He motioned to the expansive dining room. "What do you think?"

"It's a marvelous place," Ari offered. "I love that you restored an old building."

"I can't take credit for the building. It had already been redone when we came along, but the decor is all us."

"Who's *us*?" Frankie asked.

"My business partners and me. They work on the food aspects and I handle the wine."

Ari smiled. "Congratulations on your wine award."

"Thank you. It was a great honor."

"Not to be a party pooper, but do you think the outcome would've been the same if Sisters Cellars had entered?"

"You're not being a party pooper at all. I don't know what would've occurred." He shrugged. "I guess we'll never know."

Frankie set down her menu. "What would you say is the secret of your success with the malbec?"

"I think it's our fermentation. We've got a team of people who oversee the entire process."

"You mean you oversee them, don't you?" Frankie asked.

He backpedaled and said, "Of course. I do the punchdown myself and then we get it into the large steel tanks." A waiter rushed to Racy's side and whispered in his ear. He nodded and the waiter flew away.

"Ladies, I have a problem to solve. I do hope you enjoy your dinner." He strode off.

Ari asked, "Did he just say that he ages red wine in steel tanks?"

Just then their glasses of malbec arrived. They toasted to a new friendship and each took a sip. It was smooth and understated. Exactly the way Ari enjoyed it.

Frankie set her wine down. "That is good. To answer your question, yes, he did say they put the malbec in a steel tank, which, I think, is exclusively reserved for whites. Reds are barreled. I seriously doubt this wine would be as good as it is if it had aged in a steel tank, but I'm no expert. I leave the winemaking to Berto. But I don't think Racy Rider knows what the hell he's talking about."

CHAPTER TWENTY-TWO

"I'd love for you to meet Frankie, honey. She's a hoot."

"Somebody sounds like she has a little crush."

Ari suddenly felt warm and she wasn't sure if the cause was thinking again about Frankie or her fourth glass of wine. "Okay, maybe a little. She's a flirt, that's for sure."

"And how is Deputy Lacaba?"

"Rosa is doing well. She's gaining some confidence, although there's been a few missteps like losing the victim's phone."

"Yikes," Molly said.

"Yeah, the sheriff ripped her a new one. I found it, and told her that if she solves this, all will be forgotten." A breeze rolled across the patio; Ari debated running back to the room for a sweater.

"Describe what you're seeing right now," Molly said.

Ari sipped her pinot gris and stretched, hanging her long legs over the edge of the lounge chair. She'd returned from dinner with Frankie with more questions than answers. Her mind still spinning, she found the opened bottle of pinot gris in the fridge, grabbed a glass and returned to the patio.

"Well," she said to Molly, "I can't see a whole lot. It's pretty dark out there. The lights from the patio illuminate the first few rows of the grapevines, but then it's like the night just gobbles them up."

"Sounds a little creepy, babe."

Ari shivered and wrapped an arm around her middle. "Yeah, I guess it kind of is. So what's going on? Anything more about your brother?"

"No," Molly sighed. She recounted some of the frustrations with her latest security client while Ari's eyes eventually adjusted to the darkness, allowing her to see the silhouettes of the grapevines in the distance. A single point of light in the distance pierced the shadows. Mina had said that was a neighbor's back door light. It seemed much closer than it actually was.

"Babe? Are you there? I just asked you a question."

Ari sighed. "I'm sorry. The night here is rather hypnotic. It's so quiet and there aren't many stars tonight."

"You're also slurring your words," Molly said in a caustic tone. "How much have you had to drink?"

"Just a few glasses of wine."

"None of the hard stuff?"

"Nope. Not now and not at dinner."

"Good," Molly sighed.

Molly had been clean and sober for over two years, and while neither of them labeled Ari's drinking as a "problem," they were both aware that she sometimes used bourbon as her crutch.

"I'm good," she said confidently. "I'm just feeling so bad for Jane."

"It really sucks," Molly agreed, circling back to the initial topic of the phone call. "She puts herself out there for the first time and gets stepped on. I get frustrated with Jane but you know I love her, right?"

"I know you do. And right now she's sought solace with a younger woman here."

"Well, that's good, I suppose. A part of me thinks this is just Jane getting what she deserves after so many years of dumping women."

"I disagree. I think this is on Rory. Don't you think it's important to be honest? We've been down that road, remember? That was the whole Biz thing." Ari hated to mention the woman who had come between them, but she was trying to make a point.

"Of course, babe. You know I do, but other people aren't us. What you said about Cleo and Mina… If they have an open relationship and it works for them, then live and let live. Not that I think that would work for us," she added. "So you can stop thinking about that spinster-firecracker you met."

Ari laughed at the term. "I guess so," she said, sighing.

"You're losing interest in the discussion," Molly observed.

"Am not."

"Are too. You always give in when you're tired of the subject."

"I just don't debate everything for an hour."

Molly laughed. "I know. I love that about you. If I go on long enough, I win!"

"Hey!"

She laughed harder. "Love you."

"I love you."

Suddenly Ari saw a shadow in her peripheral vision, and then Dexter jumped in her lap. He wore a bright yellow sweater to ward off the chill and looked absolutely adorable. She laughed as he licked her cheek.

"What's going on now?" Molly asked, relief in her voice.

"Dexter has come to visit me. You got that cute picture I sent of him, right?"

"No, Ari."

She grinned. "No you didn't get the picture, or no, I can't have a dog?"

"The latter. I confirm receipt of your absolutely adorable pet pic, but I remain unconvinced."

"Aw, come on," she cajoled, offering Dexter a scratch behind the ears. "I guarantee if this little guy jumped in your lap you'd be swayed, especially now that he's wearing his chic and cute banana-yellow sweater."

Molly sighed. "Quite possibly that would sway me, which is why I'm glad he's twelve hundred miles away. I gotta go, got paperwork to do. Let me know if something on the case breaks or if you need to bounce ideas off me."

"Will do."

They offered a semi-mushy goodbye and Ari leaned back in the lounge chair, her gaze returning to the sky. There was one bright star, a planet she imagined, but astronomy was hardly covered in Phoenix schools or newspapers since the night sky was blanketed by light pollution.

Dexter's gaze remained focused on the vineyard. Ari stroked his head, her fingers following the curly strands of his fur. "What'cha see, Dex? Aren't you supposed to be at Mina's house? I don't think she'll like it if she calls and you don't come."

His back went straight and he emitted a low growl. He stood and Ari sat up, tracking his gaze. He sprang from the lounger and took off into the night.

"Dexter!" Ari called, but he disappeared between two rows of grapevines left of the patio.

Ari pulled herself up and waited for the world to stop spinning. "Shit," she hissed. She didn't get drunk anymore and why she'd imbibed three glasses of the gris—after the excellent malbec at dinner—was a conversation with herself—and maybe her therapist—for another time. Right now, all she cared about was Dexter.

"Dexter, come!"

She trudged down the uneven flagstone steps to find him, carefully watching the ground. She took a deep breath, dreading the idea of walking into the darkness. A gust of wind almost toppled her over. She stopped at the edge of the pea gravel, a dividing line that protected the chic shoes worn by the vineyard's guests and the rich soil that nurtured the vines and ensured those visitors returned consistently.

"Dexter?"

She closed her eyes, listening to the grape leaves ruffling in the wind.

There was a yell of pain. "Damn it!" a voice hissed.

Then a yelp.

Dexter. Someone is hurting the dog.

She barreled into the pitch-black night, jogging between the vines, slowing, listening, charging forward again. She stopped, suddenly realizing how stupid she was. She'd left her phone and its internal flashlight on the table next to the nearly empty bottle of gris. For a second she thought of Dion staggering through the production room without his phone. *Definitely ironic.*

She crouched and let her eyes adjust to the surroundings. Molly had taught her staying low was key in a game of cat and mouse. She knew she wasn't alone in the field with Dexter. Someone had cried out. Someone had sworn. Someone had smacked or kicked Dexter. *Fucking asshole will pay.*

"I know you're out here," she spat. "Only a coward hurts a little dog."

She rolled her eyes at her bravado, a nervous chill creeping up her spine. She scanned the ground but only saw the ravaged grapevines, picked clean of their fruit. Dexter whined. She sprang up and ran in a different direction, bobbing between the plants, unsure if she was predator or prey, but knowing she had to find Dexter. She tripped over something and hurtled forward, cushioning her fall with her forearms and landing face-first on the fertile soil.

Dazed, she tried to sit up, the fresh scent of earth filling her nose. The fall had knocked the wind out of her and she panted hard. Then Dexter's furry little face pressed against hers, offering slurpy kisses. She managed a smile and studied him. He seemed to be okay. He wagged his tail, wasn't limping or growling, so she imagined the danger had passed.

She strained to hear anything beyond his yips of joy. She sat up and he climbed into her lap. She closed her eyes. *No car engine. No footsteps.* Whoever had been among the grapes hadn't driven away. A pain shot through her ankle. She searched the immediate area for the thing that had tripped her. A cylindrical-shaped object rested on its side a few feet away.

"Hold on, boy," she said, gently pushing Dexter from her lap and retrieving what proved to be a coffee can with a plastic lid. She shook it lightly. It sounded half full. She prepared to remove the lid—and stopped. Something nagged at her. She looked around, realizing she wasn't sure of her exact location. The patio lights burned just east and south, but she wanted to note the exact place where she found the can.

She looked down at Dexter sitting at attention, his tail wagging across the soil. "Would you mind loaning me your sweater?" she asked as she wriggled it off him and set it atop the vine where she'd picked up the can. "Now they'll be able to find it easily." She patted him on the head, tucked the coffee can under her arm, glanced at her watch. *10:15 PM.* "Come on, Dex. I think the night is just beginning."

"A coffee can? In the vineyard? What the hell?" The exasperation in Mina's voice was clear. Apparently she'd left Jane at her house and returned to the production room. The line disconnected and ten seconds later Ari saw Mina come around the corner of the building, flashlight in hand. Dexter left Ari's side to greet her, and she scooped up the little dog, who seemed to put an instant smile on her face.

"Sorry if I was a bitch," she said with a laugh, depositing Dexter into a nearby chair. "What'd you find?"

Ari motioned to the large metal coffee can. Mina stared at it, puzzled. She shook it and said, "Huh." She peeled back the lid, froze, and immediately resealed the can. When she looked up at Ari, she was pale, her hands shaking. "When you found this can," she whispered, "was the lid on?"

"Yes. I think Dexter scared the person and they dropped it and ran away."

She scooped up Dexter and wrapped him in a hug. She kissed the top of his head and whispered something in his ear. She let him go and gazed at Ari. "You have no idea what you've done."

Ari stood there speechless while Mina's fingers flew across her phone. She had the speaker on and the ringtone sounded while she sent a text at the same time. Cleo's voice mail message began and Mina swore under her breath. When the beep sounded, Mina shouted, "Both of you get your asses out of bed and get back here. Now!"

CHAPTER TWENTY-THREE

Mina continued to call and text everyone affiliated with the vineyard, and she ordered Ari to summon Jane, Sheriff Jerome, and Deputy Lacaba. "Tell them they need to come immediately."

"What on earth is in that can?" Ari asked between calls, but Mina just shook her head.

"I only want to go through this once, but part of the story will be you reciting what happened with as many details as you can remember." She picked up the bottle of wine and studied the contents. "You drank four glasses?"

Ari shrugged. "Hey, Rosa—Deputy Lacaba—had one. I'm not drunk if that's what you're implying."

Mina said nothing as she sent another text. Ari sat down on the lounge chair, her phone calls made. The sheriff and deputy were on their way, and Jane had said she and Peri would be there soon.

Within fifteen minutes Cleo and Emily had arrived—in Emily's car. "What's going on?" Cleo demanded, ignoring Mina's hard stare.

Mina pointed to the can. "See for yourself."

Emily and Cleo exchanged a worried look and pulled up the lid. Emily gasped and Cleo resealed the lid immediately. "Holy fucking shit!" she exclaimed. She grabbed both sides of her head, and Ari thought she might fall to her knees and scream. "How in the hell..." She didn't finish her sentence but instead she stormed down the road toward the garden shed, Emily following behind her. They returned two minutes later, carrying flashlights, shovels, and rakes.

"Where was it found?" Cleo asked.

Ari pointed to the general direction. "It's over that way. I put Dexter's yellow sweater on the grapevine where I found it."

Cleo exhaled. "Thank you. That was excellent thinking." She glanced at Mina and said to Ari, "If I wasn't already in trouble for this one," she motioned to Emily, "I'd kiss you."

"Damn it, Cleo," Mina cried. "This isn't the time for jokes!"

Cleo sighed and moved close to Mina. She said nothing but Mina closed her eyes. Her shoulders relaxed and she leaned against Cleo. Ari stole a look at Emily, who looked away. Cleo kissed Mina's cheek and trudged off with Emily.

Jane and Peri arrived, and oddly, Berto and Eddie pulled up in Berto's old truck. "Found this guy walking down the road," Berto said.

"My car stalled half a mile away," Eddie growled.

"You really need to ditch that piece of shit," Mina said.

"Yeah, I know." Eddie pursed his lips and motioned to the coffee can. "What's that?"

Mina whispered to him, he nodded and jogged off to the production room. Then the orange and red lights of Sheriff Jerome's cruiser came through the main gates and pierced the dark night. Ari saw two other headlights behind him and surmised they belonged to Denise, since she was the only other employee missing.

While everyone waited for the sheriff, Jane sidled up to Ari. "What's going on? Mina sounded hysterical."

"I don't know. She opened the coffee can and looked like she'd seen a ghost. Then she started calling and texting."

Eddie returned with what looked like a fish tank, except a rubber glove was built into the left and right side respectively. Mina opened the top, placed the coffee can inside the tank, and closed the top again.

Once Sheriff Jerome and Deputy Lacaba had joined the group on the patio, Mina turned to Ari. "Ari, can you please recount what happened this evening?"

She cleared her throat. "Sure. I was enjoying some wine on the patio with Dexter on my lap. He heard a noise and ran into the vineyard. A few seconds later, I heard someone curse and Dexter yelp, like the person was hurting him. I got up and ran toward him. Then I tripped over the can. Then Dexter found me. I was trying to listen for a car or footsteps, but Dexter was so happy to see me... I wasn't sure exactly where I was, so I took off Dexter's sweater and left it on the grapevine closest to the can. I picked the can and Dexter up and came back to the patio. That's when I called Mina. It just seemed too weird for someone to be out in the vineyard in the middle of the night."

"Cleo and Emily are out there now," Mina added. They all looked toward the bobbing flashlights amid the grapevines.

"Oh, my God," Denise said. She bolted off the patio and headed toward them.

Sheriff Jerome groaned and wiped a hand over his face. "That better not be what I think it is."

"What the hell is it!" Jane roared. "Agent Orange?"

Mina stuck her hands inside the gloves and manipulated the coffee can from outside the tank. When she removed the lid, dozens of tiny green bugs flooded the tank. Jane, Ari, and Lacaba leaned closer to see them, but no one else did.

"Dios mío," Berto whispered.

"Are those aphids?" Jane asked.

"Oh, no," Eddie said. "This is far worse. Meet phylloxera. The deadliest enemy to vineyards ever known to man."

The tiny green bugs continued to flow out of the coffee can. Ari surmised there were a few hundred inside and she imagined the person Dexter scared away intended to release them in the vineyard.

"So tell us about these bugs," Jane said to Mina.

"Phylloxera feeds on the roots of grapevines, specifically grapevines whose roots haven't been grafted as a protection from the bugs."

"And yours haven't?" Ari asked.

"For the most part, no. We're almost completely an old vine vineyard, meaning most of our vines are original, planted by my uncle, which also means our vines are more vulnerable to some pests, especially phylloxera." She looked out toward the group in the vineyard. "We were beginning the process of grafting the roots in the pinot gris section, but we hadn't gotten very far."

"Can you tell us a little more about these critters?" Lacaba asked. "From the way everyone reacted, I'd have thought that can contained the plague."

"Essentially it is the plague. Phylloxera originated here in America, probably in the 1600s, but here it mainly devastated leaves, not root systems. Unfortunately, as we shared more wine with France we transported it there, and it was responsible for the worst case of blight ever recorded. Entire vineyards were lost for over a century as these bugs ate the roots of most of the old-world vines."

"How do you get rid of them?" Ari asked.

"You don't," Eddie said. "They kill everything. They're incredibly difficult to fight because they mainly destroy the roots underground. If the roots are compromised, the entire plant will suffer. The only way to bounce back is to replant with grafted roots that the phylloxera won't attack. You can't imagine how expensive that is."

Cleo, Emily, and Denise reappeared with somber looks. "Well, I can't say with absolute certainty," Cleo began, "but I don't think any of them were released. We didn't find any other coffee cans, no sign of the bugs…I think we lucked out. However, I'm going to start calling the other vineyards. They're going to want to see for themselves."

Sheriff Jerome stepped forward and placed a hand on Mina's shoulder. "From the legal perspective, it doesn't matter that the bugs were never released. If we catch whoever did this, they'll be facing jail time. As far as I'm concerned, they can sit in a cell right next to Dion's killer."

"How does someone acquire this bug?" Ari asked.

"The dark web," Emily said. Everyone looked at her. "Well, at least that's what I've heard."

Sheriff Jerome motioned to Lacaba. "Deputy, follow me, please."

They stepped away from the group, Sheriff Jerome speaking while Lacaba took notes.

Strong arms wrapped around her from behind. She turned to see Mina's grateful smile. "If that lid had come off, it probably would've ended Sisters Cellars. Almost everything would've died. So, thank you."

"Well, you're welcome, but really, Dexter is the hero. I'm guessing from what I heard that he gave that person a nasty little nip."

Mina squatted and Dexter jumped into her arms. She caressed his ears and said, "You're the best, Dex." He licked her face and she laughed. "I've had enough for one night," she announced to the group. "Until someone says otherwise, I'm going to assume we averted a disaster. Thank you all for coming so quickly. I think Sheriff Jerome and Deputy Lacaba have this under control."

She started down the hill toward the cottage. Ari glanced between the two odd couples, Peri and Jane and Emily and Cleo. While Peri and Jane headed back to the parking lot, Cleo squeezed Emily's hand and jogged until she caught up to Mina. She threw an arm around her shoulder and pulled her tight. They drifted into the moonlight, Dexter trotting alongside them, a little family again.

Emily, abandoned, stood rooted in her spot, a look of hatred on her face. She watched them until they went through the front door, and only then did she look away. When her gaze met Ari's, she'd reconstructed her customer service smile. "We can't thank you enough, Ari."

"Just glad I was in the right place at the right time."

"Yes," Emily agreed, almost hesitantly. "You were."

She turned away, her shoulders straight and her gait rigid. While she obviously had been with Cleo and wasn't confronted by Dexter in the vineyard, perhaps she was working with someone else?

Emily interrupted Sheriff Jerome and Deputy Lacaba. Ari moved a little closer and heard her say, "I need to amend the statement I gave you, Deputy Lacaba."

"You do?" the sheriff asked.

"Yes." She paused as if she were ordering the words in her mind. "When Deputy Lacaba asked me if Cleo was with me the entire night that Dion was murdered, I said yes."

She stopped talking as if what she'd said explained everything. "And?" Lacaba nudged.

"I don't think she was."

"You don't *think* she was. Does that mean you don't really know?"

Emily looked at the ground and then away. She seemed utterly morose, and Ari guessed she was fully accepting the fact that Cleo would never leave Mina and she would always be the other woman.

"Cleo and I had a late dinner around nine thirty. We went to bed, but when I woke up around two a.m., she was gone." Emily dabbed her eyes, wiping the tears streaming down her face.

"Did she tell you later about where she went?"

"She just blamed the harvest. But that didn't make any sense because the production room was closed."

"Did you press her on that?"

"No, I let it go. If she was lying to me, I figured she had her reasons. Of course I had no way of knowing about all of this." She waved her arms toward the vines and the production room. "This place has become such a farce." Her voice trembled and Ari thought she might cry again. Instead she said, "I can see why Denise wants to leave. Is there anything else you wish to ask me?"

Lacaba glanced over at Ari before she said, "Since Cleo wasn't with you during the time of Dion's death, can anyone support your claim that you were home asleep?"

"Well, I spoke with my mother on the phone. We were talking about my history of poor romantic choices."

"Was that a landline or your cell?"

"My cell, of course. But I had no reason to kill Dion."

"On the contrary, Ms. Mills. You had a very good reason for wanting him gone—you wanted his job, one you thought you were going to get since he'd obtained a new job in Portland, which you helped him secure. All that work to find out he was staying put. That had to aggravate you."

"Yes, but I wouldn't hurt anyone, especially over a dumb job. And that's the truth."

"Well, since you're finally owning the truth, why don't you admit to taking Dion's phone?"

Sheriff Jerome, spotting Ari, called, "Ms. Adams, you might just come over here and join us." Ari nodded and the sheriff said to her, "Tell Ms. Mills what you know."

Emily's expression was cold but her eyes betrayed her fear.

"I overheard you earlier today telling someone you'd hidden *it* very well, somewhere no one would find it. I assumed *it* was the phone, and since I'd already searched the storeroom, a place where no one goes, I figured that if you had taken the phone, that's where you hid it."

Her cool exterior crumbled, and Emily hunched her shoulders, dropping her chin to her chest. "He was blackmailing me."

"Who, ma'am?" Sheriff Jerome asked.

She looked up. "Dion, sir."

"About the photo of the plane ticket," Lacaba confirmed.

She nodded. "If Mina found out..."

"Did Cleo know?" Ari asked.

"Not yet. I had to make sure she loved me as much as I loved her." She gazed longingly toward Mina and Cleo's house. Several lights were on as if confirming their complete domesticity— together. "I guess I've got my answer."

"You're under arrest for obstruction of justice," Sheriff Jerome said. "Let's go."

The sheriff and Lacaba left with Emily, the sheriff reciting her rights as they walked. Eddie, Berto, and Denise remained huddled together, whispering. Ari couldn't make out what they were saying, and for the first time since her arrival she felt completely like an outsider. Not even Jane, the person at whose behest she had come, was sticking around.

A gust of wind whooshed past her and she wrapped her arms across her chest, hurrying back to the patio for her phone and jacket. A text from Jane covered her home screen. *Thank God you were on the patio! I know I'm being a shitty friend right now. Long story to tell. Please try not to judge me too harshly. Give me time, space, and grace. Love you.*

Ari exhaled. They were due to leave in thirty-six hours, so she imagined she could wait that long. Undoubtedly the return drive to the airport, when they were cloistered inside the Range Rover, would be a perfect time for Jane to spill her guts about her expired relationship with Rory, as well as whatever *thing* was going on with Peri.

Cleo. So where was she if she wasn't with Emily or Mina?

She overheard Denise say, "Of course they're connected. It's like whoever is doing this is trying to pick people off. First Dion. Now Mina—or Cleo—or both of them. Those bugs would've destroyed everything, and we'd all be out of a job too."

Dion. Mina.

Ari remembered the framed photo of the two of them in Dion's cottage. He would've done anything for her and probably died trying to help her…in some way. She closed her eyes for a second as a thought blazed forward. Dion's killer and the person who'd attempted to destroy Sisters Cellars were done for the night. Ari was now certain they were one and the same.

CHAPTER TWENTY-FOUR

Ari awoke much later than she'd intended on Saturday. The sleep paid off and the "wine fog" from the night before was gone. She'd fallen asleep thinking about Dion and Mina. He'd gone into the production room to get something—a piece of the puzzle he was missing. *A piece of the puzzle he was missing.*

She got dressed and found she had a message from John Graham. Coincidentally, he was planning on coming to Sisters Cellars Saturday morning to help with the phylloxera disaster, and he'd be happy to chat with her then.

She headed down the back stairs and slowed when she saw at least a hundred people in the vineyard. Many carried hoes, shovels, and shears and all of them wore protective booties on their feet. Their body language conveyed the same message: they were hunting.

Dexter ran up and barked. He turned in circles, his tail wagging vigorously.

"Well, Dexter, you certainly don't seem any worse after your harrowing encounter with a killer." He immediately sat at attention, his soulful eyes filled with kindness. She scratched him behind the ears. "Dex, when we discover the killer, you have my permission to bite 'em in the ass."

He seemed to smile as if he could understand. Ari had thought on many occasions that animals understood people, and she firmly believed animals were smarter than a significant percentage of the human population.

She found Cleo speaking to a man in jeans, a flannel shirt, and bright red suspenders. His long blond hair was pulled back in a ponytail and his bushy beard covered most of his face, his dirty ball cap shielding his eyes. Between them they seemed to be studying a map.

"Good morning," Cleo said when she saw Ari.

"Good morning."

The man smiled. "Hello, I'm John Graham. Cleo and Mina buy grapes from me." He stuck out his hand, which was as coarse as sandpaper when she gripped it.

"I'm Ari Adams. It's a pleasure to meet you."

His smile brightened as he recognized her name. "And you as well. I'm happy to help answer any of your questions."

Cleo looked between them. "Am I missing something?"

"I called John yesterday."

"Oh," Cleo said slowly, a puzzled expression on her face.

Ari gestured to the activity in the vineyard. "What's going on here?"

"This is a community at work," Cleo replied. "When word got around that someone attempted to release phylloxera here, every other vineyard and a few dozen community members volunteered to scour the entire vineyard and confirm our conclusion that the ground is clean."

"Wow. That's amazing."

"It is. John and I were just reviewing what areas have already been covered." Denise waved for Cleo. "Will you both excuse me?"

Ari smiled and asked John, "How long has everyone been here?"

"We arrived before daylight so we could get organized and start checking right when the sun rose. We all want to support

Cleo and Mina but we're in the middle of harvest and we need to get back to our own businesses."

"Of course. Still, it's very neighborly of you to show up."

"Well, thank you, but to be completely honest, our presence is somewhat selfish. Phylloxera makes us all cringe. If it gets in one vineyard, it won't be long until it gets into another. Think of it as plant lice. The little bugs are hardly noticeable, so if professional grape pickers wind up with a few bugs in the cuff of their pants or in the treads of their shoes, those bugs can easily relocate to another place, most likely another vineyard where the picker works. That's essentially how it wound up all over France in the 1800s."

"Well, I'm sure Mina and Cleo are grateful for the support."

He looked around. "This is actually the first time I've been here in quite a while."

"Oh?"

He rubbed his chin. "Yeah. It's hard to get around to all of my buyers, but Mina and I had a falling out a while back and we haven't spoken since."

"Well, you're here now."

He nodded. "True. But I haven't seen Mina. Eddie says she's still hopping mad, so he's off with her in the production room."

Dexter barked and wagged his tail for John. "There's a handsome boy." He leaned down and scratched Dexter's ears. "I won't say this in front of my dog Chardonnay, but you're definitely a great calendar cover dog."

"Excuse me, John, I don't want to offend you, but Mina said Dexter didn't really take to you."

John snorted. "If you haven't noticed, Dexter is Mina's baby."

Ari laughed. "Yes, I've noticed."

"And," John said, staring at Dexter, "this little man can get too big for his britches sometimes. I put him in his place about jumping on people and he didn't like it. After that he didn't jump but instead he gave me a low growl. Mina thought it was a big deal and I just saw it as a dog having a temper tantrum. If she'd left it alone, he woulda quit. Look at him now." Dexter was indeed sitting, waiting to be petted.

"I get it."

Dexter gave a little bark and ran to Cleo who appeared to be arguing with Denise.

"What questions can I answer for you?" John asked Ari.

"Well, really only one. There was that issue with the malbec grapes last year. They came late and Mina missed the Laurelwood competition this year."

John took off his ball cap and shook his head. "That was a shame and I don't know how it happened. My guy, he's known as Speedy, swears he gave Berto and Eddie a certain amount, but the weight tag said something different, and Berto got confused... It was so long ago, Ms. Adams. I'd hoped Dion would figure it out."

"What?"

"Well, he came by about a month ago and asked to see all of my weight tags... And speaking of which..." He pulled a paper from his pocket. "Here's the one for the grapes I brought today. Can you see that Mina gets it?"

"Of course. Can I ask you one more question? Where are the grapes weighed? At your place before they leave or here?"

"Well, always at the receiving place because the buyer has to claim them for tax purposes, but I like to weigh 'em myself as well. So usually twice."

"I see."

"Well, I should get going. I finished the area I was assigned. Got at least four more tons of grapes to harvest."

"Things are going well?" Ari asked.

"Almost too well. Third year in a row we'll have more grapes than we forecasted. Nothing wrong with making money, though." He stuck out his hand. "Pleasure to meet you, Ari."

"You as well."

Ari spied a coffee cart on the other side of the patio. Apparently Mina and Cleo were providing a light breakfast for everyone who'd shown up to help. She poured a cup and parked herself on a patio chair. Volunteers were starting to finish, lining up to report back to Cleo and Denise. From the body language and smiles, Ari guessed there was no sign of phylloxera.

She heard Jane's distinct laugh and had to blink twice when she saw her in dirty jeans and a long-sleeve T-shirt. She and Peri each held a rake. Ari shook her head. More than once Jane had declared she was allergic to dirt. Yet Peri had coaxed her outside... Seeing her standing in the middle of a field was a shock. It didn't add up.

And other things weren't adding up. When she saw Deputy Lacaba emerging from the vines in her jeans and a flannel shirt, she waved and joined Ari on the patio.

"I think this is all clear," Lacaba said, dropping into a chair. "I'm dead tired. When I catch whoever brought that coffee can into this vineyard, I'm going to shoot them."

"What if I were to tell you that I think that person is the same person who killed Dion?"

She leaned back. "I'm listening."

"First, we both believe Dion was in the production room to get information. Probably to help Mina, right?"

"Right. And we've established that his death was accidental since the unintentional killer was probably just trying to scare him so he wouldn't pass the test."

"Hmm. Maybe, maybe not. The killer's motive is what I've been thinking about. He or she wanted to stop Dion from getting that information. I think they figured out what Dion was doing. Yes, they wanted to scare him away that night, but not to affect his test scores. The test has nothing to do with this."

"You think that person wanted to make sure Dion didn't get that information," Lacaba said. "Son of a bitch." She motioned to the rows of grapes. "So how does the near catastrophe with the Wine Bug of Death play into this?"

"There's only one person who would be harmed by the phylloxera. Mina. This has never really had anything to do with Dion. It was always about Mina."

Lacaba nodded. "I see what you're saying. If this were about Dion, it would've ended with his death, whether or not it was intentional."

"That goes back to J.D.'s conversation with Dion. He told J.D. he was helping Mina."

Lacaba clapped her hands and stood up. "So we need to figure out what the heck Dion was doing."

"Yes."

Lacaba's phone chirped. "Shit."

"What's up?"

"My cat, Willow. She swallowed some dental floss yesterday and the vet kept her for observation, to make sure there wasn't a blockage. She wouldn't eat or drink anything in the last twelve hours. He wants me to come in and see if she'll eat for me. I'll be back as soon as I can."

"I'll think good thoughts," Ari said as Lacaba hustled toward the parking lot.

Ari looked out into the vineyard and stuck her hands in her pockets, crinkling the weight tag from John Graham. She went in search of Mina and found her out by the crusher-destemmer with two other employees.

"Take a look at next year's malbec," she said with a grin, plucking bunches of grapes from the bins.

"Here. John Graham gave this to me." She held out the tag for Mina.

"Oh, you can just toss it. Berto weighed 'em and we made a tag." She exhaled and said, "Wish we could get some consistency."

"What do you mean?"

"I mean usually we have about a third less, but this time we have significantly more."

"But that happens, right?"

"Yeah. It does. Eddie says John's struggled."

She stepped away from the machine and wiped her hands on her jeans. "I have something for you."

Ari followed her into her office. "I just have to remember where I set it..." While she hunted around, Ari scanned the brag wall, her gaze settling on the picture of Mina, Cleo, Berto, and Denise. She looked closely at the person in the background—Eddie. It wasn't accidental that he was in the picture. He was staring at the camera, trying to be in the picture without being *in* the picture. Then she noticed his hand at his side. It looked as though he was making a fist, but his middle finger was extended. *He's flipping them off!*

"Here," Mina said. "I wanted to give this to you. I know you're not leaving until tomorrow morning, but with everything that's been going on, I'd probably forget."

She handed her the 2020 Vineyard Dogs of Willamette Valley calendar. Plastered across the cover was Dexter's handsome, smiling face.

"Oh, thank you. Look how cute he is. He really deserves the cover."

"Well not everybody thought so," Mina said. "I told you about that stupid fight with John, right?"

"Yeah, but when I saw him this morning, he said Dexter was the perfect choice."

Mina made a face. "Really?" She shrugged. "Maybe he's been smoking some really great weed." They both laughed and she said, "I know this has been the weekend from hell for you on so many levels, and I have no idea where this situation will be by tomorrow morning when you leave, but I'm just so happy I met you."

The hug was natural and it suddenly didn't matter that Mina had known Jane longer and that Jane had confided in Mina first about her breakup with Rory.

"You heard Emily was arrested last night?"

"Yeah. And it broke my heart. I'm so angry and I feel horribly betrayed."

"How did Cleo take it?"

"Better than me. She knew Emily was on the edge." Mina closed her eyes. "If she was somehow involved in what happened last night…" She ran a hand through her hair.

"You look incredibly tired."

"I am."

"I don't know if anyone mentioned it, but as Emily was being arrested—"

"She denied Cleo was with her. Said she left."

Ari nodded. "How did you know?"

"Denise called and told us what happened after everybody left."

"And?"

"Cleo says Emily is making it up. She swears she was there until four a.m."

Ari cocked her head to the side. "Wow. Hell hath no fury as a woman scorned."

"No kidding." She checked her watch. "Well, I have to get back."

"Want some help?"

"Sure. C'mon." They strolled back outside, Mina still wearing a bewildered expression as she asked, "He really said Dexter belonged on the cover?" Ari nodded and she shrugged. "Well, okay. Mind blown."

Ari stared at Dexter's cute photo. She flipped through the other pages. She found John's dog, Chardonnay, featured in June, alongside John and a young man with milky skin and white-blond hair. The calendar identified him as Speedy Graham, John's nephew. She froze.

Mina stopped and turned. "Are you okay?"

"Yeah, but I need to make some phone calls now. Okay if I skip the winemaking?"

Mina's face brightened. "Are you going to solve the case?"

"Maybe."

"What can I do to help?"

"I need you to buy some grapes."

CHAPTER TWENTY-FIVE

"Sorry my car is so messy," Lacaba said as she scooped a pile of papers from the Corolla's passenger seat.

"No worries," Ari replied. "You should see my SUV on a busy day."

Ari rubbed her temple. She had a headache from perusing *all* the photos on Dion's phone and making a folder of just those pertinent to the case. It proved much easier to find visual evidence to back up a theory—now that she had one.

"So do you want to tell me why we're going to Carlotta's?"

"I have a hunch but it's just that—a hunch."

"But you have a plan?" Lacaba asked. "You're not just flying blind."

"Hmm, a little of both." She touched Lacaba's shoulder. "I know how much pressure you're under, so I wouldn't just drag you out to the middle of nowhere for a whim."

"I believe you."

She looked at the time. In a little less than six hours, with Mina's help, she was able to create a scenario and test her theory.

Carlotta's sign came into view. The sun was beginning its descent and the neon tubes glowed so brightly that Ari wondered if travelers near the Canadian border could see the sign.

Lacaba slowed behind a car backing out of a space and turned on her blinker.

Ari said, "We need to park around the back."

"Um, okay."

Ari directed her into a corner space directly behind Carlotta's vintage Mercedes. Ari had called Carlotta for confirmation on a few facts, and the more she spoke with her, the more she liked her.

Lacaba killed the ignition, turned to Ari. "Do we sit here?"

"Yeah." Ari checked her watch. 4:30 p.m. "Let's just wait and see what happens."

The deputy only lasted sixty seconds before she reached for the pile of papers she'd thrown in the back. "Can't hurt to multitask, right?"

"No, you go right ahead."

With no paperwork to occupy her, her mind wandered to something else—Jane. She felt horrible for her best friend. She felt even worse that she'd originally thought Jane was once again at fault—because it always had been Jane's fault. She routinely sabotaged relationships anytime the other person got close. Ari had thought Rory was different, someone who was a little older and wiser. Someone who could finally tame Jane. And she had done so—until she ran over Jane's heart.

Another twenty-five minutes passed. Ari started to worry nothing would come of her little plan. Lacaba had finished her work and was glancing at her watch. Ari was just about to explain everything when the deep rumble of an approaching truck silenced her. It stopped on the opposite side of the back lot. Adorning the driver's door was the Sisters Cellars logo.

"Well, what do we have here?" the deputy asked.

Eddie hopped out of the cab while Berto came around from the passenger's side and they walked toward the diner together.

Lacaba looked at Ari. "What do we do?"

"We wait."

"For how long?"

"I think this will happen quickly," Ari said with more confidence than she felt.

Ten minutes later a large, unmarked delivery truck pulled up alongside the Sisters Cellars flatbed. Three men jumped from the cab. A short, stocky Hispanic man in a denim work shirt and jeans hopped onto the flatbed. Ari recognized the second man—a pale, thin guy with white-blond hair.

Lacaba peered through the windshield. "I know him."

"You do. Picture him holding a stack of menus."

"That's the maitre'd from Racy's."

"It is. His name, or nickname, is Speedy. He's John Graham's nephew."

Lacaba jerked her head toward Ari. "Seriously? How did you find that out?"

"He's on the 2020 calendar with John and John's dog, Chardonnay."

"Got a record?"

"I wouldn't be surprised."

Speedy stationed himself between the vehicles. He wore jeans and a white button-down shirt. He looked extremely uncomfortable and stood around while the other two did most of the lifting. Ari doubted he went outside with any regularity. The third man, who had the sense to wear a felt hat with a wide brim, raised the delivery truck's back door. Only his arms were visible as the three transferred boxes of grapes from the flatbed to the delivery truck.

Lacaba leaned toward the windshield. "They're stealing Mina's grapes! Let's get 'em!"

Ari gripped her forearm. "Hold on. We need this to play out."

She sighed. She tapped on the steering wheel. "I can't believe it. Racy is stealing the grapes to make his wine. That's why he won the contest. Mina didn't have enough to make her malbec in time because Racy took them." She scrunched up her face. "That little asshole!"

Ari didn't correct Lacaba's conclusions, since she still questioned her own.

Ten minutes later all three were back in the delivery truck and preparing to leave. Ari calculated they'd taken sixty crates. The stocky guy in flannel had redistributed the remaining crates so the theft was less likely to be noticed.

"Now?" Lacaba asked.

"Give me one second." She texted Carlotta. *Bring them out now.* "Okay, pull up behind them so you box them in."

"Ten-four," Lacaba said, starting the engine and roaring across the parking lot. She got out, drew her gun, and stood behind the truck. "Gentlemen, keep your hands where I can see them and please exit the vehicle."

"What the hell?" Speedy uttered.

"I could ask you the same thing. We just witnessed you removing dozens of crates from that truck. And since I've recently become quite familiar with Sisters Cellars, I know that none of you are on their payroll."

Speedy tossed his chin toward the restaurant. "No, but they are."

They all looked at Eddie and Berto returning to the flatbed, Carlotta watching from the front door. Both men wore quizzical expressions.

"What's going on?" Eddie asked. "Carlotta said something about a flat tire."

"We just caught these men attempting to steal sixty crates of Sisters Cellars grapes."

"Seriously?" Eddie cried. He looked at Berto, who stared at the man in the wide-brimmed hat. "This is horrible!"

"For shit's sake, Eddie," Speedy said. "Just give it up."

"Give what up? I've never seen you before in my life."

Speedy's jaw dropped as he realized Eddie was going to let him swing in the wind by himself.

Ari stared at Berto. "Eddie claims not know these guys, but you do, don't you, Berto?" Berto looked at her slowly. He wore a cold stare and looked like he might hit someone. "Can you identify any of these men for us?"

Berto eyed all of them before his gaze settled on the man in the felt hat. "That's Ben Putnam, a lazy SOB who used to work for Mina."

"And now he works for you?" Lacaba asked Berto.

"No," Ari corrected. "Now he works for Eddie. Isn't that right?"

Eddie threw up his hands. "I don't know what you're talking about."

Ari turned to Lacaba. "Eddie's been stealing Mina's grapes for at least a year, long enough to ensure he had enough to create Racy's wine, Respite. He's been falsifying the weight tags and blaming Berto, or rather he's created the idea that Berto's memory is failing and that's the reason for the shortage."

"You son of a bitch," Berto growled.

Berto's fist connected with Eddie's chin and sent him reeling. Berto swore in Spanish and grabbed him by the shirt collar as he fell to his knees. The other three men and Lacaba separated them before Berto could deliver another punch.

"*Capullo*! Letting me think I'm losing my mind. You probably hid my pruning shears, laughing at me as I ran around trying to find them." Berto's eyes grew round. "You let Mina think I screwed up the count and that's why we're in deep shit with the feds. It was all you!"

Eddie continued to shake his head. "Not true, Berto. I'm sorry you're losing it. I really am. But blaming other people is pathetic."

Ari faced him. "Really? As pathetic as seeking revenge on the woman who scorned you? Nothing is as pathetic as a guy who can't take no for an answer." Eddie scowled through clenched teeth. "You just couldn't stand that Mina wouldn't promote you, that she didn't see in you what she saw in Denise. She didn't want you personally or professionally."

"You don't know what the hell you're talking about. I broke up with her."

"You've been jealous since Sisters Cellars began. I saw that newspaper article in Mina's office. You weren't invited to be in the picture on Opening Day. The one they printed above the fold. So what did you do? You stood in the background and gave them the bird. All this time and you've just been rejected and rejected."

"She's a foolish bitch," Eddie spat, his face red and his teeth bared. "Can't recognize talent when it's right in front of her. I showed her! I'm the one who created Respite, a wine that's as good as her malbec."

Lacaba suddenly laughed.

"What's so goddamn funny, deputy?"

"You think it's some kind of accomplishment to duplicate someone else's wine?" She looked at Ari. "I get it now. Dion figured it out, didn't he?"

Ari nodded. "Once he judged that wine competition and tasted Racy's wine, he suspected something fishy was happening, especially after all the problems with the Department of Agriculture."

Eddie stared upward. "I'm not saying a word. I want my attorney."

"So shut up," Lacaba spat. "You'll get one." She looked back at Ari. "How did you figure it out?"

"Once we learned the first column of Dion's table was dates and all of them coincided with grape pickups, I dug through those files from the storeroom and saw that most of the grape pickups were from John Graham, the person who supposedly was still having a feud with Mina."

"Supposedly?"

"Supposedly. Eddie was the one who kept it going. He told John that Mina was still angry about the dog calendar, and he told Mina that John was still angry. That kept them away from each other."

"And if they weren't talking, then they wouldn't figure out that Mina's grapes were short."

"Exactly. On John's end, Speedy made sure the weight tag was correct so John wouldn't suspect. Eddie forged a new weight tag after a third of the grapes had been lifted—right here in this parking lot." Ari pointed to the building. "They conveniently parked on the side where there wasn't a security camera." She touched Berto's shoulder. "The worst part is that Eddie needed a fall guy, a reason all this was happening. Eddie knew Mina had a soft spot for Berto, so he became the patsy.

"This morning when John showed up to help look for the phylloxera, he admitted Dexter deserved the cover of the magazine. He also said he'd had an overage of grapes for the last four years."

"So he was never short at all!" Berto thundered. He pointed again at Eddie. "You son of a bitch." He lurched toward a handcuffed Eddie again but Ari stepped in front of him.

"Berto, no," she said in a soft voice. "He's taken so much from you already. Don't give him reason to send you to jail with him."

Tears pooled in Berto's eyes, and he dropped his fists. "Basta," he said. "Enough."

Ari stared at a glaring Eddie. He spat on the ground and said, "I'm not saying shit without my lawyer."

"Oh, you're going to need one," Ari said. "By altering information provided to the federal government, you've committed a federal offense. Along with manslaughter."

Eddie's face fell as he connected the dots. Ari couldn't stop her lips from curling into a smile. "But you almost got caught, didn't you? That day the Ag guy showed up unannounced you were just returning from a run to John Graham's place. The Ag guy was there to check the scale. No way you could've falsified the tag with him standing there. So you made up a story of having an appointment. And the Ag guy skipped that part of the inspection as a courtesy."

"How did Dion figure it out?" Lacaba wondered.

"He did the one thing no one had done: he called John Graham to verify what Eddie was saying. He learned John held no animosity toward Mina, so he asked to see John's copies of the tags. According to John, Dion took pictures of them with his phone—"

"Which Emily stole from the conference room," Lacaba growled. "All because of her little fling. She's obstructed justice in more ways than one. I would've found those pictures with more time."

"And I was able to because I knew what to look for. Dion took photos of the weight tags and he also had pictures of the theft from last Sunday. And a video that he put in a folder titled 'Dexter.' So once Dion had the original tags from John, he wanted to compare them with the tags Mina submitted to the feds before he went and told her his suspicions. Eddie was an old friend and an old flame. Dion wasn't sure she'd believe him."

"That's why he was in the production room," Berto said. "He had to go in there to get to where those tags were stored. He wasn't going to Mina's office. He was going into the storeroom."

Ari leaned toward Eddie. "Once we compare those weight tags with the ones you signed off on, the ones Mina submitted to a *federal* agency, I have an idea more law enforcement officials will be interested in having a conversation with you about the murder of Dion Demopolous and the ongoing fraud you've perpetrated for over a year."

"I didn't murder Dion!" The bravado evaporated from Eddie's face, replaced by panic. "It was an accident. I only wanted to shake him up, make him let go of this." Tears ran down his face as he was unable to wipe them away while in handcuffs. "He should've had his phone."

"You'd already left by the time he passed out, hadn't you?" Lacaba said.

Eddie sniffled. "After he went inside the production room, I killed the power to the main door and left. I figured he'd call Mina, she'd get him out. I didn't know Dion was dead until the next morning. Really. This time I'm telling the truth."

Ari asked, "How did you know he was slipping into the production room during the quarantine?"

"I overheard him talking to Denise. I saw the note she left on the community board for him. I thought he might've figured it out. I really did just want to scare him."

"What I don't understand," Lacaba began, "is why you tried to kill the vineyard."

"I didn't do that," Eddie said with sincerity. "I've got no idea how that happened."

Lacaba looked nervously at Ari, who nodded. She stepped into his space and said, "That was you too, Eddie."

"No, it wasn't!"

"When you arrived with Berto, he said he found you walking *down* the road, not up. You said you had car trouble but you were walking away from the vineyard, not toward it. He caught you trying to leave and you had to make up a story."

"That's right," Berto said.

"Wait," Speedy said. "You did that, Eddie? You almost ruined us all!" He turned to Lacaba. "I swear, just take these handcuffs off for ten minutes and I'll save everybody a ton of money!"

"I didn't do it!" Eddie shouted. He whirled to Berto. "You got it wrong, old man."

"But I don't think Dexter got it wrong," Ari said. She looked at Lacaba. "We need to check his arms and legs."

"Do it."

Ari reached for his arm, but he pulled away. "No way!"

Lacaba grabbed his arm roughly. "Mr. Navarro, I can't even tell you how long and awful these last few days have been. But here's what you need to understand. You have no friends here. In your attempt to get revenge on Mina, you could've destroyed the entire valley and the livelihood of thousands of people."

He curled his upper lip in defiance. "I want my lawyer."

"Hey, deputy, just use your Taser," Speedy called. "We'll all deny it, won't we?"

Eddie looked around at the nods and his lip uncurled. "You wouldn't do that, would you?" he asked Lacaba.

She pulled the Taser from her belt and shrugged. "Looks to me like the votes are in, Eddie. It only hurts a little and the worst thing that could happen is it makes you impotent. But where you're going…"

"Fine, crazy bitch!" he shouted. "I've heard about you." Deputy Lacaba leaned closer and Eddie whimpered, "Just put that thing away."

Ari squatted, wrapped her hands around his left calf and squeezed. He didn't move or react, so just as she was about to squeeze his right leg, he said, "Don't. Just pull up the pant leg."

Ari rolled up his jeans to mid-calf, exposing a huge bruise and three bandages that covered the actual bite mark.

"Well, I've heard and seen enough," Lacaba said. "This is the part where I read you your rights."

"Wait," Ari said. "I have one more question. Does Racy know about this?"

"No!" Speedy shouted. "He has nothing to do with this."

Eddie nodded. "He's clueless. About most everything, really. He has no idea how to make wine. He just drinks the final product." He seemed to stand up straighter as he said, "I'm the winemaker."

"No!" Berto cried. "A true vintner, a lover of wine, would never ever harm the grapes! You attempted to murder thousands of living creatures."

Eddie stopped and hung his head. He turned to Berto and said, "I know it doesn't mean much—if anything. But I'm sorry for that."

Ari and Berto watched from the sidelines as an Oregon State Police car showed up to transport Eddie's partners in crime. Carlotta joined them outside and offered Berto and Ari a ride back to Sisters Cellars.

She filled in some holes, recounting a few incidences that in the moment had seemed harmless—Eddie hiding the truck keys from Berto, disappearing out the back door when he'd told Berto he needed to go to the restroom. It had all seemed like harmless fun.

At one point she said, "Berto, honey, I just remembered something."

"What?"

"If I were you, I'd have the police check your water bottle."

Berto looked down at the familiar lime green water bottle attached to his belt. "Why?"

"I'm thinking that maybe he's spiked it with something. That would explain a few things."

He groaned. "I wondered why I sometimes felt so weird after my lunches with him…"

Ari realized that if Eddie constantly doctored his water bottle, then that would explain some of his forgetfulness, his lethargy, his general mental fog.

Once they arrived back at the vineyard and Carlotta had departed, Berto took Ari's hand. "You know, getting old sucks." Tears flooded his eyes and he struggled for words. "Today you gave me back a part of my dignity that I thought was gone forever." He looked out at the vineyard with great pride. "This is all I've ever wanted and I'm so grateful to know I can still be a part of it. Thank you."

He squeezed her hand and wandered out into the section of the vineyard that had been in pandemonium just the night before. No doubt, Ari thought, he wanted to check on his "children" and make sure they were okay.

CHAPTER TWENTY-SIX

"When did you suspect Eddie?" Lacaba asked.

She had dropped by in her civvies once the group of grape thieves was processed. Now she and Ari enjoyed a glass of wine on the patio.

"This morning when I met John Graham. After everything I'd heard about him I was expecting a terrible bastard, but instead he was kind and forgiving. The common thread was Eddie. Putting the pieces together, he had to be the one who manipulated their relationship to control the grapes. And he was key to the other problem too. John mentioned that for the fourth year in a row he had a surplus of grapes. Again, that wasn't what Eddie had told Mina when she was shorted."

"Because he'd stolen them."

"Exactly."

"How did you know they'd take the bait this afternoon and show up at Carlotta's?"

"Because the phylloxera stunt backfired in more than one way. Eddie and Speedy were supposed to meet at Carlotta's today, but when John came to help look for the phylloxera, he just brought the grapes on his own trailer."

"Which meant that Eddie would've lost out on a chance to get more grapes to make Racy's wine."

"Exactly. So when Mina explained my theory to John, he was more than willing to put together another shipment."

Lacaba frowned. "How did he react to learning his nephew was involved?"

"As you might expect. He was crushed. His sister had hoped John could straighten out Arlen, that's Speedy's real name. Racy had also been acting as a support, but when Eddie saw a chance to make wine *and* get revenge on Mina, he offered Speedy a lot more money than he'd ever make working as a maître d'."

"You ought to see the bite Dexter gave him!" Lacaba exclaimed. "In the cruiser he admitted that his leg hurt like hell, so we stopped at the ER. Turns out it was infected."

"I can't say I feel sorry for him."

"Me either. Not even if the damn leg fell off."

Ari raised her glass. "To Dexter!"

"To Dexter!" Lacaba shook her head. "I still can't believe he almost destroyed the entire vineyard, potentially many vineyards. I read up on those little green monsters last night. They're like bedbugs only far worse." She sipped her wine and stared out at the vineyard. "I can't imagine being that angry with someone." She paused and said, "No, that's not true. I can. And I have been," she whispered.

"You said you were in the military and I just assumed you went overseas."

"I did. Two tours in Afghanistan. What I saw…"

Ari reached over and touched her forearm. "Hey, don't go there. This is a good day. You don't need to tell me."

"No, I want to tell you, at least a little." Although there were tears on her face, her eyes smoldered and she winced as if she'd just won a battle with herself. "I know what they all say about me. I know they call me Deputy Do Right. The guys play cruel jokes. Leave a stick in my locker, like I'm a stick in the mud. A box of Pampers in my trunk because they call me 'baby.' For the most part, Sheriff J keeps them in line, but he can't fight all my battles." She wiped her face with her sleeve. "One day I came in and found a blowup sex doll in the one female stall they have in the unisex bathroom. I exploded. I knew who'd done it." She looked down and said, "I went a little crazy. I took my nightstick, opened his locker and just went to town."

"On his stuff?" Ari clarified.

"Yeah, just his stuff." She took a sip of pinot. "That got me five sessions with the department psychologist. That was why I couldn't stay the other night and go to the wine tasting."

"I understand."

She sat up straighter. "I just wanted you to know."

"Thanks for trusting me." They fell silent and watched the sun disappear.

"One other thing I should say," Lacaba whispered, her voice barely audible above the breeze.

Ari cupped her ear and was rather certain Rosa said, "Thank you."

CHAPTER TWENTY-SEVEN

Mina and Cleo decided a celebration was in order. Denise and Peri drove into Eugene and picked up a Thai feast and Mina opened the first bottle of malbec. Everyone swirled and sniffed before they enjoyed the first taste. All agreed it was impeccable.

"So much better than Respite," Denise said, making a face.

"I agree," said Frankie, who'd been invited at Ari's suggestion. When she winked at Ari, Ari felt that familiar blush rising on her cheeks. She was beginning to think Frankie liked making her squirm.

Everyone was enjoying the meal when Mina stood and tapped the side of her wineglass. "May I have everyone's attention?"

The chatter dissipated and all eyes turned to her. She and Cleo stood at the head of the table, their arms wrapped around each other. Mina looked at Cleo, who said, "We want to make a few announcements. First, Mina and I realize that…well, our personal life hasn't been easy on the business or all of you."

"Or each other," Mina added.

Cleo continued. "Especially after our last choices of partners—two thieves. Both of whom are now fired and enjoying the county's jail accommodations."

The guests nodded, and Ari suspected they were still processing the loss of two friends.

"So, we're done with that," Cleo said. She pulled Mina closer and touched her cheek. "There's no one else I'd rather have. Just you, baby."

"Me too."

They kissed and the crowd cheered.

Denise stood. "Wait. Are you saying no more of this open relationship stuff?"

"That's exactly what we're saying," Cleo said.

"Fine. Then, I unquit."

Everyone laughed again and Mina hugged her.

"What are the other announcements?" Frankie asked once they broke apart.

"Well, we're announcing that each employee at Sisters Cellars will be receiving a post-harvest bonus."

"Really?" Berto asked.

"Yes." Mina grinned. "Racy Rider had a meeting with his business partners. While Racy didn't do anything wrong, he did profit from Eddie's illegal scheme."

"He never paid a dime for any of the grapes that he turned into his award-winning malbec," Cleo added. "We did."

"So he's agreed to make complete restitution for the stolen grapes, our tax penalties, and any other financial hits we took because of the theft. We're using some of that money to give each of you some cash!"

The group whooped and clapped until Denise stood. "That's great and I appreciate it, but he can't give us his medal. He can't give us back the Laurelwood."

Ari noticed there were tears in Denise's eyes and her face was stony.

Mina smiled as her own eyes pooled with tears. "No, we can't get that back." She sighed. "I guess there's only one thing to do." She picked up a bottle of Sabrosa and cried, "Win the Laurelwood next year!"

Everyone shouted and clapped until Mina silenced them. She reached behind her for another bottle of malbec, one with a red bow around the neck. "This is for our new friend, Ari. Thank you for literally saving everything. We can never repay you but we hope this is a start."

The applause surged and Ari hugged them both. As she looked out on the smiling faces, she felt the power of friendship and wished Molly were there to share and enjoy it. Her gaze landed on the next best person, Jane. Peri had her arm around Jane's shoulder and was whispering in her ear.

Once everyone had stuffed themselves with Pad Thai and they milled about chatting and enjoying the night sky, Ari went looking for Peri. She found her in the kitchen retrieving two more bottles of pinot gris.

"Hey," she said, holding up the white. "Ready for another round?"

Ari shook her head. "After last night I've had enough. I'm done. And actually, you're done too."

"Excuse me?" she asked quizzically.

"Yesterday I heard Emily talking on the phone to someone. She was telling that person to just keep up what she was doing." She stared at Peri, whose hands were shaking. Ari pointed to the bottles and said, "You might want to set those down."

Peri did so and leaned against the counter. Her face was neutral but her eyes were frightened.

"She was talking to you," Ari continued. "You were keeping tabs on me through Jane and reporting back to her."

"We didn't have anything to do with Dion's death."

"I didn't say you did. But you used Jane, someone who was very vulnerable. Someone who is my best friend."

Peri looked down at the floor and shuffled her feet. "It wasn't like that. I really like her."

"Then why?"

"Because I thought Emily was my friend. We'd been through a lot together. More than that, she controlled my life. She decided the work schedule. She decided when I got a day off, when I could have vacation—or not. She made it very clear that she would make my life miserable if I didn't help her, and my mom needs me. Emily was in love with Cleo and she just had to get Cleo to love her back. That's what she told me." She started to cry. "Look, you can have me fired and I'll wind up in some two-bit restaurant because jobs are so hard to come by here. I'm begging you. Please help me."

Ari met her gaze. "Under two conditions. The first is that you never speak with Jane again. Doesn't matter if she calls you, texts you. You don't reply."

"Okay. And the second thing?"

"I'll give you a day to tell Mina everything. And when I text her and ask if you've spoken with her, if her answer isn't yes, I'll tell her my version."

Peri nodded. Ari turned to go back to the party, and Peri said, "I'm sorry, Ari. I really am. I was hoping we could be friends."

"I was too. Maybe someday."

Once the malbec was gone—and several other bottles of wine as well—the party broke up. Berto cried when he hugged Ari. He'd thanked her a hundred more times throughout the evening and she was happy for him. Dion's death had hurt the vineyard significantly but uncovering Eddie's scheme had revitalized Berto.

As Frankie prepared to leave, she gave Ari a bear hug and a sweet kiss on the lips, which sent electricity down to Ari's toes. "I just couldn't help myself," she said, her eyes twinkling. "I hope you'll visit again, with your partner."

"I'm sure we will."

Frankie caressed her hand and whispered in her ear, "You know, not every threesome has to be like Mina and Cleo's drama fest." She winked again and floated off into the night.

Deputy Lacaba held back until most everyone was gone. She looked at Ari with a genuine smile, stuck out her hand and said, "I'm Rosa from now on. Just Rosa. It's nice to really meet you, and I hope we'll keep in touch." She shrugged. "Maybe I could call you and your girlfriend if I need to bounce around ideas?"

Ari pulled her into a hug. "Absolutely."

* * *

"You really should be driving," Jane announced. "I'm still a little hung over and all this scenery is doing nothing to keep me awake. It's like driving past endless landscape paintings at the museum. What a snooze."

"I think your sour attitude has less to do with the scenery and a lot more to do with the sucky weekend you had." Ari touched her arm. "I'm so sorry, honey."

Jane offered a tired smile. "Well, it is what it is." She took a deep breath and said, "I'm just glad my two favorite people in the world were there to help pick up the pieces of broken little me."

"Always," Ari said. Her FaceTime chimed. "Here's *my* other favorite person in the world." She tapped her phone and melted at Molly's big smile. "Hey, babe."

"Hey honey. Hi, Jane!"

"Hey!"

"I'm sorry about Rory, Jane. Next time you find a potential spouse, I'm going to perform a government-level background check and at least a twenty-four-hour surveillance."

"I'll probably hold you to that," she said.

Molly smiled at Ari. "So the winery is up and running, free of thieves and ornery little bugs, right?"

"It is. It's such a beautiful place."

"A great spot for *a wedding*," Jane said.

Molly chuckled. "I think I'll let that one go for right now."

"Good idea," Ari agreed.

"Do you think the deputy will become the sheriff?"

"Rosa didn't say for sure, but a lot of the guys were impressed with her arrests and the high stakes of the case. If nothing else I think they'll stop giving her such a hard time."

"Well, she has you to thank for that. Without you, she'd still be in that conference room, probably interviewing Dexter."

They all laughed and Ari's eyes filled with tears. "It was really hard to say goodbye to him today. He kept running around my legs so I wouldn't leave."

Molly made a funny face and scratched her chin. "Hmm. I wonder if leaving him would be less sad if you had something to come home to."

Ari laughed. "I do. I have you."

"Yeah, that's true. But now you have her, too."

"What? Who?"

Molly popped off the screen for a second, and then all Ari saw was a large brown eye. Molly refocused the phone and a cute Yorkie stared at her.

"A puppy!" Ari cried. "You got us a puppy!"

Introducing Dexter

The only biographical character in *Dying on the Vine* is Dexter, a spunky rat terrier. At eight months old, winemaker Pam Adkins carried him to work in her bib overalls. He accompanied her practically everywhere she went. He journeyed to the vineyards to pick up the grapes, always looking out the windows at the passing scenery. He'd wander the rows of vines, as if inspecting the grapes himself. He especially loved snow. He rode the forklift in the production room where the wine was made, and he greeted visitors at the Adrice tasting room in Woodinville, Washington. Even in his old age, he offered a friendly wag of the tail from his little bed that sat near the tasting room bar.

Dexter crossed the Rainbow Bridge, but Pam and her wife Julie still keep his little bed nearby, certain that he's not that far from the life he loved.

About the Author

Ann Roberts is the award-winning author of nineteen mystery, romance, and general fiction novels. Ann's most recent mystery, *Justice Calls*, was a 2019 Goldie finalist. A Goldie award winner and three-time Lambda finalist, in 2014 Ann was awarded the Alice B. Medal for her body of work. She lives in Eugene, Oregon, with her wife and a growing collection of fur kids. When Ann isn't writing her own stuff, editing someone else's, coaching a newer author, or remodeling her home, she can be found exploring Oregon's wineries or strolling along a beach, preferably near a lighthouse. To learn more about Ann, please visit her website, annroberts.net.

Bella Books, Inc.

Women. Books. Even Better Together.

P.O. Box 10543
Tallahassee, FL 32302

Phone: 800-729-4992
www.bellabooks.com